T0013070

PENGUIN B

TEACHER NARIT

Pamda Bure (aka Bunyaporn Burechittinantta) is a Bangkok-based writer. Educated in Thailand, New Zealand, Japan and Australia, she enjoys exploring many facets of cultures worldwide and drawing inspiration from them. Peripatetic and adventurous, she is never daunted and always looks for the quietly amusing, idiosyncratic side of things regardless of the situation. When not immersed in writing stories or thinking about writing one, Pamda can be found pondering existential meanings. Her life goal is to become a tango gypsy (live in a horse-drawn caravan).

Teacher Narit

Pamda Bure

PENGUIN BOOKS

An imprint of Penguin Random House

PENGUIN BOOKS

USA | Canada | UK | Ireland | Australia
New Zealand | India | South Africa | China | Southeast Asia

Penguin Books is part of the Penguin Random House group of companies
whose addresses can be found at global.penguinrandomhouse.com

Published by Penguin Random House SEA Pte Ltd
9, Changi South Street 3, Level 08-01,
Singapore 486361

First published in Penguin Books by Penguin Random House SEA 2023

ISBN 9789815058932

Typeset in Garamond by MAP Systems, Bengaluru, India

www.penguin.sg

To all the bears in my life who have been the source of my inspiration, optimism and frustration:

Sombat and Duangmanee Burechittinanta
Sarankorn Onlamool
Jarunee Mod Setthapinun
Bob Komar

Special thanks to Geoff Farries for your tutelage and for pointing out that my short story could grow into a book—without whom I would have saved six years, yet achieved nothing.

Contents

Part I

1988

Chapter 1

Darin chewed on the end of her pencil. A drop of rainwater ran off the tip of her nose and blotted out some of the words on the paper. As the ink slowly spread on the page, so did the smile on her face, for it was her most interesting contribution to the assignment so far. She laid back on the wooden daybed and wriggled her toes.

The light creeping out from the swollen clouds brought new life into her. Everything else beyond the rain-beaded glass of the bay window was obscure. There she was, floating in the dark, her reflection staring back at her. Her big downturned eyes, her damp tousled hair, the soaked-through t-shirt that clung onto her slight, boyish frame. Darin sighed at the finger-drawn heart in the condensation of the window. The raindrops beating on the tin roof were complimented by the *tap–tap–tap* of water dripping into a nearby bucket. The soi got a little lighter as the sun continued its assault on the overcast sky. Then, a rooster crowed.

This spurred Darin to copy a phrase or two from a reference sheet before casting the paper aside. And like it always did soon after sunrise, the creek of the bed, the snap of the fan's button, and the familiar sounds her mum made gently woke up the peeling paint on the walls, the old furniture, the very fabric of the rustic house. As the door creaked open, Darin sprang to her feet and called out in her brightest voice, 'Mum!'

'Dumpling,' yawned Kwantar as she ambled out in her morning dizziness. 'Oh, how many times do I have to tell you not to go out in the rain! Come here,' and she reached over to the rickety cupboard she had just passed, pulled out a towel, and cloaked Darin in it.

Darin snuggled up to her mum, trying to ignore how brittle she had become, her arms loosely wrapped around her mother's waist while her forehead just brushed her bony shoulder.

'It's going to flood, mum. The canal's spilling over onto the streets. How are you feeling?'

'Worried that if you don't go and wash your hair now, you'll catch a cold,' replied Kwantar, gently picking out a strand of hair from Darin's lips.

After having bathed and lingered over her morning congee, Darin finally headed for the door, only to find that her gumboots were not in the last place she had left them.

'Look, Dumpling. I can write a letter. You don't have to go to school, not today,' Kwantar handed over the boots she had been holding the whole time. 'The radio just says a storm's coming from the Indian Ocean.'

'But I already did it.'

'Did what?'

'His homework thingy!' Darin grumbled. A glance at the clock startled her. 'Mum, I've really got to dash.' And after having waved off her mother's offer of an umbrella, she left.

Outside, puddles had formed over the higher ground, and the low-lying areas were swamped. After some hopping, Darin joined the line, squelching up the wharf, filing onto the boat. The ferry bucked and swayed through the water. Darin perched precariously on the side rail, flushed with agitation. Behind the rice field on the other side, where the school stood, the national flag was climbing up the mast.

She jumped off the boat—well before it was safely secured to a mooring—into what she thought was a shallow puddle, but it came up to her knees. The long grass stung her legs as she negotiated her way through the passage. Soon, she found herself on open ground, the school gate looming before her. Notes of the national anthem had died down long ago. It was the third time she had been late this week.

* * *

Inside a classroom, the students hushed one another. Soon, it plunged into silence. In walked a middle-aged man with a tall and lean figure. Teacher Khatha's face was saturnine; his eyes sharp, accentuated by his sleek, tied-back hair. A stack of books under his arm on the side of his stronger left leg. In fact, Khatha's gait was not at all ugly, it merely looked as though he could not bear the weight on one side for too long. He was in his shirt as always, matching trousers, and a pair of tan loafers that were clearly in need of good of good polishing and brushing up.

The teacher soon arrived at his desk and told the class to pass up the homework from the previous lesson. As sheets were travelling up to the front, the rear door slid open. Through it, Darin traipsed in, red faced and perspiring.

'It's nice to see you're early as usual,' said Khatha, turning his wrist to glance at his watch. He was still busy flicking through a book. 'I trust you have something to hand in.'

Darin's toes curled. Tentatively, she made her way toward him, leaving a trail of muddy water in her wake. Her hands went digging into her bag and pulled out a crumpled piece of paper. Khatha scanned it and looked up at his student for the first time. There was a twitch in his solid countenance.

'Where's the other one?' he asked as he put the paper on top of a pile. 'Right, what's your excuse this time?'

Darin coughed. 'Well . . . the alarm clock must've died. I think I need a new one.'

To this, there were scattered giggles amongst the girls. Vilai, who was rocking on the rear legs of her chair, almost fell off.

'Oh, come on, Darin, that's hardly original. I'd have expected you to come up with something better than that.'

'I can explain!'

'I doubt you can, but you will. See me after class. Now to your new seat. No, you will not sit there; from now on, you will sit here.' The place indicated was at the front row, right opposite the teacher's desk. Darin used to sit next to Vilai, and they never stopped talking for a second. But that was over.

Having lost time over housekeeping, Khatha hobbled over to the blackboard and began to write:

'I'm young I'm foolish I'm dumb

So, I've come to search for life's meaning

Here, I've hoped to learn many things

But yearning shatters—

for promises were nothing but paper in the end.'

He dusted the chalk off his hands, turned to the class, and asked, 'What do you think this student meant when he wrote this in 1973?'

Most of the girls would agree that Khatha could be a real pain. He was known as Mr Pedantic throughout the school. Still, Khatha was respected by all the students as well as his fellow colleagues. Despite his sarcasm, his students found fascinating the way he brought past stories alive. So much so that it was believed that he wore the injury sustained from the 1973 uprising as more of an element of pride.

History was his subject yet he could easily teach political science instead. Khatha was once passionate about politics and a staunch advocate of democracy. But as life had mellowed him over the years, the nature of unchangeable historical events grew on him. The world of his youth might have crashed, but the dust and other remnants had yet to settle in layers under his skin. Many had moved on from 14 October 1973, but Khatha was still recounting the stories to the class, most of whom were born around the year of the event.

The rest of the class passed smoothly without incidents. By the time Darin was putting her notebook away, Khatha had already left the room.

Noticing this, she scrambled to her feet and out of the room she went and around an unobtrusive corner. Khatha was quick for a man with a limp. He cleaved his way through the crowds as he bowed his head detachedly to the teachers who addressed him along the way.

A flight of stairs soon came into view. The administration office lied just below. Khatha moved down adeptly while Darin followed close behind.

'Inside,' Khatha tilted his head and stepped into his territory.

It was not her first time in his office, or, as Darin called it— 'prison'. The room still lived up to its severe, cramped condition. Though big in size, three quarters were taken up by books, sheets, and documents that were all neatly arranged and systematically sorted in anticipation for more. Making the place even more unpleasant was Khatha's habit of sealing up the blinds that would otherwise reveal a rain garden nearby. He presently reclined into the chair; legs crossed.

'Right, come on then.'

'I got nothing to say, teacher.'

'What was that about the "I can explain" thing?'

'The truth is . . .' Darin thought, looking down at her clasping hands to avoid his gaze. Her mum was sick. But what good would that do to tell him so? He would not care. 'The truth is . . . I was worn out. My plate was full.'

'As it was with many of your classmates. So?'

'So, I couldn't complete everything. There's not enough time.'

'That was not the response I was hoping for.'

Darin bit her lower lips. Khatha stayed aloof. He tapped his pen on the table once, and twice he flipped it over.

'Listen,' began Khatha, 'we all have trade-offs, and if there's some truth in what you say, I hope you're being kept busy with worthwhile tasks. It's true, you know, that all these historical lessons aren't very practical in the real world. But they do help develop your thinking process.' A thoughtful pause and he sighed, 'Submit your homework on Monday. And mind you, this will be your last chance to scrape a pass.'

Darin found it hard to endure his half-serious, half-satirical tone. While she secretly conceded he may have a point, all she remembered was his haughty way of telling her off. 'Well, I . . .'

'Also, detention after school. You'll clean the basketball court,' Khatha cut in coldly.

Darin nodded and hesitatingly turned to go. She thought she should at least say sorry. It was hard, but she did succeed in bringing herself to it.

'Look here,' returned Khatha, 'solemn apologies won't do for me, and I am tired of explanations. Had your grades not been so poor lately, you wouldn't be here. For your own sake, get a grip. Must I say I expect better of you?'

Darin moved her head slightly in a way that was neither a nod nor a shake.

He narrowed his eyes and took the measure of Darin. 'I trust you got that. Now, that will be all. Off with you.' He then acknowledged a wai from his student and gazed at the door as it gradually swung shut. Slowly, Khatha uncrossed his legs and started to massage them in the deep recess of his office.

* * *

To the relief of many, the last bell finally sounded, and school finished. Darin was now sitting on a grandstand, hugging her knees, with a broom and a mop leaning beside her. As her classmates passed by, they would intentionally wave. Darin was raising her arm in response with exaggerated waves herself, when a series of vibrations against her back told her that someone was approaching.

'It can only be you, Vi.'

'Don't try to be clever. Tell me, what's the sentence? The usual?' Vilai lazily dropped herself down, took off her comb hairband, and slid it back up.

'Umm.'

'I knew it! Though the class had wagered on things being a lot worse,' said Vilai. She too started to wave. 'Isn't he quite capable of being half-human at times? How is your mum, by the way?'

'She's all right, I guess, keeps on talking about moving into a hospital.' Darin smiled, even though she knew that was useless.

'What? She looked so good the last time I was at your house. Wasn't it last Wednesday that she surprised us with our twinned checked dress?'

'You mean our partner-in-crime dress.'

'Yes, that. Well, what is it?'

'Well, yesterday, I saw blood-soaked tissues among the rubbish. It's frightening.'

Vilai stole a glance at her friend who looked suddenly pale. She reached out and hugged Darin for a bit. 'You poor thing.'

'I don't want to lose her, Vi.' moaned Darin. 'Anyway, shall we?'

'Shall we what?'

'Start cleaning. Because you wanted to help. That's why you're here, right? Come on Vi, lend a hand to someone down on their luck.' Darin tugged pleadingly at her friend's sleeve.

Vilai grimaced in wry amusement, but Darin knew that was a yes.

Most students had gone home. The school was quite a lonely place in the evening when it was deserted. The whole place looked like it was being compensated for a full day of nuisance and having its rest.

Darin and Vilai soon set to the task. They looked like they were having fun chasing each other about the ground. Buckets after buckets full of dust were carried away. None escaped the notice of a pair of eyes on the girls from afar.

In the room at the end of the field, Khatha was leaning against the wall, looking through the parted blinds. It was long past his workhours, but he was there anyway, buried in papers, having gone through all that was necessary.

It had been so long since the last time he had looked out. The day darkened without him noticing. His perception of the scene had altered somewhat. He could not put his finger on what lay at the root of this change, nor was he aware that his eyes softened as he watched them and wondered if he had been too hard on them all these terms?

'Vi,' whispered Darin, shortening the distance between them. 'That nurse, she's been sitting there for ages. Looks like she's waiting for someone.'

'Who? Where?'

'There, on the bench! Oh, I've got an idea,' said Darin as her eyes widened. 'Perhaps she's a ghost.'

'Don't be silly. Wait, isn't she the nurse who sometimes comes for our health check-ups?'

'Hey Vi, leave her alone!' Darin wailed, but it was too late. Vilai had darted out, and that drove her in that direction also. Khatha too was distracted. His eyes moved towards the girls before he even realized.

'Hello, can we help? We remember you,' asked Vilai.

'Thank you. But no, I'm just waiting for someone.' She leaned forward; her smattering of freckles bunched up as she smiled. 'I see you've been working very hard. Are you not going home? It's getting quite late, and a storm's coming. Look.' And she pointed at the thickening clouds. Another gust of wind presently burst through the trees lining the rear of the stand. Leaves were once again shaken off the quivering branches.

'We were just leaving,' Vilai grinned. 'We'd better go, Darin.'

'But the leaves! They're everywhere, or soon will be. Teacher Khatha will think we haven't cleaned the court!'

'Not we, Darin. You. Anyway, he won't be able to think so clearly in the rain,' reasoned Vilai impatiently. 'Now, let's go!'

'Won't he? What do you say to that, Sarvitri?' The low, steely voice came from behind. Darin and Vilai recognized it immediately. They looked at each other and slowly turned around.

'Well,' continued Khatha, who now had his jacket on and was ready to go, 'I'd say, you should go now. The storm is coming like she said.'

'We'll go now, sir,' Darin and Vilai responded uniformly as they inched away.

Khatha glanced at his students, then at his watch, and began, 'I thought you were at the hospital.'

Sarvitri smiled. 'The new nurse wanted to swap her shift. So, here I am, umbrella in hand, not knowing it'd be so windy. Will you give me your bag this time, Narit?'

'Sar, you know what I'm going to say. And please, why suddenly that joke? I am Khatha now.' The rebuke turned Sarvitri's face a shade dimmer. Khatha detected this and felt a pang of guilt. 'This is not funny. You know how it affects me,' he admitted, hoping to make up, 'Anyway, you can give me the umbrella. It could be my walking stick.'

Amid the gale, Khatha walked away arm in arm with Sarvitri, a briefcase in one hand, the umbrella dangling off it. Unbeknownst to the couple, Darin and Vilai, who had hidden in the bushes along the school gate, watched them until they were out of sight, grins spread across their respective faces.

Chapter 2

Frank Sinatra was crooning from a flashing rainbow jukebox. It was probably 'Fly Me to the Moon'. The place was unusually busy that night. Kwantar attempted to manoeuvre through the cramped bar, whose alcohol display illuminated most of the space. A familiar cluster of intoxicated men deserting their nocturnal nest blocked her path. Kwantar uneasily stepped aside to let them pass.

There he was. His legs were crossed, so were his arms. In one hand he was holding a book, in the other an unlit cigarette. He had not shaved in a while, with dark circles under his eyes, slouching before a steamed-up glass of Coca-Cola with a puddle beneath it. Yet she simpered to herself forgivingly. Today his hair was tied up in a bun, and she loved it when men wore their hair like that.

She took a long look at him, trying to hide her joy at finding him in his usual haunt. With lightness in her heart and a glow spreading across her face, she went up to where Narit had tucked himself away.

'Hmm?' She was unsure whether it was a response to the book he was reading or an acknowledgement to her question if he fancied some wine. But she soon felt his strong arm embrace her hip and draw her towards him. Kwantar did not stir as she had the first time but blushed as though influenced by the red wine whose bottle she was diffidently hugging.

Without taking his eyes off the pages, Narit muttered, 'Hello, Tar.'

'You were so sure it was me in this bar and not someone else?'

Narit looked up cheekily and said, 'Must I say I smelled your perfume, and glimpsed your legs?'

'You are pathetic!' snapped Kwantar before pushing annoyingly at her boyfriend. Narit responded with a guffaw. Having put down the bottle and slapped her purse down on the table, Kwantar squeezed herself into the folding chair opposite him, waiting for him to acknowledge her as she continued to stare.

Narit knew he had to close his book and did so before putting it on the table. Kwantar tried to size up what it was about, but its utopian-sounding title made it feel like a political discourse or hardcore philosophy.

'It's a novel by ML Krukrit Pramoj,' Narit said knowingly, hands clasped around his crossed legs. 'Come on, why do you girls get up in arms over such complimentary remarks?'

'You girls?'

'I was just pulling your leg,' Narit stopped mid-sentence, his smile distorting into a smirk. 'Tell me again, what did you say when you came in?'

'I asked if you wanted some wine, and I knew you heard me.'

'No, I didn't.'

'Yes, you did.'

'Well, if you say so.'

'And?'

'I still don't know what it's for, but why not? I'm in danger of breaking into a thirst. Let's ask for some glasses and fill her up one finger high.'

'This way, right?' asked Kwantar, illustrating her words with an index finger pointing horizontally.

'Careful there, I intend to put that into account.'

And now, it was her turn to laugh.

That laugh dissipated as Kwantar jerked awake the moment she started to nod off. She rubbed her eyes and smiled whimsically at the reminiscence. In the real world, she was already an old lady. The radio on the shelf no longer played Frank Sinatra but had been interrupted by the news of Pui Porntip crowned Miss Universe 1988. The rain still played as the soft background noise. She leaned over and turned up the volume of the radio.

* * *

The village, which was now inundated, could only be glimpsed in the flashes of intermittent lightning. Concealed potholes and water gushing from broken pipes aside, it was filled up with mud and drifting rubbish. The dustmen must have visited the area this afternoon, taking with it last week's floating mattress and other local's riddance that had run aground by her house's corner.

Darin sloshed through the gate, climbing up the steps which felt even steeper with an extra kilo of wet clothes. Her house was a simple wooden assemble, raised high enough so that the main compartment was always dry, and the open space underneath served as a common sitting area during kinder days.

'Mum, I'm home,' Darin fumbled in, knocking grit off her boots. She had gotten used to calling out to her mum now when she got back. It felt good to know that someone was there waiting, even though that feeling was sadness in disguise. Her mum's failing health had tolled the knell on her time at the textile factory. She was always home now. 'I'm so starved,' she slurred.

'Good grief, Noo Da, look at you!'

The unaccustomed voice startled Darin. A short, plump woman wrapped in a sarong stood hauntingly in the kitchen. Darin gawked openly at the tawny complexion of the woman behind the glowing circle of a lantern. 'Na . . . nana? It's aunt Nhamfah, isn't it?' exclaimed Darin happily after a short silence. 'Is it?'

'Oh, never mind who I am, you'd give your mother a fright in that state,' replied the woman. And as she pushed the door shut, the light crackled with static before it fully came on. 'Oh, finally!' Nhamfah blew off the candle and turned hesitantly around. Her thinly pencilled pantomime eyebrows made Darin burst out, 'Nana, it's really you!'

'Oh, stop gaping at me,' said Nhamfah dismissively, smiling at Darin. 'I know I've changed, and not in a good way. Bangkok can be draining at the best of times. I'll hold your bag while you remove those socks.'

'But nana, don't say that. You look fine! Have you been here long?'

'I got here just before it started to pour again, which, as you know, is barely long enough to talk about the weather itself,' Nhamfah walked back into the house with her usual loose step, rocking from side to side with her elbows sticking out. She started to giggle at herself. 'I'm sorry, just that my mind ran back to the moment your mum opened that door. She thought I was a stranger while I thought I was at the wrong house, if you know what I mean. It wasn't funny then because we were both quite shocked. Oh, how time has got the better of us. That is, to put it mildly.'

'Why do you say that?' asked Darin, stopping short at the shoe rack.

Nhamfah fluttered her hands nervously as though doing so would help her speak.

'I see,' Darin paused, a part of her started to panic. 'Mum hasn't told you? You don't know. Ah, mummy! The crossing got delayed in the gale.'

'Dumpling!' uttered Kwantar as she carried herself through the door. 'Haven't I told you . . .?'

'I know mum, the Indian Ocean storm has turned me into a piglet with frizzy hair,' said Darin enthusiastically as she was eager to relieve herself from the spot. She hustled about the house, storing things here and there. She soon poked her head around a bathroom door, 'Nana, you're staying for supper, aren't you? Please say you are. I want to hear about Bangkok.'

'Of course, she is,' Kwantar smiled, fetching the hanging apron and tying it around her gaunt waist. Her pale face brightened despite herself.

'Alright, I give in,' said Nhamfah reluctantly as if she was doing them a favour, but that was just one of her charms. She dragged out a stool and began rummaging around inside her tote bag on the table. 'You mentioned omelette before, and I'm hungry now. Here it is, I almost forgot, I've brought you some marrow soup. Shall we warm it up too?'

'Oh, yum!' exclaimed Darin as she disappeared into the bathroom.

'Give it here, Fah,' said Kwantar.

'Are you sure?'

'Absolutely. It feels nice to be useful once in a while.'

Nhamfah bit her lip. She was surprised that Kwantar was still able to make it around the house unassisted. Nhamfah approached the stove and placed the amorphous plastic bag in Kwantar's hand. 'You still wear the same things. Earrings and all,' Nhamfah commented, trying to conceal her own unease. The all too familiar jewellery, which now hung tentatively on both side her friend's face, swung a little as Kwantar turned for a pot in the dish rack. She wore them so often that they could almost be described as part of her.

Kwantar went on groping around the overhead shelf as though she did not catch Nhamfah's remark. 'Ah, here it is. Now, can I fix you some Oolong tea?'

Nhamfah placed her hand on her friend's wrist as Kwantar tried to run the tap. 'Tar, maybe it's better you sit down. You look like you are in pain.'

Kwantar turned away.

'I'm sorry, but it would be stupid if I'm to go on pretending that you look normal! Tell me what's wrong? I would've come back earlier if I'd known you were sick! Tar, you've helped me so much. Don't make me be ungrateful.'

The question cast a mournful cloud over Kwantar's eyes. She paused and slowly looked at Nhamfah to make sure she was ready for this. 'It's cancer,' she confessed. 'Oh Fah, not that face. Don't be so sorry, I'm okay with it now. It was hard to accept at first. But I've, adapted, to an extent.'

'How . . . how bad is it?' Nhamfah mumbled. Her face was hot. She was not prepared to hear something incurable. Unknowingly, she grabbed the counter for support.

'Not very promising,' Kwantar tried a fade smile. 'Cancer is either getting worse or remaining bad.'

'Don't be like that.'

'I'm not. I was just quoting the doctor. But does it matter? We all die sooner or later. I guess I don't have to be afraid of dying for very long, do I?' Kwantar seemed strikingly calm, her palms together in her lap. She was talking about death as if it was a pair of stockings she was going to lose. Despite all that, Nhamfah could still feel a world of fear in her voice.

'You're strong, it can be fought. Nothing is for certain at any rate, you mustn't give up on life.' Nhamfah waved her hands and sighed. 'What about our little imp?'

'I, well, I haven't decided,' came the answer from somewhere inside her throat. She paused to gather her breath; her voice raspy. She placed her elbows on the counter and sank her head into her hands. 'I really don't know.'

Kwantar went on to crack an egg, but it shattered into bits. She now turned around for a sponge, with a flat reserved face of a person who has learned to lock away her grief in the closet. 'Oh, Fah. What would every parent want but I wouldn't? To be there for their kids when things are difficult, and to be strong and healthy so as not to be a burden when they get old.'

Nhamfah heard Kwantar's tales from her lips and knew that she had been used to that kind of life, that she often had this lamenting tone when she could not have something. Nhamfah gazed at her friend who tried to scour off the mess repeatedly in circles. She took her by the shoulder. 'I shouldn't have asked. You go and sit down; I'll do the cleaning up and cooking.'

In the bathroom tucked behind the kitchen, Darin almost finished washing. While the clink clank clunk of cooking noises continued unabated in the background, only muffled voices and unintelligible words came through the door. Once she was sure the talk had ended, she got dressed and stepped back into the room with rosy cheeks and a twinkle in her eyes. 'Can I play chef too?'

The three of them chopped the wood into small pieces and then added dried leaves before lighting the stove. After the fire was fanned, some coals were added before the pot full of marrow was heaped on top. The soup simmered and steam rose towards the ceiling before evaporating through the half-shut windows.

'Nana,' asked Darin as she pour Sriracha sauce over her omelette. 'Are you really going to stay here for good?'

'I thought I might,' replied Nhamfah. 'I've managed to save some money. I'm just not sure if it's enough.'

'For a hair salon you mean?' Darin cut in excitedly, moving up to a half-sitting–half-lying position.

'What a memory you have!'

'Why don't you stay in Bangkok and save some more?' asked Kwantar, shuddering as the breeze whirled through the blind. She wrapped her shawl tighter around her.

Nhamfah flapped her arm in protest. 'You're pushing it, Tar. I'm getting old. I just want to rest. I had enough of being in the kitchen and all that.' Nhamfah, who was done eating, toyed with her arm during the suspended silence. 'So, Darin, do you all have to take turns cleaning the field?'

'It's a punishment.'

'A punishment, dumpling?'

'Yes mum, I forgot to do one of the Mr Pedantic's homework,' Darin sniffed.

'Wait, who's this Mr Pendantic?' Nhamfah cut in.

'He's a nightmare. Everything about him is depressing. You know, like the black coffee he gets each lunchtime, he just drinks it all in by himself in his room. We all think he's got a bit of a big head.'

Kwantar coughed to loosen her throat. 'Now you're saying that it was his fault to be a teacher. Remember, dumpling, you can't expect people to be nice all the time when you want their knowledge.'

'Yeah, and presumably, that knowledge is the button of a blouse. By the way, nana, that's one of mum's optimistic teachings—when a blouse is not commendable, speak of the excellent shape of the button,' Darin quoted.

'Well, I'm hardly surprised that comes from her,' said Nhamfah.

'Still,' continued Darin. 'I don't get it. Then, there was this nurse . . .'

'Who?'

'Nothing,' Darin scraped her plate clean. 'Anyway, if we're to wage a war on this man, first we need some dessert. An army marches on its stomach and a good pudding, don't they?'

When the night came, the rain had added a certain charm to the air. The flood meant Nhamfah would have to stay the night despite her family's home being a stone's throw away. And despite the atmosphere being perfect for sleeping, Nhamfah found it hard to close her eyes. Doing so would be dismissive of how things had turned out for her friend. But all it remained now was to wait for the morning, for the water to flow down the river, and the soil to soak up whatever fluid remained. Until then, the very same rooster that crowed each and every dawn would crow, once again heralding the start of a new day full of future memory.

Chapter 3

To Darin, passing through the first semester was like waiting for a cake to come out of the oven. The half-term break felt a little more than an extended lunch time. She had enjoyed the carefree sleeping in and fooling around with Vilai, but that had passed all too quickly and was now nothing more than a pleasant dream. Darin once again put on her uniform and set off to school. This time, she intended to turn in Khatha's homework punctually, or even arrive on the dot when history was the first period.

Khatha had been busy for a few weeks, buried in the arrangements of a new curriculum. He worked like a machine, aligning the school courses with the national examination requirements, and realigning that again with his own plans. Though the three eternally clashed, he tried earnestly to find a middle ground for them. Khatha was always up to his neck in work, but all the details were named and organized into the filing system in his head. Busy as he might be, only fools would assume he was too wrapped up in his own thoughts to notice them or their acts of mischief whenever they crossed his path.

For Kwantar, things went on as if nothing had changed through the dwindling rainy days. But Kwantar's crumbling health was a better indication of the time than the seasons past. She had recently invested in the hair salon with Nhamfah. As the shop got more popular, her friend was less often seen. But every time Nhamfah popped by, she brought with her all manners of gossip, ranging from tales of a cat stuck on a roof to somebody taking up a lover. It meant that Kwantar could at least cling onto the threads of the outside world.

Kwantar spent most of her time at home just to cope with the spasms of pain and coughing fits that sometimes brought up blood. She kept this fact away from her daughter, hoping that she was, to an extent, giving the impression that her cancer was more of an inconvenience than a life sentence. At home, Kwantar normally slumped into her normal ways just as when she wanted to lay back and have a bit of a rest. In dreams, Kwantar often saw herself, someone she now barely recognized, living so far off in the past that any connections to her having ever existed seemed false. Yet there was no regret to have been a more trusting being, only that she still wished that she could draw any picture, and it would become her future.

Today, like any other Friday, was always an exception to the rule. Kwantar now stationed herself by the casement, resolved and at peace. She closed her eyes and breathed in until the freshness filled her lungs. Her chest was giving her problems again, but Friday was always worth drinking a toast to.

Soon came the awaited sound of the gate screeching open. And a smile, that was the beauty mark on her painted lips, began to crack on Kwantar's face. She parted the cotton curtain and saw her expected visitor waving at her.

Kwantar opened the door. The man was very neat, slightly stooped, and wore the side parted hair she had suggested to him some time ago.

'Good morning, Tar,' said the visitor, his face beaming with a risen eyebrow.

'Good morning, Doctor,' said Kwantar, her voice a little more than a whisper.

'What's with all this "Doctor"?'

'That's what you are, isn't it?' Kwantar weakly chuckled.

'I feel distant when you call me that. Let's say it's difficult for we are good friends in any case.'

'All right, Anuwat,' Kwantar gave in.

'I've called to see how you're coping with the breathing. Is it still very painful after the drug I've given you?'

'I see you've made that the opening of your home visit script,' Kwantar smiled.

'It's been carefully written; I can assure you that. So, is it painful, still?'

'I can't complain. Would you like to come in first?'

'I can't now, but later when I'm back in the afternoon,' replied the doctor.

Kwantar nodded. 'Well, you know how these things are never 100 per cent.'

'Still, I ask.'

'Still, you ask.'

'I'll make sure you're alright. And you are. You look good today, Tar.' He blushed. 'Have you reconsidered what I said about the chemo? I know a friend . . .'

Kwantar gave him a dissatisfied look.

'Right . . . I understand. And, and how is Darin?'

'She's good. She's been asking about you.'

'Tell her I said "hi", will you?'

'I certainly will.'

Anuwat nodded. 'Right, I've got to go. Patients are waiting. Until this afternoon.'

'Until this afternoon,' Kwantar repeated softly, watching Anuwat disappear down the lane on his bicycle.

She soon seated herself at the sewing machine, unbound a pile of clothes, and started to run them up into nightgowns. Kwantar took on a pile a month from a go-between in Chiang Mai, but the income generated was barely enough to stop her from eating up all her savings.

The needle ran the thread in and out of the fabric pieces. She had never thought that her childhood friend should turn out to be a doctor—that plump awkward boy who did not seem to have a world. And now, someone in that notable white coat? Come to think of it, it was not entirely unimaginable. There could hardly be a gentler person who could be more needed for the profession.

Anuwat was a physician and an amateur oncologist. He was Kwantar's most sincere friend from the capital, who somehow happened to be transferred here and had decided to stay. Until a little more than a year ago, the last time he had seen her had been when he had set off to England to get his degree. Their reunion was a belated one. At that point, her cancer had already spread to the other lung.

Most of Anuwat's time was spent at the public hospital. There was already a long line of patients in front of his examination room.

'Sar,' said Anuwat gently to his nurse, with his usual subdued manner. 'Would you call in my earliest visitor?'

'Yes doctor,' replied Sarvitri as she would every morning. She was caring and always in a good mood. Anuwat would have hoped for someone more detached. But he settled for Sarvitri, largely because he was no different.

Most of Anuwat's patients were long-term ongoing cases, and he knew some of them better than he did some of his own relatives. So, even if it was Friday, he would not have the scruples to make just a perfunctory effort in his diagnosis. And had that day passed slower than he wished, Anuwat knew exactly who was delaying it.

The crowd got thinner, and the doctor finally escorted his last patient to the dispensary and dashed off. No time was to be spared for a late lunch or noticing that his white gown was still hanging off him. A short trip over the bridge and Anuwat arrived at the wooden gate of Kwantar's home. He glanced at his watch and breathed a sigh of relief.

The weather was pleasant. Kwantar was languidly bringing in her sheets from the front yard. They billowed in the breeze like the loose clothes that draped her body or the flowing strands of hair that sometimes escaped from behind her ear. Anuwat stood watching her, still and reticent.

Kwantar turned to pick up a pillowcase from the plastic basket and saw him. She smiled and received his smile in return.

'Afternoon,' said the doctor, 'I have to confess I have been observing you.' Having let himself in, Anuwat walked towards Kwantar and started removing clothes pegs.

'I didn't expect you this early. But this is a nice surprise.' Kwantar made an attempt to block the abating sun with her forearm.

'Today wasn't very busy. Perhaps people are getting healthier, and they've stopped seeing me.'

Kwantar responded by just staring knowingly at his gown and saying nothing. Anuwat noticed his coat for the first time and was suddenly self-conscious.

'Well, I forgot,' Anuwat shrugged, though looking perfectly comfortable in it. 'There are also times when I intentionally keep it on too, you know. Sometimes I just need to feel more like a doctor. But never mind me. Any plans for the afternoon?'

Kwantar paused and narrowed her eyes. 'I would've said picnic, but, given my current state, how about going to the temple? It's a full moon.'

'Why, we can grab some snacks along the way, and I think I can recall some good spots around the temple,' Anuwat said. 'Say you agree, it'll be nice, especially seeing as it's a full moon.'

Kwantar stopped folding her clothes and sighed inwardly. She nodded at last.

After a quick trip to a grocery shop, they were ready. Anuwat threw his leg over his bicycle, soon caught his peddle stroke and off they wobbled towards the outskirts. Kwantar, sitting side-saddle at the back, was clutching onto her seat fearfully as the bike shuddered over the hardened ruts of numerous carriages and buffalo. The rice swished in the gentle breeze, the same cool breeze that caressed their cheeks as they rolled along the shade of a woodland's fringe.

The double roof tiers, radiating with oranges and browns, soon peeked out from behind the waving trees. The pair turned one last corner and came to a stop. It was so serene at the gate of the temple that they could hear their own footsteps. They soon went down on their knees and started praying with jasmine garlands. The Buddha image stood tall, his long benevolent eyes gazing down. As both a witness and an audience, the clay-cast figure offered inspiration to those who had pledged to fulfil their wishes through their own effort that was besides words of appeal. Kwantar and Anuwat realized that too well, yet it was hard not to judge their own fates and 'mumbling' for more.

'Do you believe that people will see each other again in the next life if they make merit together?' asked Kwantar when they came out traipsing into the trough of the valley.

Anuwat looked far away and said, 'No, I don't.'

'Oh?'

'I believe in many things, Tar, progress for one,' Anuwat walked hands in pockets. 'Let's put it this way. I don't know about the next life, but I hope for all my wishes to take place in this one while I can feel them with this flesh and blood.' He bit his lips and soon recovered his track of thought. 'Truth is, there's little point in seeing each other in a later life yet not knowing who they once were.'

'I guess you're right. Only that the thought of us meeting again is such a comfort.'

'We could try getting to know each other again in another life. But there's nothing too broken to still try in this one. Being middle-aged, I'll admit we're halfway through it, so it won't last as long. But long enough.'

'I love your optimism, Nu, it suits you well. Shall we go and sit over there? I'm a little dizzy.' Kwantar padded dry her dripping face and pointed to a shady bower in the field.

'Let me help you.'

Bushes grew in a way that they seemed to be leaning impertinently towards them. The sound of the rushing waterfall pounding the rocks on the side of the hill could still be heard from here, with the smell of old fallen leaves on damp earth. Kwantar reclined on the curve of the trunk, looking curiously at peace with herself. She brought out a bag of foy-thong from the basket and offered some to her companion who was resting back on his arms. 'You know what I still want from the time I've left? I'd like to hear what people will be doing. Because that way, I can at least imagine something about them when I won't see them. What will you be doing?'

'Tar, you will see them yourself.' Anuwat insisted, grunting with an effort to make his honest line less grating. They had had this kind of conversation many times before. But try as they may, they were always drawn back to it for no good reason. Anuwat pushed up his glasses. Through the lens, the horizon was crisp and beautiful. He stared out and talked at the inhibited sky. 'You'll see that I'll always be a doctor. On that note, let's continue on a certainty that you will grow to be a very, very great old lady, seeing Darin make significant progresses throughout her life.'

'You're romanticizing the concept of hope again. Let's face it, though.'

'Tar, the fact that I see people die regularly doesn't make it any easier for me to see more people go. Including you.' Anuwat had involuntarily raised his voice a little, and this had startled Kwantar.

'I'm sorry,' she said promptly. 'Just that hope takes a great deal of looking after, and it would be presumptuous of me to carry it around.' She reached to touch his arm, but quickly pulled it back. Demurely, she turned her gaze away and coughed into her lace-trimmed handkerchief. 'Nu.'

'Hmm?'

'There's one thing I've been meaning to ask . . . when I die,' she began, as Anuwat took a sharp breath. 'No, please listen. I may not have another opportunity to say this. It's Darin, my daughter. You see, after I was disowned because, well, you know . . . I was on my own. I've worked so hard, hoping to win a kind of prize by getting back closer to where I was, I did not know that I already had that prize.'

'And that is Darin.'

Kwantar solemnly nodded. 'I'm setting up a kind of trust fund. And I wish, I wish, perhaps you could help me take care of that arrangement.'

Anuwat looked at Kwantar. While he felt honoured, that feeling was mixed with a more violent sense of dejection. By the tremor in her voice, he knew that she was in fact pleading behind that impassive countenance. Kwantar was pleading him. Needlessly uneased, Anuwat quickly told her not to worry and that he would take care of everything, then just as quickly, he digressed.

'What?' Kwantar interjected, not out of surprise but sheer bewilderment, that he should dismiss his awkwardness so hurriedly. In other circumstances, she would have inserted, 'Anuwat, please stop. You don't have to do it. Really.' It would have been more polite too. Yet as things had stood, she could not risk him withdrawing. She had had to let a graceful thank you slip through her tongue, with an appreciative smile thrown in.

'Oh, I mean let me tell you about someone, someone fascinating,' Anuwat cheerfully repeated his last sentence.

'Yes.'

'He's a teacher; actually, Darin should know him. His name is Khatha.'

'Oh, him, she's been relentlessly grumbling on about her Mr Pedantic since she got to secondary school.'

'I didn't know he was famous. Well, he and I, we meet at the orphanage and nursing home each weekend. You know he volunteered, so he's compassionate, all right. What bothers me is that sometimes I feel like I don't know him at all. Maybe you can solve this puzzle. I'm not boring you, am I?'

'Not at all. Do go on.'

'Right,' Anuwat, now beginning to feel settled in his new subject, swallowed down the last bit of the golden dessert and wiped his fingers with a napkin. 'The man keeps everyone at arm's length, not because his posture is flawed or anything, he's a hard one to interpret. The point is, he always looks like he's constantly brooding over something, like he needs to have something to brood over constantly. If there were no tomorrow, I think he wouldn't do anything different in that last day from if he were to live for the next 100 years.'

Kwantar was closing her eyes to the last sunray. The silence reminded her that she should say something. 'You know some people love responsibilities. They keep them occupied with the present, making them feel secure from whatever they try to hide from. I can understand him though. Nu, you must not judge him too harshly.

'Maybe it's just how he is. But I couldn't help but wonder whether there's a chance that the civil war might have caused him to morph into this creature?'

'Which one? The civil war.'

'14 October 1973. Tar, are you alright?' asked Anuwat, seeing that his companion was coughing into her fist, her breath coming out in shaky puffs.

Kwantar quickly composed herself and cleared her throat. 'No, no, I'm fine. 1973 . . . I just thought, well, it's getting rather late and cold. Will you hate me terribly if I say we go home now?' But without waiting for his response, Kwantar began bagging things up.

Anuwat, while something urged him to help her out, still tried to comprehend what had happened. But it was too late to broach the subject as he already found himself heading after her to the bicycle. They were about to set off when Kwantar drew Anuwat's attention to the field. Farmers were watering the rice, the spray creating marvellous fragments of rainbows. 'When the sun disappears, the rainbow will not be staying,' Kwantar mused. 'Nothing can remain as it is, just like what we have is not permanent.' She smoothed the skirt under her and clutched onto Anuwat's waist. 'You know, you are very annoying today, but I appreciate your eagerness that I continue to exist. It's certainly better than to die when nobody would care. Now, shall we? Darin will be home soon.'

Chapter 4

'Dumpling, wake up. The sun is way above your head,' Kwantar called out, drawing the curtains and sitting down beside her daughter. Darin twisted and jolted forwards, letting out a soft squeal. Her face was drenched in cold sweat. 'I, I dreamt, I was burned alive,' stuttered Darin.

'Silly girl, who's going to burn you? It's only Vi here.'

'Vi?' exclaimed Darin, taken aback. 'Why is she here?'

'I know who's going to burn you alive. It's teacher Khatha, right? We're meant to have a little review, remember? Before exam? Next week?' Vilai was spreading out the worksheets on the floor, her floral dress enveloping her legs.

'Oh?' Darin made a weak attempt to adjust her pyjamas' top in an effort to hide her embarrassment. 'Today?'

Vilai paused and rolled her eyes. Her flat open face with widely spaced eyes made the expression look even more ironic.

Darin sneered. Kwantar stifled her laugh that threatened to trigger a heaving fit. 'I'll let you deal with her. And Dumpling, I know you're looking forward to the market, but surely you don't want to repeat a year. Now go and wash your face. I'll cook you both some brunch.'

As the serious business of revision commenced, Vilai poked the tip of her pen against her chin, trying hard to understand what the author was saying. Darin, on the other hand, just sat there doodling, or picking at the crumbs of cake left on the plate.

So, when a cockroach sped across the floor, Darin quietly knelt down before trapping it in her hand like a goalkeeper. A victorious smirk spread on her face.

Vilai was still reading out to herself when the insect plopped onto her shoulder, struggling in its fall, and this gave Vilai an extra tingling surprise. She jumped to her feet and screamed out loud. After managing to throw the scared cockroach out of the window, she pelted Darin with crumpled-up paper balls. Paper missiles escalated to a full-on pillow fight. The old house was soon rattling with peals of laughter.

Kwantar laid back in her rocking chair, shook her head, and smiled. In this portion of the house, the ruckus was but a joyous background sound. An old classic was being crooned on the radio, while the pictures on the wall seemed to be tuning back to a time when they were so much more. In the monochromatic photographs, the new mother and her baby girl were all smiles. A much healthier Kwantar pecked her new-born on the cheek. The deep lines on her current face did not belong to the tender moment.

A blood-stained handkerchief clutched absently in one hand, Kwantar got up to switch stations. Beside the radio was a mirror in which she caught herself. Kwantar gazed in. There they were, the jewellery, which had taken their pride of place on her ears. Now they were all that was left of the memory of her consummated love.

* * *

'Hurry up, Narit, we've almost reached the top!' she shouted, waving happily in what seemed to be a small rock yard. Standing on the steep ledge of the National Park, all she was carrying was a hat and a nylon shoulder bag. Narit on the other hand, was laden with a huge backpack, a bag across one of his shoulders, and balanced on the other one was a live hen in a bamboo cage for the Muslim friends. He was trotting in a line of clammy men sacrificing what little free time they had to the painting trip of the Arts Faculty.

'Don't they all look like donkeys?' quipped Chaba, a close friend of Kwantar, as she breathed in some smelling salts. The wet towel on her head had long dried up over the course of the three-hour climb.

'Oh, hush, you have some nerve to say that! I think he's macho,' Kwantar blushed over her honeyed way of pronouncing 'macho'. But her bashfulness only prompted her friend to turn back and cry, 'Narit, Tar agreed you look like a donkey! Hey, what are you tugging at my shirt for? Narit, she said she wants to start painting before dusk so she can catch . . .' Kwantar quickly shot her hand over her friend's mouth. She smiled at Narit who was bowing low, resting his hands on his knees. As he looked up with an exhausted yet amused face, Kwantar twisted open a bottle of water and quickly began, 'Don't listen to her. Here, take a sip.'

'I just had some,' Narit replied as Chaba pretended to vomit before turning away.

'But you sweat a lot!' Kwantar scolded him. She could not resist indulging herself a little as she caught him admiring her, smiling to herself, safe in the knowledge that she had him hooked.

Metres after metres, Kwantar's each step was completed with shaky ankles and buckling knees. Yet, it was exhilarating to walk through the lush vegetation. To watch birds appear and disappear with a natural shyness, or suddenly to spot a family of monkeys crisscrossing the path and grabbing something which was not theirs—in one instance a sketching pencil tucked behind a senior's ear. Then there was Narit. He had agreed to accompany her. It was great that he was making an effort and putting his best foot forward at the beginning of the relationship.

Kwantar kept looking back at Narit making his way through the bush, worrying that he was carrying too much. He did have too much on him and, from time to time, swayed and slipped on the jagged rocks. But however often she voiced her concern, he always insisted that he was fine. 'The military conscription was worse,' he said. Much as Kwantar knew about a man's ego, she simply could not help being worried seeing him heave at the landing of each ascending slope.

'Tar,' Chaba called out to her friend, her eyes fixed on fornicating rabbits.

Before Kwantar could say anything or even giggle, somebody ahead of them shouted. 'Oi, what the hell does that silly girl think she's doing, dipping her toe in the pond? That's our drinking water!'

* * *

The pain in her chest intensified suddenly. Kwantar started to cough, soiling her dress with flecks of blood. Hearing a choking sound, Darin darted out to check on her mum. Arms still clutched at her chest, Kwantar told her daughter to stay back, trying to keep a modicum of composure to her voice as she did so. She swallowed back a mouthful of blood, then dabbed her mouth clean. 'I'm all right,' she said. And when Darin was out of sight, Kwantar started to fumble for her pill and gulped it down with a glass of water. She threw back her head and closed her eyes, waiting for the morphine to seep into her veins and quieten her nerves.

Outside, the water was filling up the riverbank as the fleecy clouds slouched across the horizon. A beautiful pink sunset was rounding out the afternoon. Darin blinked in disbelief and began to stretch. But just as the day started to dwindle, Vilai complacently slapped down the cover of a book. Darin immediately perked up.

The two friends quietly packed up and deserted the bedroom. Light-footedly they picked their way across the squeaky floorboards. But with the guitar slung across her shoulder and in her usual state of clumsiness, Darin banged the instrument against the cupboard. The deep hollow sound resurrected Kwantar from her dreamy inertia. 'Darin?' Kwantar gently rubbed somewhere under her eye. 'You're going already?'

'We were just getting ready downstairs.'

'You can just go, dumpling, I'll be fine. Nhamfah will be here any minute now,' said Kwantar, glancing at the clock above the bookshelves. 'Really, go. I don't like to be coddled all the time. Just make sure you leave the door unlocked.'

'Why? You've given aunty the key,' Darin protested.

'Oh? Yes, yes, you're right,' Kwantar paused momentarily in a state of queasiness, wondering at her poor memory. 'Well, take good care of each other. And, dumpling, don't be too late back home.'

The girls went sliding down from the stair rail, tearing down through a garden of grass and headed onto the ferry. The market that was just behind the quay was already teaming with people as though every traversable road ended there.

The shopping district was incandescently lit up under the dazzle of light bulbs. And kiosks lined facing each other, selling everything from flowers to food and modern art to handicrafts. Darin made her way to her usual corner, the shy, tucked-away patch at the edge of the meandering flow of shoppers.

'We shouldn't be doing this during the end-term, should we?' remarked Vilai as Darin started to unlock the instrument's case. 'Somebody's going to find out, and you can take all the blame. Behavioural mark, Da. It's 10 per cent, could have saved you from ruining your last semester.'

Darin shrugged. 'Just pull the plug on that. No one's that bothered. Now, help me hold this,' she said, stuffing a hat in her buddy's hand.

'What? Oh no, no, I'm not helping you,' Vilai gabbled.

'Come on, Vi. You're every inch a dear friend.'

'Bugger off.'

'Just hold it. I'm not asking you to extort, am I?'

'Okay, okay, stop nagging me,' she sighed, finding herself ruffled up as always, swaying between feeling annoyed and merciful whenever Darin played an innocent panhandler. 'I must be out of my mind,' she mumbled, standing as stiff as an electric pole with the hat held uncomfortably in front of her.

Darin started tuning her guitar with a look of fondness. Her fingers turning the pegs were becoming more accomplished now since the first day of her public play. 'I will be singing "The Star of Faith",' she informed the street. Her heart was pounding. Her blood raced towards her fingertips. Darin swished her wrist. By way of reassurance, she smiled and started to play.

As the performance unfolded, the bystanders came circling in. Darin felt at one with the lyrics of love and an unvarnished dream. Her eyes became shiny as she swayed her hips to the tune. Some individuals in the audience hummed along, and some feeble claps soon started to chime in. Then, at the last note, 'Bravo!' Vilai shrieked out triumphantly. The crowd obliged and gracefully applauded. The enjoyment dissolved in the wake of being indebted. Despite Vilai's attempt to circle amongst them, many looked down at the ground to hide their faces and stealthily merged themselves with other passers-by.

Darin flushed as the clinking coins came landing into the case. She was still bowing down to her patrons when a 20-baht note was carefully placed. Her eyes sparkled.

'This is for studying for the exam, mainly.'

Stupefied, Darin looked up, her eyebrows raised and became hidden behind her fringe. That compassionate, always smiling freckled face was somewhere in her memory.

'It would please him more than your little performance, he says.'

Darin's eyes widened and before long, her hand leapt to cover her mouth, her lungs sucked in air eternally about to exhale. This woman was the nurse, positively the one who was with Mr Pedantic. Darin deepened her focus and found Khatha's intimidating look shooting its way toward her, that sharp, deep pair of eyes. She could see in them a sort of imperative sign, of threat, plain as the cheekbones on his otherwise impassive face. Darin blinked hard and hazarded another look. Khatha had already turned away.

'Do you know about the song? It was his friend who had composed it years ago,' said Sarvitri. 'Anyway, your ballad was beautiful, and I wish you good luck,' she squeezed Darin's arm tenderly before hurrying after her beau.

Darin watched the couple until they had sauntered away into another alley. Vilai ran up, prodding her friend and asking what had happened. Darin was silent, her mind was back on Khatha and his exam. 'I'll tell you some other time. Let's go home,' she muttered. This, of course, came as a complete surprise, but more of a relief to Vilai who thought they were going to break up only when it was too late to go back home.

That night, Darin kept pinching her cheeks and slapping her face to keep her head on her neck and her eyes seeing the paragraphs as vividly separate lines. She could no longer say that she had forgotten about studying.

Chapter 5

A couple of days into the New Year, Anuwat departed early as usual for the town's orphanage and elderly nursing home. It was still dark and cold in the mountain, and the streetlights had long gone off in expectation of sunrise. Anuwat reined in his flapping jacket and paddled on through the fog.

Decades ago, at around this time of the year, his mother's final day had arrived in the unnerving stir of the wee hours. His memory of her was forever a living picture of a woman shivering on the poop deck of a Chinese junk ship. Her blue, bruised complexion hidden behind the shawl as the salty wind continued to lash. Anuwat had helplessly watched on. All the while the famine in Shantou was sluggishly sliding into the past as the ship sailed for Bangkok. They were heading to the city painted by the words of early day emigrants as heaven.

His mother was struggling with pneumonia. She was defeated. The guards gave the boat a going over before it docked for quarantine. Torches were flashed. His mother was picked out and dragged away. She was too broken to even move a muscle. Anuwat scampered after her and fought in her place. But alas, amidst the uproar of the family's protest and hollering along with deafening silence of the other shocked passengers, the frail lady was swung overboard as if she were already dead. The water made very little sound down below. Anuwat witnessed her bobbing up and down. A ravenous tide then came steamrolling over, pushing her down into the undertow that charged in the depth of the most beautiful bay he had ever seen.

Anuwat crouched lower and picked up his pace. His destination, from an illuminated speck in the distance, had gradually become a house tucked away behind a playground. The orphans were already flocking out to greet him. Anuwat gave a relieved sigh, here came the clamour that would dispel his waking nightmare.

'Doctor, doctor,' the children called out as they contested for his attention. And much the same as every week, Anuwat untiringly told them to queue up and attended to their wishes. Yes, he would stand in for their parents to whom they were delivered into this world unsolicited. Anuwat soon persuaded the gleeful bunch to go inside and proceeded into the hall. There he was amiably greeted by all the elders who were doing their morning exercises. He enquired after their week, listened to their grumbles and their repeated stories of whatever memory they had been left with to cherish.

Through a ramshackle corridor, Anuwat headed for the staff common room. He merrily entered and found Khatha all by himself, making a hot drink amidst the saturated smell of nicotine.

'Still smoking?' he remarked, sounding more than a little annoyed. 'After all these years while people are dying of cancer. Lung cancer to be precise.'

'The smell proves it. I can't get away with that, can I, doctor? By the way, I don't mind having that scribbled on my death certificate. What got into you today? It has never bothered you before,' said Khatha, without turning to see his colleague's peevish face. 'Tea or coffee?'

'Is that a question or am I to make a choice?' Anuwat bustled across the room, hastily pushing out all the hinged window screens.

'I'm making hot chocolate, that's another alternative.'

'Hot chocolate it is. Ta.'

They soon sat down at a long table at the centre of the room. Anuwat sipped at his chocolate, thinking to himself that it was a little on the bitter side. He tapped his armrest, a grandpa treading on a reflexology footpath outside captured his attention. Khatha, sitting cross-legged, facing the wall, lit up another cigarette. Wreaths of greyish smoke curled up in the air.

'How could there be so little to be had,' began Anuwat. 'After all, these people had invested the better half of their lives in their kids. All that just to end up discarded like an old pair of shoes?'

'Why mourning? This is already good, having children around.'

'They are not their real family, Khatha.'

'Well, they'll have to do. I see very little trouble in that when some people can raise their pets as family members.'

'Oh, really? These two institutions were merged together because we were short of staff more than anything else. But for goodness sake, Khatha, just come up with a better objective for running it as one.' Anuwat stared at his companion but all he got back was a groan for a reply. Anuwat turned away. With a huge journal already on his lap, he recommenced his interest in the recent findings on cancers.

Khatha stubbed out his cigarette in his typical contemplative style. 'I'd say,' he said, not one bit blind to his colleague's shift in focus. 'Concern yourself with the children. They're the future here. Actually, I've done the roadmap for you. Maybe you'd like to have a look?' Khatha pulled out a folder and limped over to Anuwat. Though taken off guard, he was nice enough to acquiesce his colleague's manner and take it. The doctor now removed the cover, went over the index before putting the papers back in again. Other staff had started to arrive, and the idle morning chitchat gradually ruffled up the subdued affair. Anuwat signalled Khatha to the meeting room.

'Tell me, Khatha,' said Anuwat, drawing in his chair. 'Do you really believe that the children will benefit from these, other than becoming articulate? These complicated subjects of yours, let me see, political science, history, poetry . . .'

'Now who's being practical! Look, I get your point,' said Khatha, leaning against the whiteboard, as was his wont in the classroom. 'But surely you don't want them to be prepared solely for physical work.'

'Ah, that's an ambitious man! Go for it then, if you think anyone is up for that.' Anuwat took off his glasses and set them down on the folder jacket. 'Not everybody is complicated like you, you know. Some people, who I dare say happen to be the majority here, just want to live simply and sufficiently. And that explains why we're here, Khatha.'

Khatha rubbed at his chin meditatively. He hovered around before seating himself down on a random stool. 'Where's this coming from? If you think I set before them some impossible ideas, you're much mistaken. I simply don't want them to be an automation.'

'You see these kids need something practical, not fantasy,' continued Anuwat. 'If you'd take into account that people become disillusioned with age, you'll see that without definite guidance, they won't know where to start walking, neither where they're heading.'

'The wanderers! Don't you think there's something charming and admirable about someone in the course of finding themselves?'

'No, I cannot risk having them become a lost cause.'

'Alas! So, you have everything mapped out for their life—growing up, working, living sufficiently, becoming an epitome of men in an agricultural nation? For them to be programmed and know exactly what they come into this world for?' Khatha furrowed, his face was fleetingly distorted. 'Factory fodder?'

'You put it rather too strongly, but yes. I'm not saying that some of them won't go to the factory. My goal is for them to at least steer clear of poverty. And that is just what we can provide— an adequate life. This is the safest path.' Anuwat sighed. 'Haven't you had first-hand experience of this, Khatha, in your past?'

Khatha looked up, stung by his words. His eyes misted over momentarily. Yet, he managed to simper. 'My past, oh yes, I wish it's buried for good.'

'Even if it's dug up, I doubt if it could make you budge at all.'

'The time was wrong for me, doctor, but I'm still willing to repeat it all over again, for all that, still.'

'You bloody masochist!'

Khatha shrugged before slipping into another transitory session of silence.

Anuwat flicked through the document again, intending to weather the storm.

The grandfather clock finally chimed and echoed through the corridor.

'Very well, I hope you give it some thought. I'm going,' and Khatha stood up.

'Khatha, you know, I've never objected to anything you've done, just take it gently.'

'Look, suppose you have a child . . .'

Anuwat forged a smile with perfect equanimity. A simple act as it was, it stripped down the tension. 'No need to suppose. I'm planning to have one for my own.'

For a moment, Khatha wondered how a real offspring would affect his stance in the argument, but when it dawned on him that Anuwat was a bachelor, he gave out a gasp of disbelief. 'Oh, get out of here! Who's the mother?'

'Bugger, can we finish this discussion later? We're running late already.'

'You can't leave me hanging like that,' cried Khatha, eyebrows furrowed. Anuwat burst out laughing.

* * *

After his morning periods, Khatha found himself straying into a nursing quarter despite his initial plan of sitting down and writing mid-year teacher evaluations. His earlier conversations with Anuwat found their way back into his mind. Something was not quite right this day, Khatha thought, his own reflection on the brown-blotched glass of display cabinets followed him as he paced around. He hated when someone reminded him of a previous life—all the degradation in his university time awash with make-believe, mishaps, colour and light, crackling just over the unbreachable wall in his memory; the fact of it being triggered disturbed him from keeping himself objectively occupied. Katha quickly dismissed it as a sort of foreboding sign and wrenched all recollections out of his mind in a snap. Through a narrow walkway, he pushed into a bungalow that was the staff common room.

The old ceiling fans were blowing out heat. The smell of a medley of northern dishes was rampant. Many were blathering on about things, which could not be too far from the scope of the residents there or the soap operas from last night. The only reason Khatha knew it was last night's drama was because Sarvitri watched it. He swept through the noisy crowd and slipped out. On a wooden bench, Khatha whipped out the remaining reports. A quick glance at the student's name and several complete paragraphs poured out into his mind. Khatha scribbled away, oblivious to the jumbled sound of children playing, of fruit flies hissing about in the garden.

Cigarette dangling from his lips, mechanically he took up the next book from the thinning stack. He read the name and retracted his pen. Ashes fell on the paper. Khatha dropped his roll-up and stamped it out. 'Darin Yuusabai,' he looked at her name again.

Darin had just failed another test. This was less a surprise than an irritation to Khatha. All the annoying answers, though not wrong, their quality was not in the range he could deign to accept. 'That's absurd,' he thought. Her time was wasted. His time too was wasted.

Just then Sarvitri turned up, squatting down before him, holding out some chopped guavas. 'Here, I had them saved for you. The room wouldn't quieten down until the others had finished with desserts.'

Khatha took a piece without uttering a word. His grip on the fruit tightened as he sank back into his pondering. 'Have I been cutting her too much slack? An orphan would have known better, dumping her studies like that . . .'

'Khatha,' called Savitri, tilting her head. 'Khatha,' she called again, as if testing her voice.

Khatha's eyes became focused.

'You look like you were miles away.'

'Sorry. What is it?'

'We're going to visit the doctor's very special patient this evening. He is admitting her to the hospital. There are some documents I have to go through with him. We can just pop by for fifteen minutes and go home together. Doctor would hate us to stay too long between them anyway.'

'Yes, that's fine,' replied Khatha self-consciously.

* * *

At the end of the day, Anuwat was the first one to be ready. He was already by his bike, looking somewhat impatient. 'Where's Sar?' he shouted as Khatha neared.

'She said she forgot her hair slide,' answered Khatha indifferently, dropping down his case. 'Let's pick up where we left off, shall we? So, who's the mother or mistress?'

'Oh, come on! Since when did you develop an interest in other people's lives? And please don't presume the whole world is hideous like you,' cried Anuwat as blood gushed to his face. 'I do not keep a lover, nor should you talk dirty about the woman whose daughter I'm planning to adopt.'

'Adopt? Can't you just usher her here like the twenty-three-something children?'

'Enough of that, I forbid you to smoke in front of me. For twenty cigarettes you smoke, I smoke one.'

'Very well,' Khatha raised his bushy eyebrows before pocketing the obnoxious pack, leaving his hand in his pocket. 'So?'

'This one's different. Go and get yourself into a proper marriage, and perhaps you'll understand.'

'You'd have me fall off my chair before hearing that. But still, I don't think so.'

'How long is this experimental living-together going to last?'

'Somebody has outlived the convention. It's 1988!' Khatha exclaimed. 'More importantly, married women become less defined.'

'Excuse me!'

Khatha shrugged and in a more solemn voice continued, 'Don't give two hoots for love. Passions bring but disillusions and mistakes. Now, can you just answer my question?'

Anuwat sighed, looking somewhat deflated. 'I've known the mother since we were children. I'm trying to stay positive, but

I fear the worst. The chances are she has weeks left. Her health is collapsing fast despite her comparative youth. She's always been a wonderful friend to me.'

'I'm sure she has.'

'A case study, Khatha. It is sad, very sad to know that one human life could be but a case study when you cannot save it.'

'And the father?' asked the teacher flatly.

'Honestly, I don't know, she won't speak to me about it. Perhaps he's dead, that'd be most likely. It'd need an utterly ruthless man to walk out on her.' Anuwat looked around and started to scuffle his foot. Powdery sand diffused and covered his oxfords. 'She's been head over heels with some chap at uni. Stooping down to be with him. Apparently, he was a bit of a loose cannon, caused all kinds of problems, and she managed to get herself disowned. Anyway, don't know what happened to that sod. The whole thing is a bit sad really.'

'Hmm! So, the woman you put on a pedestal then.'

Anuwat fixed his glasses up his nose.

Khatha coughed into his hand. 'And the girl, do you love her too?'

'She takes after her mother so much. By the way, she's at your school.'

'Her name?'

'Darin, Darin Yuusabai.'

Khatha gave a confounded chuckle. 'Ahh, her. She's a funny one all right. But I can't help but think she has so much more potential than she has realized. I'm planning to call her into my office again, as well as her parents. But now everything will be easier because it turns out he's standing right here before me.'

'My goodness!' Anuwat's eyes widened. 'That's a bit of a coincidence. But you cannot blame her. She might perform badly at school, but now you see why.'

'Yes, I suppose I do. But despite your feelings for the mother, I expect you'll be impartial in how she fares in class. Apologies, if that seemed a little hard. Ah, there she comes.' Swiftly Khatha turned to Sarvitri and shouted, 'Have you got it?'

Soon the three set off for Kwantar's home. Anuwat recovered in due time, knowing that his friend could never mean ill, it was merely his way.

Chapter 6

Like in all neighbourhoods, there were both good and bad, friendly and unfriendly people tossed in together. But the majority in this humble side of town had managed to drop by to show their sympathy towards the family. The grocer visited the house with two drooping bags filled with household stuff. The uncle next door showed up to waffle on about rehab food recipes he had heard his relative use to some effect. All of them came to express their concerns in their own ways with this one identical look in their eyes, the sorry kind that got worn at a funeral. In fact, they might be even sadder because it was the real rotting reality that they were making offerings to, not Kwantar's best portrait on the high altar.

Kwantar now sat sinking deep into her chair with a sheer blanket covering her legs and a barber cape draped around her shoulders. She held up a mirror before her as locks of her hairs fluttered and landed, some on her and some on the floor. Nhamfah was bowing low behind her friend, turning Kwantar's hair into a bob cut to simplify the upkeep.

As evening drew in, the mountains were being smothered by an impenetrable patch of fog. Food trolleys were rolling back to where they came from. Commuters were retracing their steps back home in a stream. And Kwantar started to worry about hearing the word 'tomorrow'. She thought hearing it would ensure its being there, waiting. Deep in contemplation, she

began, 'I'd never gone to bed thinking "what if I don't wake up."'
Kwantar cleared her throat to soften her grating voice. 'I guess it
was like one had never imagined that one would feel the weight
of this airy gown.'

Nhamfah let a thin section of Kwantar's hair down and ran
the scissors through it. Nhamfah kept quiet. She just listened and
tried her best to identify with her.

Snip, snip, went the blades. Occasionally, she looked up to
check if the length was level. The hair was symmetrical alright.
What Nhamfah did not plan to see was her friend's quavering
reflection in that quavering mirror. Nhamfah pulled the mirror
away in alarm. 'You know if you cry, you cannot breathe.' She
signalled Darin to go outside.

The sound of choking came seeping through the door. Darin
sank down on the terrace, bracing herself in her jumper as she
tried to ward off mosquitos. Somebody was appearing from a
corner close to her house. Darin stared harder and blurted out to
herself, 'Doctor!' She got up and stomped down the stairs.

'Hello, Darin. Are you well?'

Darin nodded.

'And your mum?'

Darin was pulling up the drop-bolt, moving her head in a way
that it was not really a shake. 'She's a little upset at the moment.'

'It's okay, I'm here.' Anuwat squeezed her shoulder gently as
he passed through, looking up towards the house.

'Hello, Darin,' greeted Sarvitri as she approached. She bent
down with her hand propped on her knee, an amiable look on her
face. Darin set about closing the gate after her, but someone else
was arriving in the queue. Darin looked up from the deep crease
at the hem of his trousers and her heart started to flip. Khatha
donned his usual overcast countenance, his eyes expressed that he
was coming in too.

Had the encounter been in the more familiar setting of the school, Darin would have just bowed and scurried by. But now all she could do was fidget. 'Teacher,' Darin stammered.

'Never mind, I'll just stay here.' Khatha gave her a quick, dour look and turned away. Darin rushed back in.

'Who's standing in front of the house?' asked Nhamfah from inside.

'It's nobody. A passer-by,' Darin answered with a straight face.

Nhamfah looked at Darin with her arms akimbo.

'It's Mr Pedantic. He came with the nurse.'

Nhamfah rolled her eyes. 'All right, just close the door quick. The flies are flocking in.'

* * *

Khatha was puffing on a cigarette as its tip started to glow in the quivering flame. Leaning casually against a wall, the star-kissed sky steered in. He took another dreamy puff. The drugged rhythm, the stubborn streak to be lost in thought through the unconscious act, then to see that high mental weight as vaporized fumes toasting the air. The self-indulgence worked like magic on an evening that was mild and velvety.

Just as he started to feel relaxed, and when there was hardly anything left in his anaesthetic mind, a huge, resounding thud from the house broke Khatha's zen-like state. He stared at the window. The door burst out before long. Sarvitri, now a grave silhouette in the framed yellow light, shouted, 'Khatha, help! The bookshelf has collapsed over her.'

Khatha quenched the tobacco fire on the peat, and off he lurched across the yard and went up in such a haste that he had half forgotten his hurting ankle.

A woman lay face down, pinned under a sizeable piece of the ruined furniture. Khatha rushed in, holding up the bulk

of what was left of a shelf in place of Anuwat, and together
with Nhamfah, put it to safety. Everybody else was trying to
scrape the area clear. 'Stay back,' Anuwat shouted, throwing
back his arm. He rolled Kwantar over gently. Her dishevelled
hair straggled across her face. He bent down, his ears next to
her mouth, his fingers touched on her throat. Sarvitri slumped
down to take her pulse.

'It's stopped!' cried Sarvitri.

Anuwat nodded, loosened her clothes, and started pumping
her chest. He pushed down and release the pressure. Her heart
contracted and expanded. Yet Kwantar remained as white as a
tuberose.

Anuwat fought down the tide of panic rising from inside and
did what he must in chronological order. Nhamfah was running
around fetching some cold water and a fan. Darin, a nervous
wreck, could only cover her mouth or clutch at her throbbing
heart. And Khatha, Khatha was guarding his distance, his back
buttressed cupboard, cool gaze fixed on the fainted lady, and
Anuwat performing mouth-to-mouth.

Kwantar's chest rose and fell as Anuwat administered CPR.
After the doctor had switched to chest compressions the second
time round, and despite the gravity of the situation, Khatha found
himself looking around the room. Scattered on the floor were
some cut-up newspaper articles, disarrayed ornaments of different
shapes and sizes, and bits of china crunched under his shoes. His
gaze was wandering among the debris when a photograph caught
his eyes. He could just make out a woman's face. He tilted his head
to get a better view.

Khatha's eyebrows knitted, and his eyes became transfixed. A
spasm of numbness started to seize him as he reached down for
the image. The porcelain pieces slid off the sheet, spinning down
onto the floor. Eyes still fixed on the photo, Khatha went to the
other side of the doctor. He moved closer to the lady, looked

back at the picture, and an inexplicable force sent him staggering a couple of steps backwards.

'Khatha, get back, she needs some air,' shouted Anuwat, pumping at Kwantar's chest. 'Khatha!' Khatha did not move. The doctor shouted again and Khatha felt somebody peel him from the spot on which he stood riveted.

With not a moment to lose, Anuwat tried breathing air into Kwantar again. After the third cycle, that long waited choke finally came. 'Tar, Tar?' tested Anuwat, padding agitatedly at the side of her face. 'Tar, can you hear me?' To this, Kwantar delivered a short groan. Anuwat produced a sigh and wiped his forehead dry with the sleeve of his shirt. He lifted her eyelids and checked her pupils. Sarvitri confirmed that her pulse was getting stronger. Exhausted, Anuwat gradually climbed up and helped himself to some water. Sarvitri took the fan and started using it to cool Kwantar's face. Her beautiful eyes were still glazed over, but the blood had started to return to her cheeks.

Everything had seemed to happen in broken sequences of pictures and static to Khatha. He gaped down at this familiar stranger, immobilized beneath him. The upper buttons of her gown were undone. Her chest was partly bare, and he could clearly see the bones through her paper-thin skin. Despite all that, her square feet, the proud, prominent, arched brows that framed her downturned eyes, the birthmark below the jawline, all those had stood the test of time. And of course, the earrings. What in hell had happened to her?

Khatha clenched his hands. His breath was short and fast. True, the fact that Kwantar being partly unconscious was a small mercy on his part. Yet, while it might prevent him from being recognized, seeing Kwantar now . . . He could feel his well-worn mask slipping as the memory of her left him stranded in shades of the past.

Kwantar wiggled her arm and her mouth parted as she produced unintelligible words. This urged Khatha to leave. As he exited, he took one final look with his grip squeezing on the door's handle. A just cause to stay remained as elusive as ever. Khatha sealed himself off at the entrance of the room.

* * *

Anuwat was back with his stethoscope. He placed the resonator here and there and plucked the equipment from his ear.

'Is mum going to be alright?' Darin asked timidly, clinging to her mum's side.

Anuwat squatted down and squeezed her hand, 'Of course, it's a fall, but she's going to be ok. She only has to rest for some time before she'll be up again and talking.'

'You promise?' said Darin wistfully. 'You really promise, doctor?'

'You'll have your mum back soon, and that is my word.' Anuwat tried a valiant smile. 'Now tell me, do I look worried?'

'A little.'

'Only a little.'

Once things started to calm down, with Kwantar transferred to her bed and the floor cleared, Anuwat's impassive face changed to one of concern. He eased himself down, mulling over what he dared not speak, if indeed he had dared to calculate it—the fear of possible effects the incident could have on Kwantar's deteriorating health.

Nhamfah yawned, and like everybody else, the adrenaline that had kept her going for some time had turned into a comatose one. Anuwat noticed this and asked everyone to go home. Nhamfah yielded at long last after stating that she would take turns nursing her friend tomorrow. Sarvitri insisted on staying and helping, saying she had nothing pressing to attend to, but perhaps Khatha might want to go and prepare for tomorrow's lessons.

'Yes, yes, but where the devil is he?'

'He's probably smoking. I'll go and find him.'

'No, it's all right. I'll do it,' said Anuwat, mostly because he needed some air too.

Khatha had been sitting below the house, still clenching the photograph. He was more than aware of his own mortality, and he knew that ageing was inevitable. But stealing a long look at her then, this was something else. Something was wrong.

Soon after Khatha got over the impact of recognizing her along with his own sentiments, the horrifying fact began to dawn on him that it was Kwantar herself, Kwantar who was his friend's dying patient.

'Ah, there you are!' cried Anuwat. 'You sit in the shadows. I can barely see you. We are in a bad way upstairs. A very bad way.'

Khatha answered with a groan in his throat. Streaks of harsh light spilled through the wooden planks above, distorting his profile.

'For Christ's sake Khatha, do try to be more cooperative. You could at least fetch Darin and Sar something to eat.'

'Is she—dying?' Khatha looked up, his voice betrayed him. 'Anuwat, do stop going round like a fly.'

'Oh, I'm sorry. But I cannot sit there and relax and feel useless.'

'So, is she dying or is she not dying?' grunted Khatha.

'Well, stop saying the word dying. That's the third time. Really Khatha, don't bother to stay if you won't stop being callous. Besides, don't make me talk of something that hardly concerns you.'

Khatha looked up, unsettled. Anuwat had his back towards him, his elbow resting high against one of the pillars. 'You're right, how could anything concern me here?' said Khatha laconically. 'I'm leaving.' He then rose from the bench, almost reaching an upright position when a thought crossed his mind, 'A meal you said?' And he swept past Anuwat like a spirit, taking all his faults and feelings in with his departure.

Khatha said what he said and started to go away. If his face and voice had not been warped by the realization, his faltering gait pathologically had. The shade at the opposite side of the lane concealed him. It was then that his legs buckled.

The slow moon had climbed and touched the top of its course. Nothing had yet stirred in the pallid casement Khatha had been giving all his attention to. The inanimation seemed forever captured. Khatha however did not lose his sense of time. He knew he had to get the bite, knew his responsibilities at school still deserved his time. Slowly his legs found what little strength they had left and straightened up under him. Khatha folded the photograph and put it into his wallet and lit another cigarette, but this time the smoke was steeped in derision, in heartache. Down a twisted path, he was soon swallowed into the umbra of the night that stretched back into his youth.

Part II

1973

Chapter 1

5th October

His fingers traced the outline of her crescent birthmark below her jawline. He narrowed his eyes and stared into the crack of dawn that gleamed through the gauze curtains. It was fresh and tantalizing, laden with promises. 'They're calling for constitution today,' he said, his head cushioned on one arm.

'Hmm? Constitution . . . another?' drowsily murmured the woman lying beside him. Her skin was white like cotton and smelt like orchids, the same orchids that she always wore in bed. Lazily she rolled over. The linen draped around her curvaceous hip while her head resting contentedly on his stomach. When he breathed in, it caressed her cheek; as he exhaled, it embraced her head. 'Politics . . . please Narit, morning is meant to be light!'

'I'm feeling quite light, as it is. All suppression will soon be lifted off the people's chests. What? Ah, it's quite a different world, is it, where your family is partly pulling the strings of the state?'

Kwantar looked up, mildly annoyed. Her shoulder-length silky hair fell, veiling half of her oval face. 'Aren't we doing all right under this paternalistic realm? It is a peaceful society at least.'

'A repressed society at the very least. The people you normally rub shoulders with maybe doing alright, while the rest of the population is not,' said Narit flatly, as though trying to tone down its meaning. As he turned his face away from the light, his gaze traced Kwantar's fingers that were lazily toying with his nipple, down to her rounded arm and the alluring arch of her back. 'The price of rice is soaring. That's ridiculous. Thailand has always been the world's rice field. Yet, we have to queue, and the rice has to be portioned. This putrid, fossilized junta needs to go.'

'Does clear blue water to sail on really exist? It wasn't there in history, nor do I feel it will be there in the future.'

'Nah, I cannot find it in the last fifteen years of history, but the future will take nothing from the past. Come closer, Tar,' and measuredly Narit drew himself up in bed. 'These eyes are great, but they'd also be good too if they could see what's hidden. Nothing is wrong with your ears, but they must choose to listen to what is right. Never shut your mouth. A voice is a vote, it counts.'

Kwantar sighed and rested her face back onto his stomach. 'Sometimes I feel like I am the normal person living amidst the insane. I'm taking a shower.'

'Suit yourself.'

Resigned, Narit reached out for the radio by his bedside and tried to tune it to his usual station. He had to tweak it a bit to get the precise shortwave he wanted.

After some tuning, the voices of the speakers came up, Narit recognized them instantly. They were Teera and Paiboon, the activists who were said to have a never-ending list of court cases for defamation.

Teera (evaporating with anger) 'The price of rice has gone crazy, and we're facing a serious shortage of sugar'

Paiboon, 'I say, this is officially a nationwide crisis. Surely, you know as well as I do, the Thais have never really cared about what justice the ruling clique employ to usurp power. But this outcry shows its most flagrant failure to dull the pain and raise the welfare of the people.'

Teera, 'Oh yes, those very sacred duties. Tyrant!'

Paiboon, 'My word, the National Student Centre is calling for a press conference today at the Volunteer Soldiers Monument. We'll be under a new sky soon.'

Teera, 'My dear fellow, you see lightening, so you think it'll rain, but that's not always true. In saying that, our brazen-faced FM Thanom is wrong to let students form a union. They're removing the system from its very root.'

Paiboon, 'Yes! Our economics and society have developed far too much for this paternalism to cater for or suppress. We'll agree to nothing short of a constitution.'

Teera, 'That's right. But what are they demanding exactly, the students?'

Paiboon, 'Oh, something extremely basic, but of course it bears invaluable significance. Let me summarize for you. First, they demand that people are to be aware and learn to cherish their civil liberties. Second, they state that a new constitution is to be promptly promulgated. And last but not least, political education is to be mandated for all citizens.'

Teera, 'I understand there'll be some kind of . . .'

Gradually, the sound of the radio faded to the back of Narit's consciousness. It had drizzled last night, and now the fresh smell of wood came through the window. The dew was still hanging at the tips of the green leaves and a light mist caressed the ground. Narit chucked his blanket aside, got up and stretched. On the wooden balcony, he lit his morning cigarette. The smell of the morning after rain got him every time.

The sound of the shower had stopped. And soon Narit felt his arm being tugged into Kwantar's embrace. She was already dressed in her flowing polka dot dress, and her full lips were painted an alluring red. 'You are cross,' she said softly, rubbing the small of his back. Then slowly she swung herself, facing him to examine his rigid countenance. 'You are not cross.'

'No, not really. Here,' Narit took a small package from his pocket, tucked it into her hand, then quickly turned away. 'Take it. It's a present.'

'What?' Kwantar grinned. 'What is it?' and excitedly unfolded the package and carefully plucked out its contents.

'If you don't like them, they can at least swell your considerable collection.'

'Earrings! Of course, I like them. I'm going to make my whole wardrobe match them.' Kwantar put on the hoop jewellery with dangling pearls. The gold shimmered splendidly in the sun. 'Narit, look this way, do I suit them?'

Narit looked at Kwantar as a rosy colour mounted her cheeks. He had to admit that she made the pieces look even more beautiful. The bold colour of her face added a sophisticated tinge to a work of art. 'You look lovely with them on.'

'And awful without?' Kwantar pouted a little playfully.

'That's hardly what I was saying.'

Kwantar knew that Narit was the sort of person who would go to great lengths just to show her something and not to tell. He loved putting his hands in his pockets and pretending to be cool. He would have her ask for things he already wanted to give. He liked looking at things, creating stories for them, then, letting her into the plots. And most important of all, she knew that what he had just said and done was just about as sweet as he could get. So, she smiled very warmly, saying thank you to him, vowing that she would wear them always.

Soon after they were done with breakfast, they loaded their bags into Kwantar's car, hopped in, and set off. Her father was expecting her before midday.

On the road below the azure sky where the clouds rolled, a valley of layered greenery laid beneath. It was so vast that all the while they were lurching on the winding tracks, Narit felt as if they were not moving at all.

'Wake up, the landscape is breathtaking,' said Narit a little loudly now that the wind was whirling its way into the car as it got exposed after coming out of a tree tunnel. He stuck out his arm and let the wind fire through his fingers. 'Our forests are getting smaller every day. Who knows, one day you might have to go to a museum to see a tree. See that sparrow, the one that just surged?'

Kwantar smiled. 'It's good you're enjoying yourself. But let me sleep during the day at least. A museum would be a marvellous idea when I wake up.' She took his hand adoringly and clasped it tight. Her head rested on the window's edge, and before long, she was asleep. 'Princess . . .' he whispered, feeling over the moon despite everything.

* * *

They arrived after Kwantar's second nap. She opened her eyes and saw the archway of her gated community before it disappeared out of sight over her head. The road soon opened into a wide crescent with all those grand houses she was only too familiar with—big, elegant gates, with name plates of the more important people in the Kingdom's higher echelons.

Narit looked around at the big houses. Though it was not his first time there, perhaps due to a rising nationalistic sentiment, Narit now felt that the ultra-rich had taken up too large a share of the wealth of this nation. He could not help thinking that if the powerful were more honest, every road in this country could have been paved with gold.

'Narit, just pull in there.' Kwantar pointed to an obscure lane close to her house.

'I know.'

'I don't want to get too close, I'm afraid . . .'

'Afraid of him leaping out with a rifle and shooting me?' Narit snorted.

'You know I could not possibly tell him. Not now. Especially at this moment when there's plenty of trouble lingering around for him to deal with.'

'Right, I'll just get out here.'

'Wait, give me a hug, will you? Just so I know that you don't mind.'

'Of course, I don't,' and he pulled her across to the driver's seat and wrapped his arms around her round shoulders. He could feel the warmth being transferred between them and knew it was mutual. He then kissed her goodbye before walking in the direction of the nearest bus stop.

* * *

Narit's lived in the Tha Maharaj area at the heart of old Bangkok. It was a three-storey rowhouse with traces of the rain that had left stains on the building while the sun had left it faded. Every home on the street looked similar. Nothing stood out, like the conformist nature of Thai society itself.

'Come quick, you're just in time for the best bits!' called out his sister, waving at him the very second Narit stepped in. Chairs scraped their legs as they were being pulled up in front of the TV.

'That lout Narong is giving an interview to the newspaper,' bawled his father, Wanchai.

Anything to do with the name Thanom-Prapat-Narong, the dictatorial elite, always put Wanchai off. Colonel Narong was the son of Field Marshal Thanom Kittikachorn who, after leading a coup against his own government in 1971, maintained his grip over the state; and the son-in-law of Praphas Charusathien, the Commander-in-Chief and the Minister of Interior.

Narit dropped his bag at the door and settled next to his mother, Yanee, at the dinner table.

' . . . A number of university professors and politicians are manipulating the students into protest. And if such an act is not considered unlawful still, I will likewise lead the military into a street protest; because they too, do not want to go to war.'

'Shameless, absolutely shameless, he means another coup!' declared his father, his face was ruddy and seemed ready to explode. 'I'm going to turn this off now. There. How dare he? Oh, look at him, he rises so high that he cannot see anything happening on the ground.'

'That's not smart, but it's good for us,' said Narit between munches of a pork bun he had just picked from the plate. 'The students will get more back up, though that will be fuelled by anger, rather than the actual goals we're demanding.'

'Hmm?' muttered his sister, Piyanuch, her head inclined to one side.

'Just look at the intellectual level of the government!' Wanchai exclaimed.

'They're clever enough to look after their interests all right, Dad.'

'Oh, their interests as he declared them to be are the pernicious threat of communism, of the Cold War, plus the fear of instability at national level. Everything is a sham turning the wheel of the coup d'état.'

'Clearly,' said Narit.

'Oh, do take a day off, Wanchai, dear,' exclaimed Yanee, coming swiftly to massage her husband's shoulders. 'You're forever adding sunshine to our days! Narit, tell him to stop.'

'Caught hunting in the national park. Dissident Ramkanhang University students kicked out. Wrapped themselves a gift of one year service extension. What's next, appointing themselves premiers, perhaps? They should all piss off!' Wanchai was intent, the muscle in his neck was twitching. He took a deep breath.

'OK, all right, I'll stop. Where were you, Narit, it's an important day. The dawn of liberty.'

'Out of the city, dashing about.'

'More faculty charity work?'

'Sort of.'

'Not seen Tar recently?'

Narit shrugged.

'I have no objection, you know. It's your happiness. But chivalric draw? There's plenty more fish in the sea, why don't you choose somebody who is less high maintenance?'

'High maintenance, dear me!' cried his mother. 'Big numbers might reflect the value of things, I read somewhere women far outnumber men. Personally, I find Tar a very sweet girl, and she's always very considerate.'

'Don't mistake me. I meant, for the nation to afford.'

Narit said nothing. It was not as if he made her sacred or could wholeheartedly accept the circumstances, but she loved him, which was why he cared so much for her. Besides Kwantar did not ask for much, she even tried to pay for meals when they went out, something Narit's male pride would not allow. So, remaining dispassionate as ever on the topic, Narit finished off the last pork bun and took the empty plate to the kitchen. Piyanuch quickly followed behind.

'What is that red thing on your shirt, brother?' she asked. Piyanuch was rarely far from his side. Being nine years apart, and as their parents were tied up in work when she was small, Narit looked after her for the most part. 'It's not lipstick, is it?'

'Must be a type of paint. Why? I wasn't home last night, so you suspect me?'

'Nope,' she replied lowering her voice, 'because I remember sister Tar's tone of lipstick.'

Narit chortled.

'Will you be back home tonight?'

'No. It's dull staying at home when a project ousting the government is on.'

'That's how you get your kicks, isn't it?'

'It's fun, true, but only on top of other things. The woe of the past. The pain of the present. The hope of the future. The bloom of democracy. Every man's opinion will be equal. You'd love that, growing up in it. Freedom is already in the air. All it needs is to get substantiated.' Narit's eyes were passionately sparked as he talked.

'How so? Whisk it until it's thick?'

'No, ignite it!'

'No one earthly man can change the world. You're not a superhero. I think you should change yourself.'

'It's not just one. All of us are putting our backs into it. It's the majority,' replied Narit, rinsing off the dish.

'Have something more, Narit,' shouted his mother through the living room. 'There're some omelette and rice in the steamer pot. They'll do your brain good, take it with you to work.'

'Here,' Piyanuch passed him a lunch box, which he then transferred the leftovers into it. Her fringe made it almost impossible to see her eyes.

'Thanks, for this,' Narit called out. But Piyanuch had fluttered off before she knew she was being appreciated.

'And Narit,' now shouted his father. 'Make sure you tutor those kids to think for themselves. Don't let them give brainwashed answers, like how Thailand should develop and prescribe industry as the only answer.'

'Yes, I know. Don't wait up. Off out.' Narit left by the back door. That evening, he did not go to tutor any of his students. They could wait. Instead, he rushed to join the planning group for tomorrow's campaign at one of their dens near Thammasat University.

* * *

'Here he comes,' announced Tohsak, a flabby guy at the fringe of the circle, rapping a board discarded on the floor.

'Where on earth have you been hiding, Narit? We all put our bloody names in,' cried Kawee, Narit's best mate, easily identified by his Elvis-like hairstyle and big collared shirts.

'Into what?' Narit was staggering in, his arms loaded with crates of beer so that he had to use his foot to swipe the door shut. After putting away the beer and reserving a bottle for himself, he walked to the inner side of the room and sat slouching down on the bed cross-legged. 'I've missed something, haven't I?'

'No, no. But I'm sure lots of hard work's been done, you know, studying anatomy,' joked a woman in flares called Neab. 'Ironic,' mused Khatha for, unlike her name, she was anything but prim and proper. 'Unbelievable, really, you're still together. Where do you fit in all your ego?' She smirked knowingly at Narit who was narrowing his eyes at her.

'Between her thighs,' replied Kawee nonchalantly before swiftly moving on. 'Oh yes, the names, they'll go into the back of the books which will be disseminated to the public tomorrow. We, the people who bequeath to the future generation the long-lost democracy.'

'We've branded a slice of history,' joined in a well-built guy by the name of Witit.

'I'm too late, apparently,' remarked Narit.

'We've got the first hundred, and now it's together. They're printing it.'

'Anyone got a draft? What's at the front?'

'The words of Rama VII when he abdicated his throne, here,' said a slender girl in the opposite corner.

Narit was dismissive. He closed his eyes and started to recite, '"I am wholeheartedly prepared to relinquish to the whole nation the authority, which I have inherited by rights. I do not, however, renounce it in favour of any particular persons or groups, to employ the authority in an arbitrary manner without heeding the true voice of the people." There, keep it. Terrific choice though.' Narit then flipped open the beer cap with a coin, and after having taken one big swill, passed it around.

'Right, shall we start thinking about the placards?' asked Kawee enthusiastically. 'Any thoughts?'

'How about: "We want a constitution,"' yelled Neab.

'Hear, hear, naked without one.'

'How inspiring, something more dramatic please.'

'Oh, your one is above all that!'

'Are you taking the piss?' asked Witit, clenching his fist and drawing back his arms.

'Boys, will you channel your energy into stuff that matters first? We have still got the painting to get on with,' scolded Neab, who had made it her business to jot down the ideas.

'What about, "Speak up, demand your rights,"' yelled another student.

'Boring, tame, moderate . . .' Narit droned. 'They're all too run of the mill. Statements. Asking, telling them to do what we want? Tut-tut. People hate being dictated to like that. Let's make them angry. Prim and prissy will not do. Don't tell them what do to. Spur them into doing it. Don't make them like us. Make them desperate to hang the government like us. So, try this. Write this down, "Country hijacked", "People's power squashed", "Our rights mutilated", "Why trammel, strip the nation free". There you go.'

'Somebody's in sparkling form,' sneered Kawee, 'Isn't that hateful?'

Narit chuckled.

'Good job our lead copywriter's here. That was awesome. Really awesome,' said Witit.

'He was just showing off,' complained Kawee. 'I could do better. Here, listen. This is dramatic, "Not protesting is female submission."'

'Get out of here!' shouted Narit, laughing all the same, amid the good-humoured booing and jeering. Soon, pencils started to fly from all corners of the room and some of them hitting Kawee hard in the head.

'Enough! I said, enough!' Tohsak rapped his discarded board again. 'Apologies to the ladies. Now move on; time is short.'

The making of the protest placards soon began. When it came to work, everybody put their more trivial bickering behind them and learned to coordinate. The poster boards and banners were soon painted, decked out in flashy colours before they were mounted to handles and poles. It was a little past midnight when every single piece stood all lined up, primed to be in the firing line.

Chapter 2

6th October

Saturday had arrived. It was a bright day and, in the distance, the Temple of the Emerald Buddha stood proudly in the sky line, the sun glinting off its pagoda. In front of it, Sanam-Luang, exulted in its lavish green, was becoming a stronghold of the protesters as they gradually amassed on its grounds. Their courage was contagious. Flags and banners rippled in the breeze, all spectacularly vivid and eye-catching.

At ten o'clock, the curtain rose, and the campaign began. 'Read all about it. Read all about it,' the group chanted as they entered the weekend market in the open field, flanked on one side by the police, and on the other, the reporters. 'Here's your invitation card to join a new country to be redesigned.'

A portion of the crowd were welcoming whereas some took the handouts half-heartedly. But it was a start. Once the first pile of leaflets got exhausted, the protesters took a break at the Volunteer Soldiers Monument while also waiting for extra supplies to come in from the publishing house. Only then did they branch out into a network, taking Bangkok from all sides—setting off from Lot Canal, Public Relation Department, the Road of 13 Department Stores and Banglumpoo Market.

Narit and his friends were in for the market. Though a couple of officers could still be spotted making sure they did not get too lonely, most newsagents had attached themselves to the main team piloted by the student leader, Theerayut Boonmee. It did not take them long on foot from the Monument to emerge into the liveliness of the place. Here, the students were welcome to share the hemmed-in streets, which were their usual confused self with no definite traffic directions for humans, strayed animals, nor carts, and the slim allay, whose ground damp with melting ice kept food and vegetables fresh in the sweltering heat. Some shopkeepers even emerged from the back of their dens and doled out snacks and bottles of water.

'I'm glad the young generation is so zealous,' said a woman with big, coiffured hair as she received the handout.

'It's the power of youth, and we mean to exploit it,' replied Narit. 'We're one up on them for that.'

'Support us,' Kawee joined in. 'It'll be for a levelled world. No more sub-class citizen branding. No more can we be left unheard. A piece of paper can be torn, but a stack of it is impregnable,' jovially he cited his majestic slogan, his quiff somehow boosted its effect.

'Oh, you already have us. We're your backup army, truly. The whole house is siding with you,' said the woman enthusiastically, glancing back at her family behind the restaurant's counter. 'We were just a little bit annoyed with the price rise initially, you see. But now, if a typhoon tore through the country, I'm sure there couldn't be a greater mess. Well, just blow the whistle and we'll be ready to march!'

'Thank you. That's very reassuring,' said Narit and with that they excused themselves. But as they turned away, the woman stood on her tiptoes and shouted, 'If you stand firm on your principles, even the typhoon cannot uproot you!' Kawee turned to nod in acknowledgment before resuming in the direction of the next block, trying at the same time to catch up with the tail of the parade.

'Good public response, eh?' remarked Kawee.

'Fantastic. It's like Songkran.'

'You sarcastic bastard.' Kawee was about to jab his fist into Narit's side, when a portly, moustached man in a double-breasted suit, climbed out of a Benz and approached them.

'A copy please,' he said, flashing a smile at the two men.

'Here you are. It'll be for a levelled world. No more sub-class citizen branding. No more can we be left unheard . . .' Kawee trailed off as the man released his grasp on the book, leaving it to drop onto the ground. 'What you're doing?'

For a brief moment, he held Kawee's gaze, unperturbed.

'Shouldn't you be giving it a good read before dismissing it like that?' said Kawee, his face blotched with redness. Slowly he squatted down to collect the book. 'Damn, all covered in dust . . .'

'What d'you want? Who are you?' Narit asked coldly.

'Someone who is a little concerned by your idealism,' said the man, wiping his hand with a silk handkerchief.

'That's touching. But we have no need for your concern.'

The man was amused, his moustache twitched as he chuckled. 'Please take one. You look like you needed it.' He offered Narit a cigarette from a case he had just taken out from the pocket of his suit. After a quick glance at the man's perfectly cut fingernails, Narit did not blink as he took the smoke without a moment's hesitation.

'I wonder,' continued the man, affectedly in his fine way of speaking. 'I wonder how certain things are full of contrasts. We protest against Japanese goods but the streets are full of their cars. We hate western influence, and again, isn't your sloppy shirt a cheap American cast-off? And dare I say it, there are even those who operate outside their social sphere in the pursuit of a bit of expensive skirt. Surely this is a whim as capricious as are the other motives, which are dead and gone.'

While he did not show it, Narit was starting to feel more than
a little uncomfortable. He flicked his half-finished cigarette towards
the man's shoes. 'Listen, my friend, why don't you get back inside
your car and fuck off? We're not going to patronize you by playing
slow. This will end sooner than you think it will.'

The man laughed; his expression became closer to a sneer.
'One man's gain is another man's loss, where then will things get
balanced? If past experience is anything to go by, you'll know that
history will not prove you heroes. It will simply repeat itself.'

'I'd love to continue this little debate of ours, but I'm rather
busy right now. I'm sure you too have more important things you
could be doing than speaking to an insignificant student like me.'

'Very brave, indeed! I'm beginning to like you, young man.'
The man laughed again, and with that, he turned his back and slid
into the backseat of his car. The vehicle soon disappeared as it
exited the roundabout.

Kawee looked askance at his friend. But all he had for a reply
was, 'A bit of a prick, isn't he?' When Narit seemed standoffish,
he knew better than to approach. So, he waited, and, when the
handouts had all been distributed, tried to catch up with his
friend's long stride.

'Hey, hang on a minute! Narit, stop. We're done. Why all the
rush?' yelled Kawee. Still Narit showed no sign of slowing down.
Kawee ran after him and pulled at his friend's shoulder.

Narit whirled round, 'Oh, it's you.'

'Did you see it?' asked Kawee, panting a little.

'See what?''

'That car's license plate.'

'Yes, toothed-wheel symbol, a military car. So?' said Narit,
intentionally picking up his pace. They were still some distance
behind the main group.

'You're sure that you don't know him?'

'No. Haven't you been listening?'

'I don't know, Narit. He seemed very interested in you. It was like he was holding back something else,' said Kawee as he gazed intently at his friend. 'Like, something aside from the protest. I know, I know, incidents like this only happen in soaps. But tell me, are things with Tar getting serious?'

'Whatever does that have to do with anything?' growled Narit, his words growing increasingly exact.

'But she ... well how should I put it? The elites are a completely different breed! None of them can be trusted, and I mean none of them.'

'Like having a terrorist affiliation, I presume.'

'You're playing with fire, Narit,' growled Kawee.

'And what do you call this?'

'Listen, everything's factored in.' Kawee carried on jogging after his friend, orchestrating his wanting for words with his flustering hands. Then he went on, 'What did he say again? He said something about chasing rich girls. Do we know any working-class guy dating a posh girl?'

'Are you a comic now? What exactly are you getting at?' snapped Narit, bringing himself to an abrupt halt. He looked his friend square in the eyes. 'Even—and that's a big even—even if that has anything to do with Tar, how would it affect what we're doing now?'

'I'd say, a great deal, Narit,' replied Kawee, his hands pressing against his friend's chest.

'For fuck's sake, me? You think I'm a child? I know it won't last, all right?' Narit paused. He looked to the ground, then measuredly turned to his friend again. 'Say what you will, it's a free world, and I won't be denying it because I could be at fault. Just don't push your strayed faith into people, Kawee. They don't live after your image.'

'Fine,' Kawee patted his friend on the back. A passive smile soon spanned gradually across his face. 'I'm just fucking with you,

you know. Feeling quite relieved now though, knowing that you intent to stay rational throughout the march. But don't get too involved. This one might get too personal, even for you.'

'Dickhead,' replied Narit. They walked on and soon fell into step with rest of the group who had just turned the market's border. Narit and friends then trooped past Daimaru, eventually rejoining the main team at Pratumwan Shopping Centre.

Two o'clock, after crossing the fashionable district where teenagers flaunted their avant-garde ensembles of kipper ties, platform soles, flares, and miniskirts, the procession crossed the bridge to the busiest wholesale area, Pratunam. The police still glued themselves adamantly to the cheery protestors. Wherever Narit chose to look, he was sure to see them patrolling around in their khaki uniforms. They had been lethargic company initially, but something much closer to an escort as the day heated up. While the group went on shouting out slogans, the officers now had their babbling walkie-talkies clenched in their hands. Over the last couple of hours, there had been a clear shift in mood.

It was not just Narit who had noticed this change. Many of the fellow protesters started to look around anxiously. Narit looked over to the steps where the high rank was standing.

The cops had stopped shuffling about or looking indifferent. Their eyes were beeping signals to one another. Fingers started to point at particular individuals. Then, in a flash, they charged.

A profound sense of confusion stole over Narit. His eyes were jumping. Most of the protestors, if they were not already been charged at, darted for the buildings or alleyways nearby. Narit pulled Kawee away from the melee and started to make a run for it, only to crash into a gang of police. They pushed each other away and swerved in different directions.

'Him!' an officer shouted from the side-line, and like a pack of rabid hounds, they swarmed after Narit, rushing past Kawee as if he was invisible. One of his pursuers jumped out and grabbed hold of the scruff of his collar. But Narit kicked out frantically and managed to slip loose. Another sprang at him, whipping out his truncheon. The first blows whizzed past his temple by a hair's breadth. But a few hits soon landed on Narit's flailing arms and stomach before he was finally finished off by an unannounced chop right across his spine. He was quickly wrestled down to the ground, landing awkwardly. A cop lunged forward and expertly tied his wrists behind his back. Wounded, and not just physically, he was soon dumped with the other wanted dissidents.

Narit could recognize only too well everyone in the bundle, all eleven of them. Some were students, but there were also lecturers, journalists, and even a politician. But what a wretched twist to the situation. The liberators, the saviours that they had been just moments ago had officially become mere hooligans in custody, now being chaperoned to the Public Security Personnel Division 2.

* * *

Looking backwards as the truck trundled through the threshold, Narit could already see a band of superintendents waiting their arrival. The car screeched to a halt, giving a strong shudder as its engine cut off at the side of a dreary maroon building. With the tailgate now unhinged, one prisoner after the other was soon snatched off. Narit cussed as he was pulled and shoved aside. He would have fallen, had the economics professor not grabbed him by the edge of his sleeve.

The group was then steered into a large room, made to stand before a long mahogany table. Glances were exchanged, but the wait dragged on. Some people had started fidgeting, while a few were visibly starting to lose their composure. But Narit, Narit had his hands in his pockets, remaining overtly aloof and seemingly bored.

After some time, three figures finally strutted in and sat themselves down at what everybody thought was the negotiating table. To Narit, it was more like pageantry, and so he turned his head down and smirked. The big man on the right wore the dark olive-green uniform that bore the insignia of Lieutenant General. The one on the left was obviously a Police General. And, of course, the middle figure was none but the famous colonel Narong Jarusatien, the heir to the regime.

The Police General sat erect, looking disinterestedly at the captives. Narong was more relaxed, with his arm thrown over the back of his chair. The General leaned forward; his eyes squinted as he scanned the individuals in the line. Once he was satisfied, he pointed at a rolled-up piece of paper at Narit and sternly directed a command to his adjutant, 'Major, that one, one–two–three–four, yes, keep it off-record. Have him locked up in a separate room. Away with him, now. We need to have a little chat with the rest.'

* * *

Narit was thrown inside an empty room, paint buckets sat on untiled floor and the aluminium ladder slouched against a wall. The latex smell accounted for stale air and dizzy atmosphere— nothing a cigarette from the back of his jeans could not fix.

Narit drew out a tube, and as the smell of nicotine shot up his nostrils, tried to comprehend the situation. Even if the upshot of peaceful protest was then to get thrashed and meted out with illustrious charges like 'suspected of being a communist' or 'congregating with intent to hold political assembly in contravention of Revolutionary Decree'—which was perfectly predictable—why has he been singled out? What additional charge was he brought in on to have been ricocheted from the usual route?

Across the room he began to walk, unaware that he was chewing on cigarette. The initial shock of the last few hours started to wear off and the pain started to take hold. He eyed his bruises, the livid purplish swelling on his right ankle, which was excruciating when he tried to roll. His other injuries were superficial. Scratches here and there and a little bleeding. He spat out the stub.

The louder albeit muffled noises of chatting and footsteps had long receded to nothing. According to his watch, the fifth hour had passed. Frustrated, Narit swiped off his shoe and flung it at the door. Wham! It was a hateful bang, a strange echo of his last thread of patience snapped. Narit laughed malevolently. What a wicked sound his pride had taken for a knock.

His throat was parched and had not been helped by puffing away half a packet of cigarettes. 'Water,' said Narit, clenching his fist tightly in an attempt of self-discipline. 'Right, how about the loo then? Great.' But the need to urinate was becoming increasingly urgent. A glimpse of the paint buckets caught his sight again, and an impression glared vividly in his mind. It was not only the latrine he had secured, but more than that, an idea. A smug flush of self-congratulation spread over his face as he took a leak.

Apart from the white paint bucket in which his urine had layered in, there was also a brown one. Narit took off his shirt and twisted it into a makeshift brush.

Gauging his canvas, the size of a wall, he rubbed his chin as he planned the layout of his art. Narit knew that his ankle was tender and unstable, but he was not mindful. Each time the pain snapped as he moved about, scaling the mental image to the actual size by putting marks here and there, he clenched his teeth, and the nagging was repressed. Resolute in his task, Narit cracked on.

From the upper right corner, Narit drew two wide parallel lines down to the middle. Paint trailed behind as it sank in. Soon a gigantic calf and foot appeared. For the big toe, he sketched an enormous head of a bald man to depict Thanom. At the second one, squared-sunglasses, egg-shaped face and double-chin for Praphat. Another one a triangular head, looking like a monkey with a moustache to illustrate Narong. He then finished by joining the fragmentary lines to complete an upward-tilted foot which was crushing down on its sole.

Below the heel, Narit daubed citizens who were already flattened to mush. But next to them on the left shortly emerged the ones who, instead of filching away from the civic affairs, had put themselves forward. Narit then stroked upward, pointy lines, arming each hand with spears. Now that normal, compromising men had to become fighters, the path seemingly paved by roses had turned into a bed of spikes. People had flocked out, not exactly to bay for blood, but in attempt to guard the tricolour flag at the far end, the nation, religions, and the king. The three petty Hitlers would have to either pay heed to the people's demand or usurp the country over piles of dead bodies. But beware where the foot fell, Thailand's future would be decided accordingly.

After a long night's work, Narit started to tire. He finally wiped the sweat off his cheekbones, his legs shaking as he struggled to stand. Yet the story told on the wall still inspired a little smirk on his jaded face. He soon hobbled back to his corner and lay down. He gazed again at his drawing before placing his arm over his eyes. It was perhaps time to get his head down and rock the ghost of his determination into a deep slumber.

Chapter 3

7th October

A whole day had gone by with nothing happening. Another night had arrived as the room sweltered from the lack of ventilation. Narit was roused from another siesta. His skin was damp with beads of sweat. His rangy limbs were cramped, his lips parched. He was also very hungry. A glance at his watch, strangely, it was a quarter to midnight.

The guards were drifting about in the passage. Some gave themselves importance and talked loudly, though the switch of tone could be very abrupt. This change was usually followed by the clicking together of heels, announcing that someone more senior had just passed by. Nothing was stimulating, no paint left in the bucket and too much piss in the other one, and to top it off, no more cigarettes. Another click of heels soon had Narit leaned closer to the gap.

'Captain! Another one will be coming in later today. When he does, take him into the room, got that?'

'Yes, sir.'

More words were then exchanged.

'That NSC won't call it quits. Asking for trouble again, pushing out a statement to shore up those prisoners, demanding their release,' groaned the first person.

'Aye, better to keep their heads down a bit, these fools,' responded his colleague. 'It's Sunday, more work for everyone!'

'Funny, the words treason and traitors are really losing their meaning these days,' lamented another. 'This one was captured right in his flat. A student, they say.'

'Another!'

'Just out of interest, anyone know what's with the one locked in the colonel's new office? Why wasn't he sent away with all the others?' asked the second man unenthusiastically.

'Nope, just to follow orders. Who knows when the wind might change?'

'You've got it all figured out, haven't you? I suppose it's part of the job to keep an eye out for whose arse to kiss. Now, tell me, is it just me who has bugger all to do today or does someone have something lined up?'

The muffled voice of the men soon receded to nothing, carried away with the footsteps as they disappeared down the corridor. Narit was alone again with only his thoughts and the pain in his leg to keep him company. He sighed dejectedly before eventually drifting into a stupor.

Before long, however, the clinking of the keys pulled Narit back to the moment. The door swung open before smashing into the wall. Narit was startled but instantly alert. He twirled over and quickly climbed to his feet.

The vision of the soldier in front of him became increasingly vivid. The man stood with his jackboots a little apart as he tried to read the story the graffiti was narrating. He had a much larger frame than an average Thai, deep chested and an oval head, smoothed over by straight hair flecked with silver. Narit knew that when he turned his way, he would see a moustache curled down at both ends, floating high above his paper-thin lips.

The man was languid, measuredly tapping his foot. And with a lazy flick of his wrist, the door was closed. 'Very well said,' began the man. 'A picture is worth a thousand words. You really do have a flair for art, Khun Narit.' And with this remark, he wagged his index finger.

Narit stepped towards the man and took a long look at him from the side. He was right, they had met before.

'So, welcome,' continued the man, accompanying his greeting with a dominant smile. 'We meet again, and yet we still haven't formally introduced ourselves. Oh, you're looking a little on the fragile side. Should I call for a doctor?'

Narit did not blink. 'Your concern for my wellbeing is touching. Am I to meet you every other day from now on? I see you're a general.'

'Excellent! I like a man with spirit,' the man sneered. 'Now, have you ever wondered why you're the lucky one while the other twelve, not counting one more for tomorrow, were sent away to the Nakhon Bangkane Constable School?'

'Yes, it would be fair to say I'm curious,' said Narit, a hint of surprise creeping into his voice. One more? Who was the other one? 'You seem to know a lot. So, may I have the pleasure of knowing what you are planning to charge me with?' Narit feigned to beg, but he could not resist for long before adding, 'Only to check if my hypothesis is correct.'

The man shook his head slightly in disapproval, then stepped forward. 'It all depends on which of the charges I have in mind you want to own up to.'

'On trying to make a positive difference, for preference, and perhaps getting a public servant to budge from his chair and do a bit of legwork.'

'Legwork? I've never been scared of hard work. In fact, I rather enjoyed being in the trenches once in a while.' The man looked almost hurt. 'One doesn't get to where I am without rolling one's sleeves up. Never mind, to be honest, we don't need to justify bringing someone in. Of course, it does help a little

when we can find something that supports our case. We raided
your house . . .'

'You raided what?!' returned Narit under his breath.

'It's a disappointment to find that your family is immaculately
clean. Thought you were just as bad as the rest of them, not
paying their due to the country.' The man drummed his fingers on
his side thoughtfully. 'Now, what does it tell you when the police
cannot come up with something honest enough? It tells you that
they'll come up with something believable.'

'Brave old world,' muttered Narit.

For a moment, the man's mask of geniality slipped. And in
that moment, Narit saw the eyes of a killer. The man smiled again.
'Have I not told you, Khun Narit, that you mean a great deal to
me? The son of esteemed civil servants and the brother of an
adorable sister. It's an understatement to say that the men were
quite taken with her.'

Narit gritted his teeth tightly.

'Now, now, it was a compliment.'

'Your regime already lost popular favour, the only thing that
legitimizes it. You're in no position to gloat,' said Narit. 'Why
don't you get to the point and tell me what's all this about.'

'I can give you a job. We could use someone like you. You're
wasting your energy on a lost cause.'

'You're insane,' Narit sneered.

'I thought as much. I don't normally do deals. But of course,
we'll talk about gratuity when you agree. Think it through, I hope
to get my answer in . . . let's say, two days, so try not to need more
than that. Now, shall we call it a night?' Without waiting for a
reply, the man then went to exit the room. The door opened to
reveal a guard standing in attention. 'He is free to go, for now.'

Narit ran after him, 'Keep your hands off my family, do you
hear me?' But just before he reached the opening, the general
suddenly appeared before him again, looking him in the eyes.

Startled, Narit took a step back. The man was not smiling now.
'No, maybe you should keep your hands off mine.'

* * *

Narit staggered out into the street, greeting the cooler air with
a mollified face. Bangkok in the wee hours was subdued. The
colourful city seemed archaic under the thin smile of the waxing
moon. The freedom was palpable but brief. The man's final
sentence reverberated in his head. He had had his suspicions, but
they had been well and truly substantiated now.

Narit's body was catching up with him. The last twenty-four
hours coupled with the constant pain in his leg soon saw him
dip down to the curb. Narit put his hands in his pockets and felt
around for some coins. He counted his money, relieved to find
that he had enough for a cab home.

A familiar lustre of light seeped through the blind on the
second floor. He pressed the bell and almost in an instant, heard
footsteps clattering down the stairs. The light on the first floor
shot through the slits of the folding gate. A yell followed.

'Bugger off! How many times do I have to tell you that my
son is not a communist? So, stop trying to frame him for being
one. Hell, it's three in the morning!'

'Dad . . . I forgot the key.'

'Narit?'

Hastily, the first layer of the gate was pushed aside and
Wanchai's drawn and haggard face appeared, the impression
strained further by the threadbare shirt and shorts he was in. He
stared at Narit, his thick eyebrows and prominent eyes were in
such a way that it expressed both dismay and relief.

'Are you not going to let me in?' said Narit after a beat.

'Ho? Right. There. Come, I'll lend you my shoulder this time.'

'You need to be to my left, sorry,' said Narit croakily.

'Look at the state you're in, moving like a zombie! Those sons of bitches,' uttered Wanchai as he propped Narit up.

Hanging over his father's neck, Narit trod in wearily. He was then left stranded for a few moments while Wanchai swept things off the wooden bed. Narit looked around the house. It was as if the room has been flipped upside down, given a good shake, and flipped back up again. The smoked green wall, the colour which had always been soothing to Narit, now looked more bereft than the colour of a deserted garden.

'I'm sorry. You're all dragged into this,' said Narit.

Wanchai tuned around, a pillow still in his grip. 'Well, you heard what I said through the door. Don't apologize.'

Having heard the noise, Piyanuch peered down the stairs. 'Mum! He's back. Brother's back!' she screamed and ran down, but her excitement disappeared when she saw Narit. She stopped short behind her father's back with her head poking out. 'Nar, you look scary.'

'That's mild. Thought you'd go for something worse. Have you been crying?'

Piyanuch came forward, unassured. Her tears had dried, leaving white marks on her cheeks. Her head was bending low as she began to murmur. 'That's not mild. It's terrible.'

'Silly girl, don't be melodramatic, hmm?' Narit stroked her head affectionately.

'Don't . . . I just washed my hair.'

'Haha, okay. I really smell bad, don't I?'

She nodded.

'Now, will my little sister be more friendly and bring me some water?'

Piyanuch nodded again. She was leaving for the kitchen when Yanee entered the living room, agitated.

'You should have at least called! Haven't I told you not to get too involved!' she burst out at last. 'We were really afraid. A friend of yours rang up and said you were taken away. Who knows how many hours I've spent on the loo or watching telly in case there was news of you. Well, there wasn't. But here you are.'

'You're right, mum, I really should have called,' Narit looked at his mother, her hair dishevelled more than usual.

Yanee was shaking. She shrugged hesitantly, sat down, and held out her hand to touch her son's smudged arm. 'What have they done to my boy? What's that? It looks—well, it doesn't look well.'

'Tell us what happened,' demanded his father, pulling out a chair and sitting down.

'Loads of accidents and misunderstandings. That's all, and that's why I'm out. I know this won't cut it, but it's enough that I went through it. You don't need to go through it too, for today at least.'

Wanchai gazed at Narit. 'Well, I guess the choice is yours. I suppose I should stop asking, and we should all go to the hospital.'

'Let me be here for now, please. I'm happy to have come home.'

'Tomorrow then.'

'Tomorrow is the mid-term exam.'

'Well, just re-take the bloody subject next semester, or be forever hospitalized!'

'Come on, dad,' Narit protested. 'You're exaggerating.'

'Just look at your ankle and tell me if it looks like a normal human's, bent like that?'

Yanee suddenly stood up. 'Narit, dad's right. You need to see a doctor. No, don't object. I'm the boss now.' Yanee then went on to make several phone calls. She soon returned and declared, 'I guess we'll have to make do with the first aid kit for now. Wanchai, will you go to the hospital now and queue up for him so he can have some rest?'

'Right. I'll get ready,' replied Wanchai. He dashed upstairs and was back soon, dressed for work. He thrusted his feet in his laced shoes and moved at a brisk pace out of the house.

Yanee hid her concerned face in her hands before sliding them down to her chin. 'Tar was here looking for you some hours ago. She was really looking for you Narit, as if she knew you were coming back.'

Narit responded with a raise of eyebrows, as he took a pint of water from his sister, thinking, 'No, things are coming full circle.'

So much seemed to have happened in the past few days. Narit felt that he was caught in transit between morphing situations. But being surrounded by his family, right here, he tried to enjoy the precious moment of a brave warrior who was being welcomed home. Though nothing was news, he felt he had never looked at them this carefully before. Had he been too busy growing up that something staple like this should have been taken for granted and overlooked?

Chapter 4

8th October

'Kawee? Kawee, it's me.'

'Huh?' came a distant voice through the receiver.

'Don't you recognize my voice?'

'What?'

'It's Narit.'

'Oh, pull the other one.'

'No really, it's me. Listen, I wanted to know what happened and what's next.'

'N . . . Narit!?' said Kawee a little less sleepily. 'H . . . How on earth can you be calling me?'

'There's no reason why I cannot use my own phone. Just answer.'

'Your phone? You mean the call isn't tapped?' he breathed.

'Kawee, give me a break!'

'Hang on, so you're really out!?' Kawee erupted, his voice now filled with agitation and the urge to make sense of the situation. 'We thought you were in Nakhone Bangkane already. We were just going to come and get you.'

'Yes, but I'm not there. They captured a wrong guy, all right? They probably thought I was this Reich Minister of Public Enlightenment and Propaganda. So, look, if it's me you wanted to see, just get on your damn bike and pick me up. You know my place.'

'That's a relief, but what about the others?'

'You're the one who's had access to the news all this while, you must have a better idea than I do. So?'

Kawee yawned and paused for a moment and after what seemed to be a long contemplation, said, 'Fine, we are petitioning for their release. There'll be a meeting at one at the grand auditorium to visit those who were towed away. Let's see, what else, oh and I heard exams will be put off. They're going to seal up all classrooms this evening.'

'What did you say? No exam? That's a result. Come in fifteen. I need to go to hospital first. Then we can go to the uni.'

'It's 5 in the morning!'

'The sooner the better.'

'Bloody hell, Narit, don't, don't hang up on—'

Narit had hardly slept. His brain had been humming away, waking him every so often to acknowledge that he was aware of it, of all his fears and wonders, of the young man inside him that he struggled to hide from the world. He could not help but feel that his experience in prison had formed a cornerstone of his manhood and that it meant he could face everything now like an adult.

Not long after Narit got dressed, he heard a motorbike. Knowing that it must be his friend, he snatched up his wallet and bolted out of the house, gesturing for his friend to cut out the blare. Kawee was making a U-turn. His quiff was noticeable even when looking from the other side of the road in the dark.

Narit quickly locked the glass door and was about to leave, but a dark contour at the back of the house made him stop and take a second glance. From the size of the silhouette, Narit knew it was his sister. She was still, perhaps observing him or simply too uncertain to make a move. He held a forefinger over his mouth.

The figure seemed to be yielding and soon disappeared. She must have tiptoed back upstairs.

'Fuck, Narit, what happened? It looks like you've been in the wars!' Kawee, who was leaning casually against his Vespa, rushed to his friend's aid. 'Wasn't that your sister?'

'Why?' snapped Narit as he reached the sidewalk.

'Wow, she looks all grown up now. She certainly didn't look like that the last time I saw her.'

'I'll pretend you didn't say that.'

'Right, more importantly, what's with that leg?'

'It doesn't really matter; we're going to hospital. Anyway, I knew you'd come.'

'Well, I've come for an entirely different reason.'

'Oh?' Narit pressed down on Kawee's shoulders as he clumsily threw his damaged leg over the seat.

'A-ha.'

'Wait, let me guess,' Narit smirked. 'Because you needed me to write a speech.'

'Don't be so damn smug. You dumbwit, this Tarzan-with-a-dodgy-leg attitude won't get you very far,' Kawee quipped and twisted the handlebar abruptly. Narit was almost thrown off and had to seize his friend's waist. Kawee jeered and twisted the handle further. The engine jerked as the bike accelerated to full throttle.

* * *

The business at the hospital finished, giving Narit and his bundled-up foot just enough time to join the gathering. Contrary to the usual solemnity of the first examination day, Thammasat University was teeming with excitable students, especially with the thirteenth arrest warrant decreed. Every notice board was covered with posters bashing the government. Large sheets after large sheets of paper overlaid the walls in a broad span resembling a collage. The campus was being turned into a harbour for the rights of human and citizens.

Coming only a short distance from Tah-Prajan Gate, the Faculty of Arts stood starkly on the left side—two eight-storey grid buildings with a porch and a three-storey one surrounded a square yard in the middle of which rose a bodhi tree.

With the bike properly parked, Kawee took off his helmet and was arranging his hair when it struck him that his friend might need helping.

'I'm okay,' said Narit, trying to hide the irritation from his voice as Kawee held out his hand.

'Fine. I'm just trying to be nice. Seeing you hobble around like an old man with a crutch for prop almost makes me feel sorry for you.'

Narit scoffed but proceeded to lower himself down in the spreading shadow of the gigantic tree. His mind was saturated with his father's shouting at the door the previous night. He said he was proud of what he was doing. With his legs now stretch, Narit closed his eyes and took a deep breath in. 'You know, right? This Bodhi-yard is going to be an epitaph for our fight for democracy.'

'So it seems. The tree will outlive us all. Almost a century old, it was there even before Thammasat,' returned Kawee, looking higher up to the outstretched branches, which grasped at the sky. 'Gosh this we-are-God government just won't give a damn. What?'

Suddenly Narit thrust his crutch at Kawee. 'Hold it,' he said, picking out a folded paper from his breast pocket before flicking it at his friend. 'I wrote it at the hospital while you were dozing off.'

'Whoa, what's this crap? Ouh, a speech.' Kawee mumble-read the page. Words rapidly rolled together into one continuous and totally unintelligible sound. His eyes swept back and forth down to the bottom line. 'Because unlike youth, wisdom is no longer wasted on the young,' Kawee cited and looked up at last. 'This is the work of a true wordsmith. Bravo, I'm glad my sacrifice of waking up in the early morning wasn't entirely wasted.'

'You're welcome.'

'How about you? Now that we're gliding in the same jet stream, what would you sacrifice, Narit?'

Narit was silent for a moment, knowing exactly what his friend was getting at, again. He signed deeply and scolded, 'Are you blind? Look at my ankle.'

'No offense, all right?'

'Look here, Kawee, a smooth life bothered only with easy decisions seems to me purposeless. It's stagnant. I think I could live with any consequences when forced. I choose what my gut tells me while I can. Wars are expensive. It's usual. It's normal.'

'Yes, my friend, and it will make you pay through the nose. Wouldn't be surprised if you get damaged so badly before things even get going.'

'Ha! Might I know then what intelligent solution could my friend be contemplating for me? Look, if a musician can't think of one, he better restrict his thoughts to lyrics and notes.'

Kawee raised his eyebrows. 'Fine.' And Kawee pulled up his trousers, also reclining idly onto the bed of the tree's formidable roots.

Narit lit up a cigarette dubiously. 'I'm sorry. It was harsh, but I did mean it. Honestly, why don't you write a song? A powerful song to mobilize the masses.'

'I don't know,' replied Kawee. His expression eased up a little in the interest that the idea had induced. 'I ran into a composer's block recently.'

'Give it a go. You're tipped for success, more or less.'

'Just stop buttering me up. Right, it's time.' Kawee sprang up and after seeing Narit still throwing his gaze into the distance, remarked, 'You're not coming to the convention?'

'I don't think so. Don't like being interrogated. Besides I've done my part—that speech in your hands.'

'Everybody was worried about you, you could just pop by . . .'

'Nah, I have some other things on my mind this afternoon.'

'Like what?'

'Like having lunch with me,' a delicate, feminine voice broke in from behind. Narit looked at her and saw the usual makeup and the dangling earrings. But something was different. He just could not tell whether it was owing to the powdering or the intense hue of a citron bucket hat she was under.

Narit smiled weakly at her, and when he did, her eyes softened. 'That's a sound alternative.'

'Hi Kawee,' greeted Kwantar as buoyantly as she could. 'Perhaps you might want to come too?'

Awkwardly Kawee stood on the spot and, as he did so, quickly stole a glance at her. He was never pleased to see Kwantar. He had been indifferent the first few months as he had assumed that she would not be around for too long, but as the relationship had blossomed, his indifference turned into something closer to dislike. She was a humiliation to their cause. The fact that he was now made to feel like an intruder did not bother him. He was going anyway and eagerly so. Kawee excused himself.

'He could at least pretend to like me,' Kwantar sat down.

'Believe me, Tar, that was him on his best behaviour,' said Narit, looking at Kwantar's curly hair and failing in his attempt to resist reaching out and stroking it.

Kwantar looked at the cast but refrained from saying a word. Somebody else must have come up with these concerns, and she knew Narit hated concerns. Most of the time she found it best to let him act as if he was okay, though it was difficult to try to overlook such an obvious injury. Narit was like that. He carried everything himself.

'Lunch, you said?'

'Umm,' she nodded.

'Is it far?'

'Very.'

'And will that be compromised by spoon-feeding service?'

'I'm afraid not,' Kwantar giggled. 'Let's get a cab, hmm? I want to go to Bann Ai Din.'

Narit lit a cigarette. 'Why not. Actually . . . no, nothing. You know what, let's get a cab.'

'I'll find one. No, don't get up, please wait there.' But as Kwantar was walking away, she felt a tug at the hem of her skirt. 'What, what is it? I won't be too long.'

'Give me your bag, it's new. I want to see it, leave it with me.'

Knowing what Narit meant, Kwantar caressed his neck fondly. 'Is it very difficult for you to say "Let me carry it for you?"'

Narit chuckled, 'Yes, very.' With this, it was as the day connected seamlessly with the day they came back from the trip.

* * *

The restaurant, tucked away in a quiet soi of Sukhumvit, was reputed for being defiantly laid back in the buzz of Bangkok. High bamboo trees on both sides reached towards each other, forming a curve of a pathway. The ground was lined with hedges and shrubs. An assortment of pictures adorned the exterior wall at the far end, on top of which the old gable roof ran wildly along.

'Come,' said Kwantar as she slipped through the alcove. A graceful motion, the way her clothes move against her skin—a picture of beauty as ever. A few times she stopped and bent down to cherish a small flower, delaying here and there for her fella to catch up. She turned, 'The tortoise doesn't always win, you know.'

'Am I a tortoise now? By the way, when did I ever ask you to wait?'

'You didn't? I thought you looked like you wanted me to. And it looks like I'm being appreciated.' Kwantar slowly traced back her steps and when she reached her boyfriend, laced her arms around him. 'Here, you're going to escort me in.'

On the terrace, they sat themselves at the first table. The waitress soon showed up with a lunch card from which Kwantar ordered spaghetti puttanesca for the both of them. Now with her chin in her hand, she leaned against the table as was her wont. Narit, on the other hand, shortly found his mind elsewhere. Despite this, he still managed to mumble phrases like 'Oh,' 'Really', and 'I see' at the right intervals as Kwantar delivered her news. Kwantar thought it was encouraging enough to carry on mentioning the swing dancing lesson she had taken up, as well as her upcoming trip to Europe. That was until it was obvious that she had lost him completely. Kwantar waved her hand and Narit's eyes focused back on her.

'What was it you were thinking of, hmm?' she purred, crossing her arms on the table, before throwing herself back in her chair. 'You weren't listening to a word I was saying. Please, stop staring. Hasn't anyone told you that it's rude? Even with those eyes, you know you won't level with me, don't you?'

Narit chuckled and diverted his gaze. 'Well, you are wrong. I did pay attention to what you said, enough to notice that you haven't mentioned anything about how you knew I was out.'

Kwantar bit her lips nervously and turned her head.

Narit sighed. 'Did you have anything to do with my release?

'Could we maybe talk about this later? Let's not ruin lunch,' replied Kwantar

'Look. . .'

'Narit, please, leave it for now,' Kwantar snapped, exasperatedly tucking her loose locks of hair behind her ears. 'Just let me enjoy what I got right now, with you, with your baggy shirt and all.

That's the situation. You're safe.' The last words came out under her breathe.

Narit stared at her, blinking only once in the bright sunlight. He stopped toying with his cigarette carton. 'Look, I just spent the night in a cell, forgive me if I want to know a little more about what happened. Is that so bad?'

Kwantar gave an incredulous look. 'Don't be so stupid.'

Narit reached out for his water and took a sip. 'Tar, I was the only one let out. The others are still in. We were all arrested for the same political reason.'

'You were not taken away because of that,' Kwantar cut in, sitting up and arranging her beige skirt so that it spread out properly.

Narit's eyes widened, laden with embarrassment for the importance he imagined himself of to be for the campaign. 'I see,' he muttered and looked away again, deflated. His suspicion was now confirmed.

'I'm sorry,' said Kwantar. 'I didn't mean to hurt you.'

'No, don't say that, Tar. The big soldier with the moustache, who was he? Your father? A relative?'

'What? You mean you actually spoke to my uncle? What did he say?'

'He wanted me to jump ship,' replied Narit in a steely voice.

'He said that?' asked Kwantar, bewildered, then began to rub her arms in agitation. 'It's just his little game. He's having fun. He just wants to control me and ridicule you. No, don't you even think about it, Narit. Narit, listen, avoid going against him. It's a war you'll never win.'

'Well, maybe. But the playing field is even. We may thrash the government before they thrash us.'

'I am one of them, Narit,' scowled Kwantar. 'Maybe you think my clan is like that of those Nazi's architecting the Holocaust, but they raised me. I may not like my family all that much and wish them to be different, but they are my blood.'

Narit looked at her from under his furrowed eyebrows, hands laced on his lap. 'And what do you want, Tar? You don't have to live this lie, you know. It can still be the truth even if you commit to it a little late.'

'Narit!'

Narit once again reached out for his water and took another sip. 'Tar, it bothers me, a lot, that I can't see the future. I'm—I'm sorry, but this isn't working.'

Narit could almost feel Kwantar's heart sink. He grabbed the chair's arms and made as if to rise. Kwantar winced and, despite everything, managed to mumble, 'But you promised.'

'I never promised. I couldn't, not about us. I only said as long as possible, remember?'

Kwantar's face twitched in acknowledgement.

'I am sorry,' Narit apologized softly and lowered himself down. Not knowing how to channel the frustration, which began to surge, he resorted to the familiar and lit a cigarette.

Many drags later, Kwantar had still not recovered. Food was served, but she kept toying with her fork. It was then that they noticed a middle-aged man at the side of the table. He wore his trousers high around his generous girth. In his hand was a half-full jug of water. 'I knew it was you,' he hissed through his teeth, leaning closer towards Kwantar. 'You little bitch!' And from nowhere he emptied the contents of the jug, splashing it all over her body. 'Your wretched family took them all from me. All!'

Hearing this, Narit shot to his feet and swung a punch at the man, his fist connecting squarely with his jaw. He slumped forward onto the table, his knees hitting the brick ground. His fists clenched. Kwantar was taken aback.

The man slowly climbed to his feet, a corner of his mouth now twitching uncontrollably.

'Who do you think you . . .' Narit growled but stopped mid-sentence. He accepted, however involuntarily, that there may be some sense in this man's rage. And yet in a lower voice, he rasped, 'Take it back. I said, take it back.'

As Narit took a step forward, Kwantar slid off her chair and moved towards the man. 'I'm sorry,' she said. She held her hand out to the man, but he slapped it away.

The man turned his head from her gaze and shuffled away to the exit. Narit was at a loss as his anger was quickly replaced with embarrassment for what he had done. Kwantar was crying.

'Hey,' muttered Narit, pulling in her head to his shoulder and drawing her trembling body into his. 'You know what, take my shirt and get changed. You don't want to catch pneumonia.'

With very little to say, Narit sent Kwantar home in a cab while he himself insisted on returning to university after overhearing the incoming diners talking vengefully about the leaked minutes. From them, he learned that there had been a conference at the Ministry of Interior, and that the session had reached a consensus: 'Communism had insinuated itself into the student movement, and it is thus vital that two per cent of hundreds of thousands of students are to be sacrificed for the viability of this nation.'

In response, the students wrapped up the day with a furious mission of locking up all the classrooms, chaining doors, plugging plaster into keyholes and cutting off the electricity. The exams were to be postponed indefinitely until all the detainees were to be released, absolved of all blame.

Chapter 5

9th October

Next morning, the front pages were more or less taken up by the story of Thammasat's cancelled exams. Narit leaned on his good foot in front of the newsstand and smirked at the variations of the same headlines.

Today was only his second day, but he had found a way to manage despite only having just one fully functioning leg. Narit grabbed one of the broadsheets, put it in his jeans' back pocket, and started to wander into the paddy market looking for something for his sister. Piyanuch had not been well since last night, so Narit stayed home.

His sister was still lying in the same position she had been when he had left. Narit set down his morning shopping and went over to his father's favourite spot, the rocking chair opposite the TV. Due to his height, he had to slide close to the edge so that his neck rested precisely on the curve of the back support. He soon discovered that he could still sit crossed legged with no extra pain. Comfortable, Narit pulled out the paper and spread it before him. A cartoon about the protest arrested his wandering sight.

Narit threw himself back gently and the chair set about rocking. 'Democracy and a mask. Hmm, could either be—must not blab about democracy—or democracy with no arguments, or both.'

'Ha!' snorted Narit, his head still dipped into the paper. Then, with not much else in the remaining pages, he refolded the paper along its creases, and chucked it below the bed where all sorts of printed paper were stored. A whimper startled him.

'Nuch, what's the matter?' asked Narit. And as soon as he had managed to gingerly shift his body to the bed, Piyanuch came ducking towards him and received the comfort of his arm around her shoulder.

'You've grown up a lot, you know. You can't just climb on me like before.' Narit then hoisted his sister up by the arms, 'Up, come now, missy. You know what, let's have breakfast. Nobody is any good without food in their tummy. All right to get up and help yourself?' Narit asked, smiling softly when Piyanuch shook her head back at him. 'Never mind, I'll do it.'

After a bowl of soybean milk and some deep-fried dough, Piyanuch sat watching her big brother reading. 'Say something. It's quiet, Nar.'

Narit thrust his thumb between the pages. 'Still afraid to be on your own after all these years?'

Piyanuch pouted.

'What can I say, sister. You don't like listening to what I read. Why don't we go back to our normal way, and you tell me stories?'

Disheartened, Piyanuch reached for a pillow large enough that she could hug and rest her chin on.

'I'm at your disposal, sister. But I cannot always guess what you're thinking,' Narit was about to resume his read but ended up wrestling with himself. Eventually, he gestured for Piyanuch to come closer. 'You know, don't you, that I meant, "Tell me what's going on?"'

'I dreamed. What if someone comes after me, Nar?'

Narit was startled, but his face was rigid as ever. Now his sister had come up with this question that he had in his mind for a few days. He looked down at his sister. 'Why are you saying that?'

'I don't know.'

Narit nodded to himself. 'I'll take care of you, Nuch.'

'You weren't in my dreams, though.'

'I must be somewhere.'

Piyanuch shook her head again.

'So, what happened?'

'I woke up and saw you.'

'There. Have I not told you I must be somewhere,' said Narit, relieved. 'You're not angry that I was late?'

Piyanuch shrugged. 'Thanks for staying behind,' she said, hoping this would make up for her brother missing anything first-hand at this crucial time. She knew that nothing could be worse for him now than to be perceived by others as a fair-weather comrade.

Sound of the metal door clanging soon had both turned towards its direction. Having recognized the boyish appearance and her basketball shoes, Narit gave a knowing smirk while Piyanuch's memory took longer to return. Uncertainty flitted across her face before she blurted out, 'Racha.'

'Just look who's here,' said Narit, fumbling in his pocket for a key and throwing it at the folding gate. 'Sorry but you will have to let yourself in.'

'Lovely hospitality,' replied Racha as the padlock snapped open. 'Came back from Thammasat just now. They were sort of talking about your crippled luck and betting whether you would hobble your way back up there.'

'What's your money on?'

She grinned, sitting down with her legs wide apart. 'Oh, it doesn't really matter; we all lost the bet.'

'I didn't mean to be sick,' Piyanuch protested, still clinging onto Narit.

'So, it's officially started.'

'Go on,' Narit encouraged.

'We've got the huge banners hung across the gate declaring something like "Is Thammasat Dead?"'

'Ha! Why not!'

'Yeah, I know, this is child's play compared to the Chinese one. But don't "Ha! Why not!" We were missing our copywriter!'

'It can be helped. So, you're back from China for good?'

'I went to Hong Kong, Narit, and Hong Kong is British.'

'Yes, yes, I know it's just my wistful wanting of the Little Red Book. Would be interesting to be rightly persecuted just for once.'

'You still have a questionable sense of humour. Anyway, on the Chinese note, not sure if I would prefer the way things work here much either. In China, you manipulate people into believing a certain thing to rectify your faults. In Thailand, you modify laws to make cheating legal altogether,' Racha paused for a moment before continuing. 'Anyway, your speech was cool, and by that, I mean gripping. You know I like the part about the *mai-pen-rai* Thais winking at corruption as long as they can do business as usual.'

'It's a pretty obvious observation.'

'They were hanging on your every word, like you'd cast a spell or something,' said Racha, mimicking a sorcerer with nimble fingers. 'Imagine, ten thousand of them and in this drizzle, shining with this fire in . . .'

'Oh, put a sock in it!'

Piyanuch had fallen asleep after the talk had shown no sign of changing direction. Narit gently shored up her head and eased a pillow underneath it.

* * *

As dusk departed and darkness set in, Wanchai and Yanee arrived home from the revenue bureau. He was wearing a simple shirt and carried a suit folded over his forearm, off which a bag seemed to hang, too heavy for its weight. His salt-and-pepper hair painstakingly flattened by a greasy product. She was in a white fitted dress with big, coiffured hair, walking wearily in two-inch high heels, well protected under an oversized umbrella that was being held by her husband.

Narit made an attempt to haul himself up, but Racha had already reached the door and was helping his parents to unload. Wanchai and Yanee were pleased to see her and insisted that she stayed for supper.

Everything was familial at the table, the TV was on, and there were no middle spoons. After general chitchat about Racha's long absence and asking about their children's conditions, Wanchai commenced his dinner ritual of lamenting his role at work. He aired his complaints that the cabinet reshuffle, for the third time in the year, would jeopardize the livelihood of state employees. He said he was too jaded to cater to the needs of every new head and smoothen the path for his or her designated climbers. Again, he spoke for both of them and again concluded that life goes on.

As usual, Yanee tried hard to deflect attention to other things that were better suited for dinner when guests were present. Wanchai, on the other hand, believed such topics were necessary for the horror of the system to be drilled in and ingrained into the next generation.

Narit once asked his mother why she so frequently turned a blind eye to the injustice of the world. Yanee simply answered, 'I go mad if I didn't.' That was his mother. He knew too well she could only bear so much but she was quiescent and dutiful. Though when he posed the same question to his father, Wanchai sighed, 'Having a family is not an advantage, son. It's something that makes you proud but it also makes you rational.'

'You want to be rational?'

'It's either you are, or you are not. Live while you can, people don't become rational by choice, Narit. I want everyone to be happy. Besides,' he continued, taking swigs from his beer, 'the dirty job will have to be done anyway. If I don't do it, somebody else will have to. Somebody more vulnerable.'

That night, just as the table was being cleared, Kawee turned up with a guitar. The whole house took this as an opportunity to retire upstairs. The three friends moved outside to a small metal table under a stained awning, gaily set up for Maekhong whisky and a good supply of cigarettes.

'So, Kawee, bring us up to speed,' said Narit.

'Oh, I didn't know you cared. But let me tell you, it's been raining for an eternity, and the students are still jamming in the Bodhi-yard and the balconies of the eighth floor buildings. Unbelievable,' started Kawee, pouring the liquor and a dash of brown sugar into a bucket of iced Coca-Cola. Racha yanked in a fork, got the mixture blended. Three straws darted in. 'Me, I can believe it as long as it's not happening in our last term,' continued Kawee after a long suck on his straw. 'What will you guys do after this, by the way?'

'Definitely not job hunting; white-collar worker, meh!' replied Racha, her handsome face resting in her hand. 'Something that doesn't nail me down to anything fixed, perhaps.'

'Narit?'

'A professor.'

'A cigarette junkie, you mean.' And the two started to laugh. Narit was amused. He looked at the charring tips of the guilty warrant as its trails of smoke whiffed past his hair. 'Come on, Narit,' insisted Kawee.

'It doesn't look like my area, does it? But I'm expanding into it, you'll see.' Narit sucked up the drink in a mouthful before gulping it down. 'So, a future musician, have you already composed something for us?'

Kawee smirked. 'You bet.'

Narit spread out his hands as an invitation for a show, but Racha interrupted. 'Anyone got an idea why that girl keeps looking at us?'

'What girl?' Narit and Kawee spoke up at the same time.

'Over there,' said Racha, and she jerked her head in the direction of the closing lottery shop across the street. 'Why don't we bring her in? She looks lonely. I bet she could use some friends.'

'I bet she's a hooker,' chuckled Kawee.

'She's not,' Narit protested, aridly returning the girl's neutral gaze. 'Her skirt's too long.'

'Well, a woman all by herself at this hour of the night doesn't look that decent to me,' Kawee disagreed. 'But why not, as long as she can vote for my music.'

'Go talk to her, Narit.'

Narit scoffed. 'I've grown past one of those nights, Rach. Though I hardly mind if you want her here.'

'He's practising abstinence,' derided Kawee.

'Ab- what? That's a darn fine word, but you must be sick,' Racha nudged Narit with her elbow. 'Oh, come on, you stick in the mud.'

'Oh, just go Rach, don't mind him. He's conceived his way to becoming a father with that miss third year whose name we shouldn't mention. And now he does little else.'

Narit rolled his eyes, but his lungs were too full of smoke to answer. While keeping track of Racha going across the street, Kawee unzipped his guitar case and started to warm up his fingers. Racha ran into the rain, dodged a couple of cars across the street, water splashing under her feet. Her target appeared to be rather alarmed. As Racha began talking to her, the girl started to hug the curious package nervously.

It was not long before Racha was towing the young girl after her by the arm. 'Hey, Narit, got yourself a fan, hah?' Racha shouted midway back.

Narit raised his eyebrows, somewhat mystified as Racha settled the girl in her seat.

'For your rehearsal, Kawee, which we're sure will be as charming as ever, may I present our guest, Miss Sarvitri.'

Sarvitri was meek. She was not the most talkative of people and occasionally her fingers would twiddle something non-existent. Once or twice, she stole a glimpse at each one of them, otherwise she kept her eyes low and her freckled face hidden behind the curtain of her straight long hair.

After some gentle probing, they learned that she was a sort of house girl; that night she had come on an errand for her stepmother; and that the sugar-palm cake was a debt of gratitude to Narit who had been moonlighting as a tutor. Sarvitri's stepbrother had scored another A, and this simple letter meant the world to the family.

When asked why she was reluctant to approach them, Sarvitri blandly said that she was afraid and did not know how to. To this, Narit produced an exaggerated grimace and pronounced, 'Well, people do say I look a bit serious sometimes, but I didn't realize I was frightening.'

'What?' asked Sarvitri after a motorcycle had sped past them, creating ear-piecing noises.

'Nothing.'

'So, Sarvitri,' said Kawee, turning abruptly austere, 'tell us this so we can be on more friendly terms. The field marshal Thanom Kittikajon just proclaimed that Article 17 of the Rule by Decree will be applied to the accused. What d'you make of that?'

Sarvitri looked up and a puzzled expression swept over her face.

Racha looked at her with a cunning eye, 'Article 17 gives the PM absolute power, unconstrained by any legitimate legal procedures.'

'I mean, could anything they do affect us personally?' asked Sarvitri apologetically.

'Of course!' cried Racha, slapping the table. 'Kawee, you should've told her that the field marshal had also waved his staff at the sky and called, "Let it pour down all night!" That's why your clothes are damp.'

Narit chuckled. He could always tell when his friends were starting to toy with their victim a little too much. A change of topic was called for. 'Can we call you Sar for short?' Narit leaned forward a little.

Sarvitri pulled back visibly. Still, she nodded.

Narit then took the conversation in a more mundane direction, asking her questions like 'All right, Sar, why have I never seen you before at the house?' or 'Do you mind if we all have the cake now?' The move away from politics helped. Her spine had unstraightened itself slightly and Sarvitri soon gave her first diffident smile, albeit a stray one. The talk soon cleaved its path to Kawee's song, which he had named 'The Star of Faith'.

Chapter 6

10th October

It was like any other morning. People stood huddled around the bus stop, hoping that their ride would stop closer to where they were so they could be the first one to get in. Piyanuch had recovered. In fact, she was positively cheerful having her brother wait to see her off. She had been perching on the edge of the pavement, humming softly to herself the whole time. Soon she began to swing her bag about before dumping it down, using it as a sort of stool.

'If you insist on sitting on the street,' began Narit from behind a kind of journal, 'I will throw coins at you. Besides, don't sit on books, its disrespectful. You know how the old saying goes.'

'Why, is sitting on books really going to make me stupid? Really Nar, my legs have gone stiff,' Piyanuch groaned. Narit raised his eyebrows in response, but it did nothing to deter her. 'You must have a third eye, because I haven't seen you looking at me once.'

'I know. I'm psychic.'

Piyanuch bit her lip. 'The bus will never come. What exactly are we waiting for?'

'For a chance to go to school, of course. I thought that was obvious.' Narit diverted his eyes to his sister. Seeing that her face was dappled with dissatisfaction, he put away the book. 'Many things have strayed off track, it's true, but you stay on yours, all right?'

'That's not fair,' replied Piyanuch, picking up her bag.

'Things have been more than fair for you, so don't complain. Have you any idea how many girls want to go to school but can't?' asked Narit, his tone started to grow more deliberate. 'There was this girl I met. She does odd jobs at home. The house is where she lives and works. The house is all she knows and probably the principal place where her experience will lie. Each day she buckles down to the things she's dictated to do and has to accommodate herself within the time allotted to her. She's never free to choose her own food, let alone discover who she is. She's even ashamed to admit that she does have something she really likes. A bit sad, don't you think?'

'Just like Cinderella.'

Narit smirked. 'Yes. But perhaps without the happy ending. There's no guarantee of that in life.'

'Why doesn't she just leave?' asked Piyanuch.

'Indeed why?'

'Because she is scared. Changes might be worse?'

'Good, you're not as daft as you look. People are often scared of what they don't know. When you have very little education, you'd often give in to outside forces because you don't know enough to go against them.'

Piyanuch scratched her head. 'If you are telling a story, you're not supposed to tell its moral.'

Narit chuckled dryly. 'Hey, look,' and he grabbed her shoulder and turned her gently around, 'any of those your bus?'

'Typical, we wait for ages and then they all come at the same time.'

A blue bus approached and pulled in, while the other was careening on its way. Narit tweaked his sister's chin affectionately, agreeing to her pleas that he would see her at dinner. They waved and said their goodbyes. Piyanuch swayed in the aisle as the bus hurtled away.

Narit turned around and began retracing his steps back home. As he drew closer, he stopped to rest his aching shoulder, once again bothered by the thought of the impressionable, hapless woman he met the previous night. What if a person like her, and not him, was prototypical? How could democracy foster in an environment full of people like this? How could an election make Thailand a democratic country when at least fifty-odd per cent was just like her, guilty of being innocent?

As he was hobbling along and his mind bustling with thoughts of the day's speech, a car screeched up the sidewalk. Narit's grip on his crutch tightened. A door swung into his path and caught his arm. He fought to remain calm. A familiar voice sung out from inside, 'Do kindly step in, Khun Narit.'

Narit knew the voice. The memory that today was meant for another meet and greet quickly made its way back to him. He looked around and saw many of those who live close-by doing a poor job of trying not to look.

'Do join me,' pressed the voice. 'That's the spirit.'

Narit hesitated a moment, then cursed himself for doing so.

Ducking down into the car was like going into a cave. The curtains were thick and perfectly fitted so that everything seemed to be in shades of grey. Apart from the chauffeur, there was no one save for the moustached man dressed in an immaculate pinstriped suit, his back partially against a door.

'Well, I must say it's nice to see you again. How's the leg?' The man didn't wait for a response. He glanced down at a pile of documents resting on his lap, absently scanning over them. Narit eased back into his seat and feigned patience.

'Not so talkative today, are we?' said the man as he licked his thumb and flipped a page.

'Well, you seem to enjoy listening to yourself.'

The man's lips distended into a smile, 'I'm afraid that is pathological. My poor niece is forever complaining that I talk too much. I hope you don't find it too annoying. Anyway, I'd like you to meet someone. It's more of a social visit. But of course, you're free to say no if you're finding this situation somewhat intimidating.'

Narit gritted his teeth. 'No, not at all. Although I have to add that I can't be too long, my fellow students will be expecting me back later on. For your information, the crowd's getting larger. I bet we'll have to move to the football field by tonight.'

'My goodness, that sounds exciting.' The man smirked and his mouth rounded to say something else but the phrases in the documents stole his attention. 'Now, if you do excuse me, I have a spot of work to do. It makes sense if I try to get a bit done during our travel.' With that, he nodded to his driver and the car pulled away.

The journey passed in plain silence that hung above the soft sputtering of the engine and the man's murmurs, which escaped from time to time. Narit was grateful that his presence was being ignored.

Despite himself, Narit could not help but be impressed with his current mode of transport. It was the nicest car he had ever been in, uninterrupted, a bit like a train that had its own track. Via a transceiver, the driver would occasionally make brief interactions with whom Narit assumed were traffic police. Many parts of Bangkok were being held back behind red lights but the car Narit was in was not one of them.

Through the heavily tinted windscreen, Narit took some comfort in the fact that he could recognize every turn. This feeling however was short-lived as it started to dawn on him that they were heading towards a place he was only too familiar with. So, when the car parked and the door was opened, Narit was already prepared to have his hunch confirmed. Despite the familiarity, it was actually the first time he had been inside the rare walls. Shifting his eyes from the vast expanse of the symmetrical lawn, Narit fixed his gaze upon Kwantar's home.

Narit felt the pressure of a hand on his back as a man moved him in the direction of the house.

'Please, don't put your hand on Khun Narit. He's our guest,' urged the host.

So, with no further manhandling and his crutch left in the car, Narit limped his way inside. A well-groomed, expressionless butler guided him through the foyer and oak-panelled corridors before they stepped into an oval room with ceiling-high emerald drapes.

* * *

Narit entered the room. A morning sun meant that he was exposed to a warm shard of light that had pierced the gap between the curtains. Narit squinted. In a corner, cloaked in a relative shadow, Narit could just about make out a figure. A silhouette of a man sitting behind a huge table on the mezzanine. Clicking sounds preceded him. He was flicking the beads of an abacus as he went over his calculations in a tiny book. It was the man again? But that couldn't be right as he was after him as he walked in. Narit squinted again, realizing it was not the man after all, but an incredibly good imitation of him. He was a similar size. However, this man's hair was not flecked with silver, and as he looked up, Narit could see his jaw was squarer.

'You'll like this boy, Tot,' chimed in a voice, as its owner appeared right behind his elbow. He languidly ascended the stairs, unbuttoned his wide lapel suit and sat down on an armchair across from his doppelgänger. They were clearly twins. 'He's not what you might call refined. But nowadays who cares about background. He has what it takes, though I'm not so sure whether he has the desire to realize it.'

With one final flourish of his pen, Tot flipped his book to a close and pushed his abacus aside. He leaned forward, his rolled-up sleeves exposed toned forearms. He beckoned for Narit to join them. 'Allow me to apologize on behalf of my brother. He gets a little carried away sometimes, don't you, Teera?' began Tot, his eyes fixed on Narit, who was yet to attack the climb, at the boy's chiselled face and rigid stare.

Teera sat back with a cup of hot tea. 'You have to love his arrogance. He's been very consistent in that sense. Do come up, Khun Narit.'

Narit clenched his teeth, his knuckles whitened as he grabbed the teak rail, and despite the considerable pain in his ankle, eventually made it to the top. He stood upright facing the two men, a little disconcerted.

Although they looked almost comical sitting side by side in the room like that, Narit didn't doubt for a second that they had blood on their hands. While his kidnapper was well-built and dressed conspicuously, his brother was slightly trimmer, more introverted, and definitely one of those lucky people who grew well into their look. The two men were placid, surfing on the tension the atmosphere carried.

Tot slowly stood to his feet and walked over to a small table and poured himself a drink from a glass decanter. He turned around, took a sip, and then spoke. 'Planning for the protest going well?'

'Very well, thank you,' said Narit.

'How about your studies? I hear that you're an intelligent young man. It seems a pity your academic pursuits must take a back seat right now.'

Something about this man's polite and cool manner almost had him convinced for a moment that he was a more reasonable man than his brother. Narit's bewilderment had kept him quiet. That was, until Tot remarked to his twin, his tone now hoarse without inflection, 'A toothless fool of a working-class hero, a beacon of light? Listen Teera, I'm not giving away my daughter so passively as I gave you her mother.'

'Well, that's a pity. It's true Kwantar can't be replaced. But she can hardly be blamed, you let her have everything.'

'So, what do you want to mould him into?' continued Tot.

'Mould?' Teera puckered, 'I'd say forge. There's nothing pliable with this one.'

'Yes, I can see that. He carries a fire within him.'

'The question is, can we douse those flames? There's a range of possibilities, but I'll have to check. You're aware of how things are. The queue is pretty lengthy right now,' replied Teera, bending over, pouring himself some more tea.

Tot nodded. 'I say, find him something with a bit of status, something that will avoid any embarrassment for my Kwantar. But please, not a professor. You know how these people can hardly make ends meet doing some biased research projects.'

Narit clenched his fists. What on earth were they on about? What kind of family was this? Suddenly, something inside had him sneer and blurt out, 'Excuse me, what have you or Tar got to do with it? I'm not water in your squalid watering can that you could just pour over your empire tree. Not me, not in any lifetime.'

'So, Tot? Hear that? Not too bad, is he?'

Tot rubbed his chin.

Teera snapped his fingers. 'I'm thinking, office. I'm thinking, paperwork. Administration, how's that?'

'Nice!' Narit broke in again. 'When do I start?'

'Oh, such a wit. You may want to be a little more careful with that mouth of yours. And please, don't interrupt us again.'

'Or what?'

'Or I'll rip your fucking throat out,' Teera responded, slamming his fist down on the table. A smile quickly spread across his face. 'Oh dear, I seemed to have lost my temper a little. Do forgive me.'

Narit clearly sensed the danger he was in now. Enough was enough. He was turning for the descending stairs when Teera continued, 'What is he, to have a mind of his own, but satisfied to be just an employee of sorts? His house is on a leasehold. His parents are . . . extras around the ministry. And his sister, did I tell you about his sister, Tot? I saw her this morning.'

Narit pivoted around in a whoosh; rage consumed him. He made a beeline towards Teera, but the man was ready for him. His hand shot out and snatched him by his collar.

'Easy now,' whispered Teera, then added almost sweetly, 'and I'll be nice and make sure she won't die of internal injuries. How about that, hmm?' And swiftly, he sent Narit flailing through the air before he had a chance to react. He hit the ground hard, smashing into the wall with the remaining momentum. He remained still and quietened.

Teera clasped his hands to disguise his glee as he paced back and forth. A complacent look came to the surface but momentarily dissolved into a more cunning one once when Narit stirred.

Narit gritted his teeth and quickly corrected himself for having winced. Slowly he dragged himself up the small table. The placemat was accidentally pulled, causing the decanter to slide and fall and without being completely destroyed, spill half its content on the floor. No one seemed bothered. His ankle must have twisted again, but Narit managed to steady himself, as sternly as the display cupboard he was leaning against. Deeply he inhaled and exclaimed, 'You, you wankers huddle up in your hole and fantasize the world is at your feet. You trample on the carpet of other's insecurities and bankroll this petty vanity of yours? But it won't be in the role of the great, will it, that you'll trip and fall? This time we will give you a lesson, and we will be brief.'

The men were silent, attentive but not expressive. Narit was unfettered and considered himself somewhat successful that their bantering had ceased. 'So, tell me if you'll lose your heart before you'll lose your head.'

'Oh dear,' Teera rubbed his chin and resumed his conversation with Tot. 'I wonder if this is prepared. Well, I'm starting to think he would make a good spokesman. Wasn't that smooth?'

Tot wriggled his foot for a moment and cleared his throat. 'We'd lose our heads first.'

'What now?' Narit rebuffed.

'We would lose our heads first. It was a question, was it not?' said Tot, sitting up slightly. 'Let me tell you, young man, things are more, shall I say established, ingrained than you're capable of seeing. Permanent interest is permanent. The aim of politics doesn't come and go but could easily be redefined to accommodate the interest of the most recent ruling class. Running for seats in the house is making an investment. Office time is payback period and beyond. You think a politician is a representative; no, it's a personal business, the taking of turns on national fortune. And it's not us who are at fault. It's democracy that condones us, that legitimizes us . . .'

A phone rang from the other end of the room, cutting off Tot's last words. The men tuned in curiously and grew somewhat less indolent as the butler pounded up the stairs. Eventually he arrived, palpitated and announced, 'General, the home secretary for you.'

Teera held up his hand as he went to another room, and so a recession seemed to have been called for. Immediately Tot started to converse with his butler in a hushed tone before resuming his session with the figures in the book. Narit's presence had receded into being a piece of furniture, a strip of wallpaper that was forever in the room, that no one no longer cared to notice. The pain in his ankle was excruciating.

It was not long before the door clicked open again. Teera was back whispering to his big brother, who in turn nodded in acknowledgement and observed his watch.

'Now, Khun Narit, let us get straight to the point,' Teera stepped forward. His face in the light was parched and hardened, his posture almost elegant. 'Which is, do you intend to continue to be my niece's toy, a dreamy boy, or would you rather stop feeding off my family and do something productive?'

'Why don't you simply step away, hmm? That would be wise, wouldn't it? My Kwantar, she's mine,' Tot declared. 'Step back a hundred paces and see if you could melt into our already exceptional picture without being a disgrace.'

'You will do as we say from now on or fuck off,' added Teera conclusively.

Narit rubbed his forehead with the back of his sleeve and laughed bitterly. 'Are your eyes there only to do up your face? Is it not clear to you that it is I who stooped down to be in the relationship? Dumping her would be easier to bear, after all.' The lines appeared to be quick and seemingly insensitive. When Narit finished talking, he thought he would see them look surprised, but he was mistaken. Every detail on those faces, from the smiling eyes to the distortion at their mouths' corners, expressed but a winning demeanour. Teera started to clap, and the sound grew louder, louder, and louder.

'Bravo, Bravo!' he clamoured triumphantly. 'Told you he's a fool. My! This is such a happy ending!'

Tot raised his eyebrows sedately.

'Kwan, my dear. He had chosen. It's finished. You can come out.'

'That's enough for now, Teera. She doesn't need to see this,' said the father before he made his way towards the door. He quietly exited.

Behind the grand armchair was a sliding door slightly ajar. And from behind that door, muffled sobbing could be heard.

Chapter 7

11th October

The running tap. The sound of water in the metal sink. The stained mirror and the face in it that stared back at him with blood shot eyes. A short moment seemed infinite.

Drops of water were dripping off Narit's stiff jaw. His hair slapped back to expose his wide forehead. He wiped his face against the sleeve of his shirt and as he did so, caught a whiff of stale beer. It comforted him. His face now dry, he stared once again into the mirror. The tap was still running.

'This was it,' he told himself. This would be the last time he ran over the whole sorry affair in his head before he attempted to push it back to the farthest recesses of his mind.

So yesterday once more. The crying drew him hesitantly closer towards the door. He drifted past its threshold, passing the old maid, wishing again that he had been more decisive at leaving. A chair lay on its side and there he found Kwantar on the floor, embracing herself in an attempt to hold still. Her reaction, it did not surprise him in itself, but left him horrified, nonetheless.

Narit gripped onto the doorframe. He looked at her, but no word would come. Kwantar slowly raised her head until her eyes met his. He ventured a step forward but then hesitated, hoping she was strong enough to get up on her own.

Kwantar clutched at her chest and with a tremor in her voice, muttered. 'Goodbye, Narit.'

Narit looked to the floor, shaking his head dejectedly.

'You think I'd agreed to this, any of this. I . . . I wanted no part. And you . . . Why did you have to give me up? You gave me up behind my back! I never thought we could be over. How can you let that word define us . . . ever?'

'Tar . . .'

Kwantar shook her head. 'I really like you Narit, even now I just want you to hold me, and believe me, I know how pathetic that sounds.' She then tried desperately to strangle a sob but failed. She took a deep breath, then slowly breathed out. Her arm that had covered her face dropped to reveal a look of resolve. 'No, I understand. I do. I really do. Leave now, Narit. Just go while you still have the strength to do so.'

Narit shut his eyes tight and turned the other way.

'Well! A man's got to do what's a man's got to do. No way you can argue with that,' came a voice from behind him. Narit barely registered it. It drifted past him and dissipated like cigarette smoke. Teera was standing in the doorway. 'Look at what you have done to my beautiful niece. Are you happy now?'

The water was still running. The cheering and vigorous stage talking still filled the football field of Thammasat. Narit shook his head, turned off the tap, and made his way out of the toilet. He drifted past the medical tent and made his way back to his table. Kawee was still lazing away in a pensive manner. A biro in his hand and a half-blank sheet of paper stretched before him. Racha soon burst into view, crossing over the bench and straddling the seat. Narit sat down.

'Ahimsa, ahimsa!' broke out Kawee, slamming down his Coca-Cola can. 'Fancy ourselves Gandhian now, do we?'

'Weren't you listening?' chimed in Racha. 'The talks with the government flopped. We'll be stretching our legs soon enough. Narit, tell him to chill out.'

'Chill out, Kawee,' Narit complied vacantly.

'That's right, we're in marvellous shape with all these donation funds gushing in.' Racha patted Kawee's shoulder consolingly and turned to Narit. 'Narit, Narit, what's wrong with you? You've been staring at that scrap of paper for a heck of a long time. Seksan's been made MC, and he's already running out of gags.'

'This thing takes time, all right? I'd be skeptical if you could get it done faster.' Narit looked up and attempted a weak smile. 'I'm joking. You can have it in half an hour.'

'Good on you to be irreplaceable.'

Narit forced a conceited smile. 'I wouldn't count on that.'

'Oh, but I do, and I'll continue to do so. Anyway, gotta go. A coordinator's gotta keep things circulating to achieve blossoming democracy!' And with this, Racha bounced off into the distance.

Kawee resumed his musing. It was so strange because usually you could not shut him up. At length, Narit was tempted to ask, and did so casually while still writing. 'More than me, Kawee, Rach should've posed you that question: what's wrong with you?'

'Nought,' replied Kawee sedately, now rolling a can of soda between his palms. 'Though I must say, you're a fine one to talk. Are you not feeling the slightest bit guilty that you didn't show up yesterday? I thought we were all in this together.'

'Look, I meant to come.'

Kawee shrugged. 'If it were me, I would've felt awful. It's like you start off with something you mean to finish, but then can't be bothered to see it through to its conclusion. You always used to say one should choose what one's conscience tells one while one can.'

'Well, I guess I was right. I guess I believed it at the time. But don't say that to me now,' said Narit, steadily shifting his concentration back to scribbling and editing.

Kawee shot the can at the nearby rubbish at the end of the table. It hit and bounced on the rim before going through the hole. Narit pretended he was still engrossed in his scribbling.

'It's driving me mad to leave my grandma in the hospital alone,' Kawee went on. 'The doctor thinks it was a heart attack. Still, I never miss a day here. I was never like that before all this started. Does this make me hard hearted?'

'What?' Narit looked up, still feigning slight disinterest. 'Take care. I'm probably the wrong person to be asking that question right now. You'd better go to her though. Well, I'm done.'

Leaving Kawee to himself again, Narit fought the worsening pain in the ankle and made his way past the nonstop incoming flow of supplies, and to the backstage. His colleagues were delighted as usual as he appeared brandishing the paper. Narit on the other hand felt awful. Though he wavered at first, he eventually managed to tell them he wanted to bow out of his role as lead copywriter as many things had now outgrown his present mobility. Yet Narit still wanted to be involved, the same way he wanted to be a role model, rather than a caricature of it. So, he told them that he would ditch the title but he would write for them all the same. This ceased their protest.

After barging through the swarming front line, Narit settled at the hem of the field. Rather than finding a movement composed simply of the country's newer blood, he witnessed how most people, when given the chance, prove more aware and more complex than he expected. The white- and blue-collar workers who had finished their working day began to mix with the students, now sitting packed cheek by jowl singing Kawee's 'Star of Faith'. But there was more to this than just an increased number to a solid sixty thousand. It was the idea that writ large, the union consisted of all social stratums, the high morale and the empowered crowd.

As evening rolled out, word began to circulate that the cabinet were meeting in another emergency session at Suan Ruamrudee. The speculation was later confirmed with the birth of the Riot Control Force, with FM Praphat Jurasuthian acting as the bigshot at the helm.

And when the night kicked in, the kinetic atmosphere gradually relaxed and started to slow its pace. Some students provided parodies along with other forms of entertainment on the stage, turning anger to humour, taking the edge off what had been an emotionally charged day. And with less political stress, going to bed became a realistic option. Those who had travelled far had already set about rolling out their mats and pillows, while others who lived closer by were packing up. The field transformed into a patchwork quilt of makeshift camps.

Narit too was taking off. Though he could put on a healthy show amongst friends and remain sane for the most of it, things were getting a little bit too much for him. He yearned for somewhere calm, somewhere he could hear himself. However, he could not face home quite yet.

* * *

The crutch felt a part of him now. On and on he moved forward, past junctions, crossings, and down the streets. At long last, Narit discovered himself on a soft green turf sloping into the Chao-phaya River where, on the other side, the gilded skyline glowed around the spires of the Temple of Dawn. The wind swept his skin, billowing into his shirts. The grass below him was too short to dance in sync with anything, but it was soft. The vague moonlight diffused through the clouds, some falling on the river's quiet flows, seldom was it disturbed by boats.

Being on the cusp of two of life's phases, one of which had wreaked havoc, was to be vulnerable. A part of him insisted on punishing itself. Narit took a handful of grass and clenched his fist. He shut his eyes tighter. A solitary tear rolled down his cheek. It must have been the wind that his eyes were parched and burning so.

'Will she at all care that it was just a game?' Narit asked himself, immediately feeling pathetic for having thought so. Regret was never the flipside of rewind. As the taste of her faded, the last three-and-a-half years had started to mean so much. The days in them had tripled in importance. Amidst the abundant bushes of tamarind trees, the crickets were singing, dearly resonating with one another. In vain Narit looked for them. They were there, but, as with the answer he sought, the task of locating was an exercise of futility.

Contemplatively, Narit sat up and started to toss whatever he could pluck from the earth into the river. Every time some dirt landed on it, the water splattered and rippled. Narit grew hateful that all the dirt kept drowning. He was really hoping that it would stay afloat.

'D'you intend to the fill the river?'

Narit looked around for the source of the shy, unassured voice. Just behind him he found a familiar girl standing pigeon-toed, arms awkward.

'It's you,' said Narit, drawing his eyebrows thoughtfully. 'Sarvitri.'

'Sarvitri. I'm never good at names. Forgive me,' replied Narit, his head turned back to the moonlit river involuntarily as though he had forgotten that he already had company.

'Why . . . why are you here?' asked Sarvitri shyly in a way making it almost imperceptible though it was good enough to catch Narit's attention.

Narit turned to look at her again. His face expressed surprise that she was still there. 'Sorry. You say what? I wasn't listening. I'm sorry. Won't you sit down?'

She blushed. Still, she picked her way and settled herself at a conservative distance, making sure that her pleated skirt covered her legs.

'So, what did you say?' began Narit.

'Nothing. Well, I said, I wondered, why you're here in the dark.'

'I should be the one asking that question. I'm fine.'

Sarvitri nodded timidly, 'Me, I come here twice a week. I mean I like taking a walk. I didn't plan to see you.'

'Nor I you,' said Narit, lighting his cigarette and lowering his head back onto the ground. Trails of smoke seeped out from his mouth and tarried before they withered away. 'Sometimes I only need a single cigarette to keep me going, but that's sometimes. You see, a part of me has become rather disorganized. But it's just the beginning of the end. Where do people go from the end, I wonder?'

'From the end?' Sarvitri blinked, looking at Narit suspiciously. 'Are you heartbroken?'

'Do I look it?'

Sarvitri nodded again. 'Like a character from a story a mum would read to her child.'

'Story. Stories are full of morals. What's the moral of the story?'

'Love was once a good thing to sniff at.'

Narit laughed incredulously. 'Fair does. I must look really pitiful that you can tell.'

'You look unhappy.'

Sarvitri then asked Narit what she had wanted to ask since that night. Narit shrugged and started to tell her about the cause and some details of the damage to his leg. He told her that some minor bone had partially cracked, and that there was a big risk that the joint surface would not heal properly, in other words, a chance of lifelong arthritis. But Narit downplayed this, adding that when the worst came to the worst, it should only be a little painful when putting too much pressure on it.

'What is that?' asked Sarvitri reluctantly, pointing at a red circle the size of a coin on the cast of Narit's outer ankle.

'Oh, this? It's the doctor's mark. He told me if I don't give it a rest or move about too much, and if blood seeps and defuses beyond the circle, from here, it has to be chopped off.'

Sarvitri's eyes widened.

'Just joking. It's my sister. She circled it, the broken location.'

October was the month of fine weather and the overture to starrier nights, a fine allure cajoling the two to immerse themselves freely in discussion. Narit did most of the talking while Sarvitri sat wide-eyed, listening to anything Narit had to say.

They went on a long while simply chatting, before Sarvitri realized that it was late and perhaps time for her to be heading home. But Narit proposed that if it was not too late, they should aim to complete her usual route. Sarvitri agreed.

The whole way, Sarvitri kept her head down, feeling uncomfortable with herself. But by projecting her eyes at the floor, she knew precisely when it was not smooth, levelled, or slippery and pleaded with Narit to be careful. Narit always replied that he was fine, trying every time to persuade her to look at something else. It was unusual that he took no offence, because normally he would have been furious to be viewed as helpless or be showered with kindness. But with her, he did not know why the well-natured fussing over him came across as endearing. Perhaps he felt safe to be uncomplicated with her. Perhaps because she had nothing to be vain of, and so neither had he.

The road finally parted. Despite Narit's insistence, Sarvitri steadfastly refused to be walked home. Accepting defeat, Narit said his goodbyes and so they went their separate ways.

Chapter 8

12th October

With the escalation of the political sit in, every inch of Thammasat sagged under the weight of a massive crowd. It was becoming something of a trend, and it was phenomenal. Still Narit had mixed feelings about leaving as the protest was chipping away at another milestone. He kept packing his bag and unpacking it. Out of hundreds of thousands, an outbound trickle of a drained, disconcerted man could not hurt anyone. No one but a man's conscience.

Now in Hua-Lum-Pong's ticket line, Narit reached out for the book he had begun the day before. But soon his fingers were starting to turn the pages mechanically or even two sheets at a time. It only confirmed his inability to indulge in the escapism of the written word. Narit resigned, and more than a little exasperated, he tucked it away.

The queue was not particularly long. But while two members of staff engaged in a blathering session, the only one actually doing anything behind the counter was going overboard with her determination to provide a masterclass in customer service. Conversation with the sallow old lady seemed to enthrall anyone who made it to the ticket window.

Narit's eyes were drawn to the hat of a man enjoying his turn before him. It had a flappy sweeping rim, a high crown that seemed to have a life of its own. Narit found the man's idea of fashion amusing for a while, but this faded as the wait became inordinately prolonged. But just as he began contemplating a polite protest, the man started to move away.

'Morning, sir,' the elderly saleswoman greeted Narit as he bent down to her level. She had a rare, sincere look which, despite the yellow teeth, was a welcoming sight.

'I'd like a round-trip ticket to, well, to go on any train that will depart soon.'

'Needing a change of air, sir? Plenty of those're going out. It's morning. Give me some ideas of the kind of place you need to be in. I was once a locomotive driver myself, you know, the first female ever. Can give you recommendations.' And she winked her left eye at Narit. 'You a hill or a sea person?'

'Hill.'

'Lovely. But even if you say the sea, I'll tell you, you could have the sea up there too, the sea fog in the valleys. But you got to be lucky enough though. Kao-Koh, Phetchabun, that's the place.' And she nodded approvingly to herself.

'Not sure about being lucky, but Phetchabun would do me very well.'

The old woman looked up from her stationary pile as if to check whether Narit was as sure as his words were. She worked her fingers. They grazed over ticket books but stopped at one with an orange cover. 'How about historical sites? The Hindu Phanom Rung Temple, Burirum?'

'It's not exactly the time of year when the sun blazes through all the fifteen doorways, is it?'

'No, no, but it's magical nonetheless.'

Narit raised an eyebrow in interest, still he replied, 'Pity that I have chosen.'

'As you wish, young lad,' she leaned over. 'Be careful, the hill is full of spells, so don't forget your ride back. Here're your tickets. Your ride leaves at 5.30 a.m.'

Narit looked at the clock and moved on to the platform. The sign for Phetchabun was a huge one. But the moment he set himself down, the old conductor ambled forward and called for boarding. Narit slung his backpack on again and went to pass him his ticket.

'Wait no, no,' the conductor protested as he glimpsed the crumpled paper. 'You wait over there, there.'

'What? This train's going to Phetchabun? isn't it. Me too.'

'You're not. Look here,' and he stabbed the ticket with his index finger.

Narit's brows furrowed at where he pointed. He was somewhat dazed when he read: Burirum, 5.30, Platform 3. 'Well, I . . .' he stumbled. 'There must be some mistake.'

The old man waved and once again jerked his finger at the terminal nearby. 'There's nothing I can do. You're supposed to check your ticket earlier.'

Conceding the conductor was in the right, Narit staggered to the correct seating section. Buriram was an interesting place anyhow. He had never been there. His outbound trip was usually with Tar, and she was never into ruins or arts. So, this could end up being okay as long as he got to go somewhere.

Outside was still grey and glum. Narit boarded the train and stuffed his bag under the seat. As the train started to fill, by a cynical twist of fate, Narit saw the man with the funny hat picking his way onto his carriage. Although dressed like a country bumpkin, something about his mannerisms betrayed him. He carried himself with a confidence of a man who was used to being in control, and before Narit realized, his mind had gone on the Phetchabun journey. It drifted onto the smell of the last rain in the woods, and to the waterfall where a small rainbow played amidst the spray. Somebody gave an audible sigh and thudded down beside him. From the corner of his eye, he could tell it was the hat man.

* * *

Whistles were soon blowing. The engine sputtered to a start. The boiler shrieked even louder. And the train finally set off towards the east. From the stifling air of the capital and past the industrial fringe, it slowly made its way into the countryside dotted with old farmhouses nestling in the rich paddy fields. Plot after plot arranged into scenic patterns. Marshes were glinting in the sun. Birds were racing in the air. And booths at stops were colourfully signposted and packed with seasonal fruits and handicrafts. The countryside was breathtakingly refreshing. The trip was starting to look like it would be a good one.

Narit, arms on the windowsill, was amused as he shifted his gaze between near and far objects. When he looked at the bushes lying on the undefined wayside, they vanished almost the moment he set eyes on them. But when he looked at the boulders on the hill slope in the background, they were there until the earth curved away. Maybe this was like everything in life, the further he looked, the more stable things would be. But then, that would be counting too much on the taste of life being tame. He unbuttoned his shirt and threw back his head. Again, he started to drift off.

A million times she had sneaked up and snuggled her cheek against his back. 'Guess who?' she used to say. Narit heard it now less than a whisper, the same way her body warmth against his had chilled. He could almost feel her pressure change as she breathed and be seduced by the feeling it called for. What was he thinking of, to try and relive the memory whose tangibility had been lost? What was he doing all this time, had he not been prepared to be sad?

Hours had passed on the track. The midday heat had his face dripping, his ankle extra itchy in the cast. And what little breeze there was fluttered in through the window in warm waves. His neighbour was shifting restlessly in the connecting seat again. Narit sighed and started counting to ten. But before he could make sense of the man's latest fidgeting, words took over.

'Hi,' said he, in his husky voice, and pulled down the hat. The descending brim revealed a full, rounded forehead of tousled hair. His triangular eyebrows were floating high like clouds, way above the glasses that were so small, their legs tore between his bat-like ears. 'I know you're on the window seat and therefore entitled to exercise your right over the shades. But will you draw the curtain? The sun's been bugging me for some time. It's getting too hot for a hat.'

To this, Narit obliged and made no fuss, seeing it as an opportunity to bring the short conversation to a close.

'So, we're both escaping the capital. Going to the temple, I assume?'

Narit narrowed his eyes and turned back, admitting as coolly as he could, 'Yes, I intended to.'

'Oh? Wonderful. Though too bad you will not see the complete carved lintel.'

'Ah, that. The Narai Banthomsin Lintel. What a shame.'

'Exactly, a shame to a Mr Alsdolf. Legal thief! "Thanks to the special privileges enjoyed by the US forces."'

'Exactly!' exclaimed Narit. The issue got him sitting a little upright. He knew about the quote. The sentence was propagated by The People of Thailand in an attempt to retrieve the smuggled ancient artefact. Narit continued, 'UNESCO is pointless.'

'True, true,' responded the man with more than a hint of contempt. And after he went into the particulars of how the agency had screwed Thailand, he craned his neck to look at Narit's book, peeking from his bag. 'That book, Hobbes' *Leviathan*, isn't it? What a choice. The state holding a crosier and backed by force. Or the Thai version of it, a gun and backed by force.'

Narit was surprised again but this time managed to stay on guard for any turn of talk. The aging man now pressed his lips tight, eyes glazed over behind his spectacles. 'Though I believe it's not life in the state of nature that is poor, nasty, brutish, and short, but life of struggling against the altering powerful faces.'

'Here we go,' Narit muttered, knowing this would be long and passionate, something he desperately needed a break from. 'To be honest, I'd rather not discuss politics.'

'Are you afraid I'm going to reason you out of your mind, my young revolutionary friend?' he said challengingly, leaning towards Narit. "We're the little people, check. We're students, we're junior, we're to inherit the country, but we're not to be heard. We don't have a voice, okay? Well, we do!" Beautiful writing!' The man soon reclined back into his seat. 'OK, OK. I admit it. I was at the protest, and I'm a fan of your column in the University Magazine. The phrases touch me in a way I cannot tell you.'

Narit sighed inwardly. 'You're addressing the wrong person.'

'I'm sure as hell not.'

'Look, I prefer a day off.'

The man rolled his eyes. 'Aren't all the young so quick to judge and do things so impulsively these days? Jumping and skipping as if by doing so they can fast-forward the world. Do consider the risk of civil war. It took King Rama V thirty-one years to abolish the slavery system. He accomplished that without bloodshed. Think about that,' and he blew his nose into a tissue. 'Mind you, were I in your shoes, I'd avoid orchestrating a chimera for the crowd to flock after. Avoid giving them the rhythm to move. When they hear a waltz, they waltz. Their number is like a hired gun you manipulate to strike your goal.'

'You're aware that it's very insulting to imply those people are being naive fools! Experience is but a slow way to learn,' Narit retorted.

'Well, no, not fools, but naive, yes, and that includes you too. Wake up. Where is this romantic la-la land? Vision is one thing. But imagination is an attribute of the inexperienced. It would've been a fairy tale if people do the dying and you get away with the notion of being a murderer.'

Narit suddenly broke into a paroxysm of laughter, going so far as to clutch his stomach. Soon, however, he corrected himself with a fair attempt for an apology. 'Yes, all you're saying is based on the supposition that my generation won't make it in the world. But we know what it has in store for us, democracy. All men are going to be truly equal before law.'

'That's rubbish,' the man rocked his head to boost the effects of his words. 'You're wrong. All men are not equal because something of a democratic decree enables it. In the west, constitution is sacred. It doesn't change so easily. But here, constitution is still a living document. A rule book that can be ripped up and rewritten. Don't buy it, democracy.'

'With respect, are you out of your mind? Who are you anyway?'

The man rolled his eyes and looked away with a smile playing about his lips. 'I'll tell you a scenario. Where's the land most populated?'

'Well, in the North-east,' replied Narit, hesitantly.

'Aha. From there, I'll fish you an ordinary man. He's minimally educated. He has to eat, he doesn't read much, he has to work. He's got a family, burden, and debts. Leaving the house to vote costs a lot. The petrol for the bike. The cost of eating out. And the child—can't leave him home, so he needs to go too. The kid wants snacks, and if he sees a toy, he yells for it too. Now, the time, you lose the time. An insurmountable opportunity cost for farming, harvesting. And that's that area's general means of living. Think, what have they got to vote for? Long years have passed, and the area they've always been living on is still called the countryside.'

The man paused and picked at his straw hat contemplatively. 'You see, there are countless reasons those high erect pricks want the grassroots to remain stupid. There is always a need for somebody cheap to wash your clothes, to clean your house. Thais are snobbish, supercilious. And I tell you, without further improvement in education, democracy will only be a bypass to a sleazier political business in this country. People will be winched to the ballot box, lured by the smell of money. It works well with the strong gratuity system of the land.'

Narit did not respond immediately. There was a degree of sense in what the man was saying. But to admit it was to admit his ideological faith had lost its stance. He shook his head, 'You choose to be neutral when it requires you to go with the correct flow. You're staying behind the time when now is the moment to make changes. You preached your points, and it sounds really cliché-ridden.'

The man adjusted his glasses.

'The last train's leaving soon. You'll be missing out,' continued Narit. 'Personally, I see no point in turning this into an argument. Now, if you don't mind, I would appreciate it if I were left alone.'

'I see. You think I'm mocking you, but I'm actually trying to help,' his eyebrows raised. He looked somewhat hurt.

'Yes. But please, can you perhaps find someone a little more willing to impart your words of wisdom? What's your name?'

'Santirat.'

'Mine is Narit. A truly rare occasion meeting you. I'm moving to the front row. Excuse me.'

Santirat was taken aback for a moment as Narit collected his things and squeezed himself out to the aisle.

'Hey,' said Santirat. 'Don't forget your crutch too. The front row is reserved for the disabled.'

Narit tarried on the spot for a moment. He looked back and forth and saw no other places empty. The priority section would have been too small to fit his pride, but it was imperative his ego be accommodating now. Lightly Narit replied. 'Well, I fit the criteria.'

The man picked the stick from the floor and handed it over. He whispered, 'Listen, I've been there, done that, and trust me, it is overrated. Tread carefully and tread quietly. Some goals are achieved much more affectively when you pick your fights and play the long game.'

Narit took the stick the moment Santirat let go of it. He paused. 'Listen, I'm sure some of what you're saying have some value. But at the risk of repeating myself, you're talking to the wrong person. I no longer have anything to do with the Union.'

Chapter 9

13th October Morning: The Interlude

It was early morning and Narit had a date with a millennium-old castle. After he had pored over the guide book the previous night, he was confident that the Khmer civilization would help put a much-needed spring in his step, or figuratively speaking anyway. All in all, he was very much looking forward to sitting on the lamp-filled staircase where flowers dripped off every step. Perhaps enjoying a coffee and simply chilling out in the splender of the site. The weather was mild. The lower land of the unkempt, humble orchard of the hostel seemed to just beg for him to lie down and smoke. He did not resist.

Having puffed one last dreamy puff, Narit equipped himself with a map and some snacks. He was all set to hit the Chaleom Phrakiat district, the land that bedded Pranom-Rung Mount, the lost historical park.

After a wobbly journey on rocky ground, for all the bumps and teeth-jarring potholes, Narit came to stand on what was once a volcano, and shortly after, the cruciform platform, a thousand years after the first brick had been placed. Burirum's first rays of sunshine were still at bay. Khmer's vibe and divine sense of history loaded the atmosphere. His mind raced back in time, attempting to tune into a forgotten era.

Pranom-Rung Park was far from bustling today, but it still attracted a good number of sightseers and the white-clad devout. Like all the newly arrived, Narit started off by tracing the wide processional walkway to get the first peek of the main temple. But there was not much to see initially, as it slid all the way towards the back of a rambler stretch and hid behind large splashes of green. The three conical roof and carved spire blended unobtrusively with the rest of the construction that was built of laterite stone.

After a long climb up a cascading stairway, however, the building looked as if it were glittering, as if it were infused with magic. The forecourt of the castle itself was meticulous with details sorting themselves out in the light. Square bricks of rosy shades were stacked next to each other, producing an intricate pattern for the wall. The architecture was so massive that it filled the width of the view.

Most people had the misconception that this place was built for the king, but the king's palace was made of teak. This was the place for worship. This was the residence of Shiva, the god of all gods who by choice dwelled on earth.

Narit looked around. Beyond two lotus pools that straddled the entrance, directly confronting him was the King Cobra Bridge. Belief had it to be the path of rainbows from earth towards heaven. Narit threw his eyes further and was lured instantly through the fifteen doors that aligned themselves into a tunnel. The light broke halfway. Narit found it inconsolable that the site was not constructed on a turning plate.

Stepping over the bridge into the celestial gallery was like stepping through a portal. Conversation echoed. The wind willowed through the window boxes peeking out. Narit soon came out into a flood of light, finding himself in the inner layer of the castle. The Heaven.

Narit tried to drink things in. The conical tower that he had seen before was in fact storeys of contracting roofs. Along the wall, pieces of stone were elaborately carved and connected to create stories from Hindu epics. A big jigsaw of Shiva dancing with ten arms could be seen on the sunrise-side of the main pavilion. Upon recognizing this, and on sober reflection, Narit joined his palms at chest level. He prayed to the supreme god to dance in the rhythm that would resonate with the will of the people. He wished the god could actually give the beat. He bowed.

Down below, right on the door frame, was a gap next to a decorated sandstone. This must be the place of the looted Narai Banthomsin lintel. Narit whipped out the guidebook, thumbed through it, and looked again for the missing picture, which recounted the story of creation. There he was, Shiva, or Narai as he was known in Thai, reclining on the serpent Shesha in the cosmic ocean. Looking at the deserted space again, and though it was a crying shame that the other lintel was left without its pair, having noticed Shiva's large, suggestive smile on the photo, Narit thought perhaps he was having a great time dreaming in America. He then headed into the main hall.

Narit had found out about this just yesterday. Still, he was intrigued to see the actual statue spouting from the centre of the room, and realize what it was and what it signified. The brahmin would pour water over it during the ceremony. That water would become holy and flow down and out through the nearby trench for the peasants to worship.

The imitation of Shiva's phallus standing proudly on a pedestal was huge, thick, and lit in a way that made it look unapologetically bare and severe. This chunk of stone was different because everything else was loaded with fine features. Apart from the dome-like cap, the statue was plain and fairly crude in appearance. If he had not been aware of its existence previously, it would have never crossed his mind that this was actually a man's pride and joy. And to think this was the only thing that stood in the way when light shone through the gate. Narit circled it one more time before zigzagging through some foreigners posing for photos, deep in thought. No doubt Shiva was the all-powerful to keep it hard like that for centuries.

Leaving via the exit ramp, Narit took the same bridge back down. But as his free foot set to land, a push surged from behind. Narit lurched and stumbled all the way down. His knees buckled, but with the stronger leg, he was quick enough to reach out and prevent himself from a sprawling crash.

Now on the lowly earth, he scrambled to turn round, more than a little disconcerted. But there was nobody there, nothing. Only the hollow doorways that stood like sentry, silent witnesses to an unseen act.

'The hill is full of spells.' Perhaps the booking clerk had not been joking after all. Narit ran his hand through his hair, chuckling, and promised himself to get his unsteady leg looked at again when he returned to Bangkok. He collected his crutch.

The whole idea of Elysium on earth did a lot to persuade Narit that he could actually be closer to God. With his inappropriate thoughts, he might be less than angelic, a mere trespasser in heaven, but he was there, and that was it. Buriram was a cultural city, wreathed in by a large belt of hills to the south. Though crammed with other castles and hidden temples whose looks alone were very tempting, Narit was resolved in leaving. A day shied away from all news had left him excited again to see how progress had notched up the headlines.

* * *

Another train ride and Narit was back, recharged and in high spirits. The capital was still clothed in its unfathomable charm, as ever tending to the flickering aura that surrounded the smiles of its people. Though the smiles were somewhat strained at the moment, in sickness and in health, Narit loved the city all the same.

From the station, Narit hopped on a motorcycle taxi for the final leg of the journey. As the bike fumed its way towards the centre of the city, Narit quickly realized that things have really picked up pace since his departure. He felt like kicking himself for being weak and thinking he needed some time to lick his wounds.

Several roads were blocked off. Rolls of barbed wire and panels of jersey walls were drawn abreast Internal Security Operations Command. The fire brigade clearly had its hands full. The riot police were sashaying about, hogging the sidewalks. Narit could not be sure whether it was more to cover the government's arse or to hype up the impression of oncoming violence.

A lane away from home, the driver requested that Narit got off. He could not cleave through any more as the street was curbed into a bottleneck. The suburb was familiar, yet Narit felt completely lost. Democracy Monument was there with all its petal-liked structures embracing the constitutional centrepiece. But it was dying. A grave black flag was fluttering at the apex. Narit's eyes went hard. His hairs stood on end at the sight.

Rest in peace, years of eternal rape had ended.

The road and the roundabout were submerged. Seething masses of students swamped the mourning boulevard. National flags were waving. Buddhist wheel-of-life flags were waving. Placards rode ubiquitously on the buzzing tides, the portraits of the king and the queen floated wherever he looked. The main truck, squatting in the centre, was fixed with speakers that could barely be heard. Seksan was up there on show, overseeing the crowd occupying the traffic circle. Narit could recognize him by his cloth cap and the emotional way he threw his arms around. The general mood was high. It was impossible not to feel the impact of the people's message—get out, tyrant.

Curious as to what had instigated the current phenomenon, Narit adeptly swung over to the food and medical tents to inquire, but all the staff were busy handing out drinks or smelling salts. So, he went onward to a group of high school girls.

Narit probed further and finally learned that the University Federation had presented the government with an ultimatum the previous evening. Both parties had met again this noon for the final negotiation. It had not worked out.

'So, they messed with us again,' said Narit, his words drowned out by the protesters. 'They messed with us,' he shouted.

'Ah, yes, we've been played for fools again. Here, listen up, they said they'd let our guys out on bail,' the girl yelled back, half of her face obscured by her cap.

'On bail!? That means we have to stand trial on the communist and treason charges afterwards?'

She nodded. 'After their release, the Office of Higher Education told us to call it quits. But it's too late. Who'd fall for this bullshit appeasement ploy? Come, brother, join us!'

'Soon.'

'I'll get a move on if I were you,' said the capped girl.

A sly grin broke across his face. 'Well, I've got to run ahead to my house first. Can't be too late, I can see no end to the procession.'

'Oh, Thammasat is bursting! We'll be gushing out into the river before you know it! The roads have filled up all the way to Sanam-Luang.'

'All the way to Sanam-Laung?' repeated Narit excitedly. 'All right, you take care. In case there's a crackdown, you don't want to end up like me.'

Narit took a detour through the seams of crowds. Nothing else but zeal had caused his face to be flushed so. He flicked up his wrist, it was 4.15 p.m. His family must be huddled round the dinner table by this time.

* * *

The house appeared the way it had always been, but as he approached, Narit started to sense something was not quite right. The telly was off. Normally he would hear the sound of idle family chitchat complemented by the voice of this newsman humming away all by himself.

Narit paused at the rust-eaten folding door and hung back a moment. He was unsure whether he wanted to walk into the midst of it, so he stepped to the far side of the door and peered in.

'Wanchai . . .'

'Come on, it's an occasion, for our daughter. This is ridiculous. Surely, we can fork out for it. A celebration.' Wanchai eyeballed his wife. He dropped his spoon and pushed away his plate angrily.

'Don't smack your lips, Nuch, and eat some more of your broccoli, you hardly touched it.' Yanee snapped.

'I'm stuffed.'

'What do you mean you are stuffed? You know you'd better finish your plate clean. You don't want to grow up and have a boyfriend with a face full of pimples, do you?'

'She said she's full . . .' groaned Wanchai.

'It's fine, dad. I can have a bit more.' Piyanuch held out her plate with jittery hands. Yanee took it. But the flat ceramic ended up being placed in front of herself.

'What's got into you now? Nuch, will you go to your room and read now? Please.'

Piyanuch scuttled away but hid just behind the loo's partition.

Wanchai prowled the room, stopping closer to the entrance. Narit could see him a lot more clearly here. On his well-worn face he spotted a look of contrition. His father ran his hands down his face, his skin drooped with the movement. 'It's your attitude, nit-picking me unceasingly. Why can't you support my decision? I cannot take much more of this, really, I can't.'

'You really want me to speak my mind?'

'Oh, do it!'

Yanee flinched. 'Oh, do sit down first, will you? It's dizzying.'

Wanchai pulled up a chair and sat down at an uncomfortable gap.

Yanee drained her tea in one gulp and sat up straight. 'Just one signature. Just another turn of a blind eye. You always do it, so often you should've by now thought your sight's impaired!' Yanee shook her head. 'Can't you wait a bit more? Nuch's still in secondary school, and Narit, you know he dreams of being a professor, he needs further education. Life's meant to be enjoyed after retirement.'

Wanchai turned inward. The gloom deepened, then oozed out of him. 'Leave it with me.'

'Leave it with you? Maybe tomorrow I'll be sacked too, and what are we to do? Sing in the streets? We've got nothing to fix anything. You can bank on that. Our generation will find a depository a befitting place one of these days.'

'I'm proud of my age. Don't talk like we have one foot in the grave already. It's morbid.'

'How can you think more of yourself all of the sudden? You were always so eager to have children. What's really so wrong with a bit of dirt? If I were you, I'd accept the gift. I have nothing to be ashamed of. These are the hands I brought up my children with.'

Wanchai slammed a plate. It bounced a bit and came down reeling on its bottom. 'You pin that on me? Why did you sign then? I asked you not to. The country's changing. Don't you think your name would pop up in the blacklist? The amount's frighteningly huge this time. They know they'd be booted out. They wanted to rake it in with this last project.'

Narit turned away and bore his back against a column. He hated it when they argued. So, towards the kerb he drifted, stalling for time.

The sound of cheering started to fill the street. Several groups of people marched past him. They held hands or laced arms. In intimidating rows, they walked, in an enthusiastic tone they chanted. They waved at him. He waved back.

Soon the metal shutter squeaked opened behind him. His dad came traipsing through.

'Narit? What're you doing out here? I thought you'd be shouting into the mic with all the shepherds.'

Narit shrugged. 'No, dad, you know I'm not big on being in the limelight. I prefer my stint backstage. But I'm no longer responsible for the writing side of things, or officially anyway. I said I'd still write for them, but to be honest, I think they feel I let them down.'

Wanchai took the news very casually, or at least seemingly so. He did not even hesitate as he sealed the door closed behind them. 'How's your leg?' he asked.

'It is what it is.'

'I see. Listen, I won't judge your reasons, but perhaps making rash decisions is a genetic thing.' A rueful twist appeared on his face. Keys tinkled in his trouser pocket as Wanchai withdrew some plastic bags and a towel. 'They say these things help with the tear gas. Get up and let's go. Old men rule today.'

The door made a noise again. It was his sister, and before he knew it, her arms were wrapped around his neck.

'Don't tell me you're coming,' bellowed Wanchai, but his words were lost.

'I missed you, Nar.'

'Don't be ridiculous. It was just one night,' replied Narit, ruffling his sister's hair affectionately.

'You're not angry anymore, daddy?'

'Who says I was angry? I was not angry. Just . . . frustrated. Well, trying to get over being.'

'Hormonal,' added Narit, smiling as he rose to his feet.

'Is that the same thing as a midlife crisis? Nar, wait, where are you going now? Can I come too?'

'NO!' Wanchai hollered.

Piyanuch winced. 'Please, I might not be thirteen and cannot yet vote. But this is like voting, isn't it? Nar, you always say I have to go to school, but this's a kind of learning, isn't it?'

'No, no, no,' Wanchai wagged his finger, 'It's dangerous.'

'Let her come, dad. She's small, we can sandwich her between us,' suggested Narit with a quick wink and clasping Nuch to his side. 'Besides, I can't see it turning violent anyway. They're not stupid. It'll just be a military show at any rate.'

Wanchai, as if suffering from laryngitis, was not sure how to react to his daughter looking at him pleadingly. He gave in, reluctantly nodding at last. 'All right, all right, you can come. But, and that's a big but, at the first hint that things might get a bit nasty, we're to return home immediately. Do you understand?'

'Thank you!'

'OK, now go inside and drop off your bag, son. Tell your mother about Nuch coming too, seeing as it was your idea.'

Narit disappeared and came back out not long after.

'So?'

'That didn't go down well. I suggest we make haste,' Narit replied.

It was only a short walk before they touched down on Rajchadamneon Boulevard, the area once foreseen to take after Champs-Élysées. Though the road was not as fancy, it was equally symbolic and spiritually significant. Narit firmly thought it was a road that incarnated people with such spirits, such force. Anywhere else, the protest would go flat. Rajchadamneon was an escalator. The road moved under the crowd. The crowd whizzed on its explosive drive. On it, Thailand could be propelled into the future at full blast.

Never in the nation's history was there this large a gathering, attended by a good five-hundred thousand. All wanted to bequeath their children the land where there was freedom and happiness in every grain of soil; to let them realize for themselves why 'he who lives in this land is a lucky man.'

Lucky, yes, the country had everything. A willing workforce, natural and financial resources, history, tradition, and the king who worked for no known bounds for his subjects. Too lucky, so everybody said, that God envied this land of the golden axe that he sent a whole tribe of crooked politicians to balance things out.

The protesters, now possessed by Seksan's gift of the gab, fearlessly crawled after the speaker truck like ants after pudding. Forward they walked. Forward they ran. The head of the procession was already turning towards the Royal Plaza. Narit trailed along with his father and sister.

A huge national flag came surfing from behind them. Everybody tried to get their hands on it. They reached up and passed it over. Wanchai gave his daughter a lift so she could have a go at it too. Piyanuch was mesmerized as the river of colours ran over her fingertips. The cloth gently rippled. Streetlights beamed down. The blue, red, and white suffused radiant faces.

The old city emerged again as the gigantic sheet crept away. Numerous ministries and old houses lined up on both sides. Though there were some who had erred on the side of caution and locked themselves in their homes, a greater number had opened up and were whistling.

Passing Makkawan Junction, the space became a tight squeeze. Air was scarce. A few had fainted. Wanchai too had lost a bit of colour. Leapfrogging lanes, Narit ushered him towards the outskirts of the throng. Piyanuch picked up a leaflet from the street and started to flap it in her father's face. The three found themselves at a corner dammed up by barriers with an opening to a smaller driveway. Though offered comparatively generous space, they were exposed as they stood in the line of fire.

The policemen were in full combat armour. Behind the rows stood government house and before them were protesters hurling insults and exuding angry kinesis. Narit credited the shields that they still stood to attention with their emotions hardly dented.

Spotlights soon shifted on a group of students who barged through with paper marionettes of the three military bigwigs. Narit, Piyanuch, and Wanchai watched on.

The group had formed circle, blithely clapping, prancing, and dancing around the manipulators. 'Whoa, Whao Whao,' sounded the chorus. The spherical line then started to play the fool. The puppeteers were gesticulating obscenely, shaking their rears in defiance. The show became even more jocular as they started to mock the police mimicking monkeys. Hands alternately blocked the ears, the eyes, and the mouth. 'Whao Whao, Whao Whao,' they kept hollering.

The spectators were laughing and booing. Piyanuch blushed and ducked her head into Narit's stomach. A good number had clamoured for the marionettes to be burned. Wanchai, becoming caught up in the spirit of his comrades, echoed the majority, 'Hear, hear.' Narit quickly chose to connive. He pinched a match box from his breast pocket, and pitched it to the bandleader, who then capered along, brandishing it at arm's length. Narit pulled his sister closer.

The assemblage cheered as the match hit the striking surface and fire sparked up brightly. The cremation began. The flames flared, and the smoke belched out and lingered. Bit by bit the papery puppets started to crinkle and curl from the toe up before their bodies were charcoaled and began to disintegrate. The crowd who must have fancied themselves in a carnival was elated in patriotic frenzy.

Narit gave the group a big hand when they bowed. And after receiving a personal gratitude from the band's head for the matches, he moved on.

It was only a little later that the lines stopped. By now the Royal Plaza was a bursting point, and so the mob had started to camp out on the street, waiting for further orders.

'Well, dad, I think I'll go and see if Kawee is there somewhere. Hopefully he'll be nice and give me some insights on what is going on. Maybe it's a good idea to take Nuch home now?'

'Don't worry, we'll get going soon.'

'Okay. I'll catch you at home then. Goodbye, Nuch, I won't be too long.' Narit then got up but stopped short of departing, 'And dad, please don't worry about money. We'll be just fine. We'll manage.'

Narit compressed himself and meander through whatever space he saw. His head bobbed out of sight as he disappeared.

Now from where he was, it was still impossible to recognize who was up on the stage, let alone hear what he was saying over the hubbub. The leading truck, though becoming bigger against the equestrian statue of Rama V the Great, was still a tiny rectangle that could sit in his palm.

The sound of a portable radio could be heard in the distance, Narit spotted the source and approached the group cluttered around it. Somebody muttered it was a rerun, but to Narit it was news.

'. . . Furthermore, there is an unknown third party attempting to infiltrate the student group. These communists are believed to be equipped with heavy weapons and are prepared to incite violence. In view of the growing unrest, it is therefore a matter of urgency that the government demands the student demonstration to be dissolved. This is to allow the police force to single out suspects and bring the situation under control.'

'Bullshit. Did they really think that something sounding more like a script in a play, delivered like daily news on the radio, can breathe a breath of myth into this crowd?' Narit thought and reeled away. The radio gradually quietened behind his back as he pushed on. Soon however, Narit had second thoughts as he started to notice nudging, people elbowing at each other's arms, and talks in lower voices. That scrutinizing look of the neighbours and the curiosity of what was being said. And to top it all were those rumours that the gutters were choking with the student federation representatives' bodies, with their brains minced, reeking and hidden under camouflage canvass.

What if chaos really neared? What if what was thought to be a short heroic adventure had morphed into an impossibly heavy responsibility as the protesters started to believe that they were placed here as prey for an intended incident?

The union was not experienced enough to herd this many people. Collapsing order would justify a crackdown. There was no way they would pass on an opportunity like that. The junta would have their way because of the protest, not in spite of it.

Narit was not sure what to make of the situation and instead began to be haunted by the hat man's take on the world. His words could not be a prophecy. But even if it were, the civil war had better remunerate generously.

The space became much denser as Narit neared the main truck. There, on the stage, Kawee was singing when the blare of car horns suddenly shot in from behind. Narit turned and saw a taxi trying to creep its way through. The vocational students who volunteered as guards immediately poured in and started to charge at the invader. They banged on the windows, fervidly rocking the car from both sides. A man stumbled out and somebody shouted, 'That's Sombat Thumrongthunyawong, the secretary of the Uni Fed!'

His curiosity burning, despite his legs now stiff and heavy, Narit gathered up his pace and surfaced just in time to see Sombat hurriedly mounting the platform, snatching the microphone off Kawee's mouth. Narit glanced at his watch and saw it was already 9.00 p.m.

The guy was knackered, his chest was heaving up and down. He cleared his throat and, in a rasping voice, began to address the patient crowd. First, he thanked them for not believing in rumours and insisted that they should listen for news solely from the Fed. He then informed them that a ceasefire with the government had already been called for, and after an audience with the king, there would be a committee member coming to convey the royal tutelage to the protesters.

The students applauded.

Sombat coughed again, muffling the sound with a handkerchief. He soon crumpled it away and waved for silence.

'Comrades. Comrades. As a result of the agreement, our captured brothers and sisters have now been released. They are released, freed of any conditions manacled to their legs!'

The crowd cheered at the news euphorically. Clapping and happy shouting pervaded the grisly atmosphere.

Sombat now repeated his wave that looked more like a salute, 'In turn, the University Federation had agreed to the government terms that it would finish drafting the constitution by October next year.'

To this, all the protestors looked quizzically to the adjacent persons. Then, as if reading from a script, they chanted in unison, 'No way, no way. We want constitution earlier than that!'

'Pathetic,' Narit shouted. 'This is nothing but a patched-up effort of a deeply-flawed truce!'

'The extent of time is considered reasonable . . .' Sombat's voice trailed off as anger stormed over. He opened his mouth again, but before he could pronounce anything, his body twirled like a spinning top. His spine folded as he dipped on his knees, hitting his head against the platform and fainting.

Narit did not stay to watch. He went straight on to the leader camp and entered unchecked and without much of a fuss. Many of the guards and ex-colleagues he bumped into were friendly as they still thought he was very much involved in the campaign. He finally spotted Kawee in a corner, backing away to allow the staff with the technical know-how to deal with the confusion.

'Hey,' Narit cocked his head at his friend. 'Hey,' Narit shouted again, trying to make himself heard. But Kawee just kept on tweaking at his guitar strings. 'I can see things are going bloody okay without me. Don't get mad.'

'I'm not,' Kawee grunted. 'You have no right to be here.'

'It's hardly a fortress given how accessible it is.'

'That guy,' Kawee stared at Seksan sitting opposite him, 'like everyone around here, he hasn't slept in two days. Have you any idea how miraculous it is that we're still in the game?'

'Narit!' Racha was making her way towards them. Narit noticed from the lack of enthusiasm in her voice that even she had lost that invincible blitheness. 'I knew you won't miss the big day. We really are in a bad shape. Perhaps you can help sort things out.'

'It's just Narit, Rach. He can't flourish a wand, tapping here tapping there and snap, things improve.'

Racha sighed as Kawee turned away. 'Where have you been, Narit?' asked Racha, 'Tar came asking after you yesterday. She looked subdued and distraught, I think. Dressed like a boy and self-consciously looking around as if somebody's gonna jump on her.'

'What?'

'Kwantar, your girlfriend, came asking after you.'

'Where is she now?'

'How on earth would I know?'

Narit was silent for a moment before he responded out of expediency, 'Yes, you're correct.'

After Sombat had been spirited away, Narit noticed things had quietened down considerably as if the protesters had taken Sombat's news and fall as some kind of bad omen. The flapping of tents could just be heard as protesters talked in hushed tones amongst themselves. The stage now looked somewhat neglected, left to struggle on its own during this period of transition.

'How many kilometres do you reckon we filled? Everybody
agrees we cannot hold back the masses anymore,' Racha exhaled
and hauled herself to her feet. 'Day by day, it's multiplying. The
situation was never meant to escalate this fast. It slipped...,
getting out of hand. The pressure to act is overwhelming. We
have no choice but to march. Can you believe it, the idea that we
were in control is a joke. There are people here who just want
blood. People are scared.'

Narit nodded. 'Tell me, is there anybody behind these idiots
who are worming themselves into the crowd?'

'We don't know,' said Racha. 'Everything is on the table, and
it is too early to rule anything out. Seksan has ordered rigorous
scrutiny.'

Narit wiped the sweat from his face with his shirtsleeve. He
squatted down, besides Kawee, 'Do me a favour, pal. Stop looking
like you haven't shat for days.'

'What're you doing. Bugger off,' barked Kawee, quickly
rearranging his Elvis pompadour.

'All right, all right,' yielded Narit, hands up.

'Look, be serious, Narit,' replied Kawee. 'We're cut off. We
know all but rumours.'

'Okay.'

'Haven't you got it? It was never part of the plan that we
move from the monument,' explained Racha. She lowered her
voice to a whisper, 'The situation between Seksan and Sombat is
becoming frayed.'

'Oh Sombat!' hissed Kawee.

'Shh,' shushed Racha.

'Well, what does he know?' continued Kawee in a lower voice.
'He's such an aristocrat. Went on a talk-show tour and wiped
himself clean with this bullshit agreement, a year into drafting!'

'Oh, not again!' Racha sprang to her feet. 'Stop making him
a patsy.'

'He killed the protest. Victory has never been so close,' Kawee was turning red.

'Narit, you see, the whole point is, we don't know what's happening with the negotiating team. It's not as if we have the phone wired here.'

'Rach, that's not the point! The point is, it's despicable that we're kept rocking back and forth on this diabolical pendulum. We need action.'

'There. Bingo, we found our instigator,' Narit pointed his index finger at Kawee. 'Somebody needs to trade in his life for that to happen.'

'He doesn't know shit, Narit,' Racha took her turn. 'Really, according to Sombat, the thirteen prisoners are released, and so we've scored our goal. Somebody should opt for a disband soon, and for goodness' sake, stop skating on this thin ice. It's self-torment. People will soon say you keep the mob around so the brutes can't tow us out so easily.'

'No, no disband. We started this. We, the trailblazers, won't stop until we win.'

Narit sighed.

Out of the blue Kawee laughed, Adam's apple vibrating deep in his throat, 'Tell me, my friends, what if the negotiating representatives are really dead? The brutes will be on our heels. They'll get us in this darkness, yes?'

Narit shrugged, Kawee must be really freaking out to think he would win one moment and die the next. Racha said, 'Well, it's dreadful to think my name will outlive me, enshrined somewhere at the side of a piece of historical crap.'

Hours dragged on. Tension kept heaping on top of its own towering layers. The communication with the Feds had gone insanely silent. Time after time the group turned to the radio, yet it consistently failed to confirm the fate of the representatives. Every time it started to hum a caution against the third party trying to instigate uproar, someone would angrily turn it off. Narit got the feeling that one more run of this and the poor device would be beyond repair.

Signs of tiredness and short temper were engraved on faces. Here and there a great many were fidgeting or smoking. Seksan, who had been picking at his jeans, suddenly jumped up and paced pensively amidst the heady cloud of nicotine.

'Sek!' shouted a guy from an entry point. He dashed in and grabbed Seksan by the arm. Seksan looked at his friend, as the latter struggled to catch his breath. 'What?' shouted Seksan. 'The reps . . . the reps,' gasped the guy. 'They're dead!' he exploded.

'What . . . Dead? Who says? You're sure?' Taking a moment to compose himself, Seksan quickly checked the source and summoned the team into a ring. Loud and clear he declared that it was obvious now that what was to happen next would be the protestors being hunted down. They must therefore be proactive and move towards Chitralada Palace for the protective wing of the monarchy.

Narit was soon caught up in the improvised preparation for the changing plan. Confusion reigned as people sitting away from the truck had no idea of the strategic manoeuvre. Still, they went with it. It soon occurred to Narit that he had better slip out to check if Wanchai and Nuch had gone home. There was no one at the spot where they were sitting.

Chapter 10

14ᵗʰ October

The clock had started its new round. The Royal Anthem blared out as the students once again started to move forth. By the time Narit re-checked in at the HQ, it had already moved to the front of the King's residence. He entered the area and saw Seksan locked in an embrace with Thirayuth Boonme, the movement's forerunner who had been set free by the agreement.

The two quickly entered into a serious talk, looking hot and flustered. Thirayuth soon had Seksan in tow as they headed to another corner of the palace. Narit followed them with his eyes, witnessing what he was certain was a tough grilling about the inevitable lack of communication and misunderstanding.

Looking around Narit realized he was more or less alone. Kawee was not there, neither was Racha. Narit sat down and tried to ease pressure off his leg. There before him stood the King's residence looped in by a moat, fences, and trees. A contract builder used to tell him that Chitralada was no stereotypical palace. It was hardly a home and was more like a huge agricultural laboratory for national research. There were farms with cows, pigs, and poultry, experimental rice fields, processing factories, and much more. Opposite the residence was the Dusit Zoo, a transformation of what was once the Royal Botanic Garden up until the reign of Rama VIII.

A messenger presently rushed over to report something to a student responsible for security. Having heard him out and learning that Seksan was in a meeting, he brought the news to Narit. He told him that there was an attack not very far from the protesters around the Makkawan Marble Bridge. A man had been struck in the back of his head by a brick. Though he was not badly hurt, he was briefly unconscious.

'You'll probably need to find out his identity and report it to the police,' said Narit.

'To the police? But we hate them.'

'Do it properly. I'll go up to announce this. People need to take precautions and be careful. Seksan should be back soon, report any progress to him directly.'

Having notified the crowd amidst the anxious chatter, Narit stepped down with a speaker clamped to his side, wobbling a little. He was frazzled himself.

'Oi, was that you, Narit?' a voice took Narit by surprise. After gazing into the crowd for a few moments, Narit saw someone whom he recognized as the chairman of the Silpakorn University Student Association, motioning him to come over. The round-faced man was with the other Fed representatives behind the palace's gate. Picnicking? Narit squinted. At first, he could not believe his eyes, these people were supposed to be ghosts. Seksan proclaimed them dead. Narit went over reservedly. Sandwiches, hotdogs, breads packed the quarter. Narit remarked, 'We thought you were killed.'

'That's absurd. What else have you been told?' exclaimed the chairman, munching on a sausage. 'Here, take some, straight from the royal pantry.'

'No, thanks,' Narit lowered himself down at the outer edge of the ring.

The guy guzzled a Coca-Cola and let out a sigh. 'What a day! This was meant to have been finished ages ago. I'm not in the least clued up on what Seksan's getting at. Coming here, camping here . . .'

'Look,' said Narit. 'It would've been nice were we actually told something. But nothing came through, nothing except the news that you guys died.'

'You should know better than to believe lazy rumours.'

'Yes, yes, but we didn't know that it wasn't the truth,' Narit protested. 'So naturally we thought we're next on the list, and it was a very compromised position back there. Seksan just wanted to cover for these innocent people. That's why we're here.'

'No, no, that's not why you're here. You guys are here because Seksan is a communist. He wants to see a war,' the chairman then jerked his head in the direction of Seksan who was shouting angrily on the other side. 'Heard that? The wound's infected, you've got to drain the pus out.'

'Seriously?' cried a neighbouring lady, racking up her hair into a ponytail.

Narit leaned over. 'Look, if somebody has enough energy for that, it's not us, all right? We're all spent.'

'Why then have your group moved from the Democracy Monument at all? That wasn't our plan. We're looking to avoid open conflict and coming here to squeeze, what did he call it?' he snapped his fingers a couple of times, 'The pus won't help steer us in that direction, will it? Be diplomatic, goddamnit. A year is a good length. Constitution is not some prêt-à-porter.'

'All right, it's not.'

'You see, you don't barricade these people in with guns and cut them no cat flap. Do that and you may well get a taste of shellfire.'

'I said all right,' acquiesced Narit, struggling with his temper. 'It's easy to say now, not so easy before, correct? I mean what've you been doing, eating al fresco?'

Mr Chairman tossed his food away and shook his head. 'This is pointless. Why don't we start telling these kids it's time to go home?'

'I couldn't agree more,' broke in the woman, 'I think the best way to go is to invite a king's representative to come out and read His Majesty's words. With this many people, there's gonna be a hell of a lot of confusion. No one's gonna believe anyone easily.'

'Yes, I was thinking on that too,' the chairman nodded.

With an exasperated sigh, Narit began to hoist himself up from where he sat.

'Hey where are you going?'

'I don't know,' replied Narit. 'But you know what, I'll have some sandwiches.'

Narit hurled himself back onto his clutch and went away. As he wolfed down the soft layers of bread and ham, Seksan was already on the cruising truck talking people into going home. The speakers around the palace came to life as a voice rattled out creating a substantial amount of static. Narit stopped to listen. It did not take long for things to quieten down. It was the public relations department reading out the royal tutelage.

'While the elders have a vast pool of experience in their possession, the juveniles have ideas and energy. If both generations can learn to take advantage of each other's strengths and make up for the other's weaknesses, the country will progress towards future along the road of optimism.

Students who have been tested and selected, who will one day become specialists in the field of their choice, equipped with both conscience and knowledge, knowing right from wrong will no doubt realize that when you have put forward your demand and achieved reasonable goals, it is only right that you now return to normal circumstances and return order to ordinary citizens.'

After hearing and accepting the words of King Bhumipol, the students set out to sing the Royal Anthem as a body. Despite a collective feeling of disappointment and frustration, their love and respect for the king came first. It was hard not to be affected by the moment, so many people singing the same lyrics in unison. Narit joined in.

From the moment the students bowed at the end of the song, the demonstration had been officially terminated. Nobody could any longer be held accountable to anyone. Not the University Federation, not the Thammasat Student Union, not Seksan, no one. There were no more leaders, no more followers, simply students, each treading their own chosen route towards home.

'So, we get our guys back, that's it?' Narit thought. This was going to be a bitter pill to swallow. On one hand it was tempting to think the Thais were entering another period of political recycling. They had learned to come to another painful compromise. On the other, a small selfish part of him was already thinking about his life as a graduate-to-be, a possibility of an apprenticeship at the Uni. He inwardly cursed himself for his badly timed optimism. All of this, for what?

Narit yawned for what seemed like the hundredth time as he ambled along. He sucked at his cigarette as the growing amber singed and broiled up at the end. He blew out the smoke. The inhalant became so thick a fume that it seemed Narit was walking in and then through it. As the miasma of smog receded, a street urchin who had been in his way seconds ago popped up in front of him, looking at him squarely in the face. A shirt, a gritty pair of jeans, and hair shorter than Racha. But the boy was no boy. Narit was riveted to the ground. Kwantar was demure.

They locked eyes, reticent.

She should not be doing this and prolonging the bitterness between them. True, he had been worrying about her, but it was already done, and he could not possibly undo it.

Narit breathed something incomprehensible and lugged himself aside. He clenched his fists and tried to make a step forward, but at the edge of his visual field, her tears were welling up. Yet, and yet, he closed his eyes and managed to make that step and strode away.

The dark buildings, the rundown quarters, the pale streetlamp all watched over him. Narit choked back his emotion and continued to walk.

'So, after all this time . . .' Kwantar panted, rushing to catch up, 'I have the rug pulled up from underneath me, is that it?'

Narit came to an abrupt pause and turned towards her with his best poker face. 'Can you please let this finish quietly?'

Kwantar kept her countenance directed towards the ground. She shook her head solemnly.

'Tar, you've got to stop doing this. It isn't healthy.' Narit took a deep breath in, leaning on stubborn rationale. It would have cut him down to his soul, still he said in a low key voice. 'Have some pride and go home. You're safer there.'

Kwantar slapped him in the face before her body started to tremor in shock.

Narit swallowed hard. 'I'm terrible, but I've never painted myself as good. So don't look at me now and think I'm somebody else.'

Her eyes became hardened in disbelief. 'I don't think you are somebody else, Narit. I think you're being too much of yourself with very little thought for others.'

Her voice was quivering. Narit was stern, seemingly stonewalling her.

Kwantar ran her arm past her eyes, smearing her face with another film of tears. 'You're supposed to make it up and not say these silly things to hurt me. You know how difficult it was for me to come here? You of all people. You didn't even put up a fight! You should have snatched my hand and dragged me out by force!'

Narit covered his face and sighed. 'How could I take you away from your family? I have nothing compared to them.'

Kwantar paused to compose herself. 'The world is a cruel place. Why is it so judgemental? Why do you conform, Narit?'

'I . . .' Narit was taken aback, angling his face away before it began to wasp. 'I don't know. Perhaps I'm messed up, broken like the rest of this world. I am sorry. Please go home,' and he quickly turned around.

Swinging his crutch, he strode away as quickly as he could as though he wanted to shake off his own shadow. Everything seemed to have gone blurry. Every sound seemed to be reduced to a distant rumble behind the wall of the world close by. His injury did little to slow down his pace. The cigarette, tonged between his fingers, had burnt down to the stub. The frail flakes left a trail and memories stalked.

Once consciousness started to sink in, Narit suddenly found himself absorbed into a tempestuous massive swarm. 'What the hell is going on?' Narit asked himself. The mob was throwing itself against the police line in a bid to steamroll its way through. The riot controllers kept crushing back, sworn by their duty to block that specific section of Rama V Road.

Before Narit could decide upon his own actions, another angry human wave surged against him, bearing him forward, hitting against the offensive line. Narit, urged by a sense of loyalty to his compatriots, gritted his teeth and exerted his force.

An officer seemingly in charge of the police gesticulated savagely in the direction of the students. Men in uniform pushed back, forcing the line to recede. However, their success was short lived as the students thundered back in, taking back the territory.

From somewhere, Narit vaguely heard Seksan futilely yelling for both sides to cease. The ex-commander's voice was soon lost in the shrieking of sirens and screams of the combatants as violence prevailed.

The clash intensified. Narit was somehow thrust so close to the forefront that his hands came into contact with a policeman's glass shield. It was so crowded that it did not matter anymore if he lost his balance. There was nowhere to fall.

The stench of hot, angry tiredness assaulted his nostrils. Caught up in the madness, Narit had lost all track of time. The heat and smell of sweat was making it difficult for him to breathe. Events had taken place at a frenetic pace until now, but the sheer tumult had his eyes seeing double and the rate at which Narit could process the frames became twice slower. He stuck with the momentum and just kept pushing, pushing, and pushing and—Bam!

A tear gas grenade landed amidst the throng. The sound of panic screams filled the air. White fumes, explosive gun shells, stabbing eye pain, and horror sent the students tumbling into the palace's moat en masse. Through the chaos, the police snatched the opportunity and ran after the dispersed crowd, whacking those who lagged behind with their truncheons and shields.

Without quite knowing how he had got there, Narit now found himself waist-deep in water. His eyes were burning, and there was a sharp pain in his ankle. He struggled hard to crawl ashore. But his arm failed him repeatedly, and he kept flailing back into the brown water.

'Here, take my hand,' shouted a man, before he started to drag him onto the bank.

'Thanks . . . Thirayuth?'

'Hurry, we'd better climb into the palace premises and take shelter,' Thirayuth hollered, 'Climb the wall! Quick, they're starting to fire!'

Amidst the yelling and disarray, Narit suddenly remembered about Kwantar. 'They've declared war on us! They've betrayed us!' Some students shouted. 'There'll be a massacre!' Anger was now suppressing fear, and there were those who were not yet done fighting.

Narit could hardly open his eyes, but his blurry remaining one could still see enough for him to make his way back in the direction of Democracy Monument. Narit limped down the streets. The macabre buildings on both sides whizzed past. His heart was thumping in his chest. In the middle of the road where they had encountered each other, Narit was looking at an empty space.

Narit turned on the spot, clutching at his leg. He had almost completed a circle when he thought he spotted a body collapse on the ground. He went hastily to the corner, rolling the person over on their back. The cap peeled off her head. His stomach dropped.

She was pale. Her breathing was shallow. He reached out with a trembling hand to touch her. Her cheek was cold. 'Tar. Can you hear me, Tar?' he called, frantically tapping on her face. No response. He felt her pulse; it was weak.

His palms sweating, his breathing fast, Narit checked hurriedly for any trace of attack. But there was less than a scratch on her forehead. 'Tar, talk to me,' Narit shook her by the shoulder.

'Please, say she has just fainted,' Narit quickly unbuttoned her shirt, seized the cap, and started to fan her. And as he began doing so, he thought of the nearest hospital. But it was then that Kwantar's face started to regain colour. Her eyelids soon twitched and lifted. Narit choked back his relief. Still shaking, he leaned down to kiss her on the forehead. 'Tar, what have you done? You're too much trouble,' he whispered, gathering her close to his chest, feeling her body quietly bucked and heaved.

Narit helped Kwantar sit up slowly. She still looked confused, but no longer at death's door. His relief was short-lived as his consciousness shifted back to tear bombs and danger. Narit studied the surroundings. While the violence has not reached them yet, sooner rather than later, the maelstrom was sure to gather pace. His eyes flitted rapidly from one direction to another as he pulled Kwantar onto her feet. Adrenaline acting as a temporary shot of morphine, Narit dragged Kwantar to an alley nearby, not yet realizing that he had long lost his crutch.

Not far away was a mini hay market where all the setting up materials were still covered and packed away. The floor was damp and unwelcoming. Narit found a mat and rolled it on the ground. Kwantar's body crumpled down onto it. He located a tap, turned it on to splash the water over tear-gassed eyes. He then crouched down next to Kwantar and twisted open a bottle of water he had found abandoned nearby.

'We should be safe here,' said Narit softly, handing the bottle to her. But Kwantar, staring blankly an ice box, did not respond. 'Look Tar, I am sorry. I shouldn't have walked away. Will you believe me still if I say I want to keep you safe from this?'

Kwantar was silent.

'Will you please talk to me, Tar?' Narit ran his fingers through his hair. 'It's war out there. How much longer are you going to keep this up?'

Kwantar kept still but finally replied in a detached tone, 'I'll be fine. You know who my uncle is.'

Narit gave a big sigh and stood up, vexed. 'I know who your uncle is, but do all of them? What if you get hit by a stray bullet? Will he be able to resurrect you?' He paused, his voice starting to break. 'Can you please go home? Tar, look at me, I'm serious. I know you're angry.'

Kwantar sat forward and looked at Narit challengingly.

'Fine, however you feel, I take it that you feel better. Look, I'll be honest. This conflict could get really bad. Fuck.' Narit massaged his eyes. He hated feeling out of control. 'Tar, this is not a game. Do be reasonable. I can't make you go home, and I can't leave you here either. I simply can't risk it. What do you suppose I do?'

Eventually Kwantar gave a resigned sigh and said somewhat irritably, 'What do you suppose I do? I had a feeling that things would turn violent. I came here to warn you.'

'Excuse me!? Did you just say you knew this was going to happen?' He turned away and waited for the rattling feeling to subside. 'What, what are you saying, Tar? How can you wait for this insanity to unfold carrying that knowledge? Those people are unarmed and scared shitless.'

'Are you suggesting I conspired against your group?'

Narit rolled his eyes, but Kwantar went on, her hand on her chest. 'I could have spared myself the danger, but I chose to find you, to warn you. And you're right. I could have been hit by a stray bullet for that.' Kwantar paused. 'Really, what do you suppose I do with that information? Seksan could not stop it. Who am I to prevent it? I certainly don't want anyone to get hurt. You can't blame me for that. I wasn't waiting to see a war unfold!' Kwantar looked strangely vulnerable with that haircut. Narit wanted to step closer to her, but it was miserably hard even to utter a thing.

'They're here. There're here to kill us!' The abject fear in the voice was unmistakable. A number of vocational students were racing past the alley entrance, carrying wooden sticks. 'Our comrades are hurt. Our comrades are beaten!' they yelled at the top of their lungs.

Narit watched them swerve round the corner towards Thammasat University and gravely turned towards Kwantar. He bit his lip and lingered for a moment. 'I was being pathetic,' he looked down and took a deep breath. 'I know what I said cannot be forgotten, but I want you to remember this too, that I regret it, because it's important. It won't happen again. But please, please go home, Tar. I have to go.'

'Narit, don't,' Kwantar pleaded. 'It's not worth it.'

'I didn't hear your answer.'

'No!' Kwantar frowned.

'Then, I'll have to take you to my place. You'll be safe there.'

'Let go of me Narit. You're hurting me. Look first at the shape you're in.'

'I'm sorry, but time's running short. There's no other way.'

Narit took off towards Rachadamnoen on his wobbly ankle, dragging the struggling Kwantar behind him. A couple more steps to the road, Narit became stuck in his shoes. Kwantar slipped off. Through the mist of the first light of the day, lines of tanks and artilleries emerged at the end of the boulevard.

Before them, the battlefield was clearly divided and chartered. The students were spread along the side of the Royal Hotel, stretching for the length of the road and presumably all the way back to the Uni. The military were stationed at the opposite junction before Phra Pin Klao Bridge, bunching around its killing machines.

Narit looked at Kwantar. She was still in a bad way. 'You all right? We can cross towards Thammasat, there's still time, I think. Just bear with me for a moment.' He took her by the shoulder and led her careering along the inner line of the pavement.

Ahead of them, students were taunting the soldiers, waving huge national flags like matadors. They called for answers as to why the government denied the country its most basic right of freedom and stop racketeering its citizens at the end of a gun.

After some running, Narit and Kwantar made their way around the monument. They came to a standstill upon running into a hive of activity a little way from the Royal Hotel. Young men were either busy mixing Molotov cocktails or stuffing clothes into the necks of the bottles.

'Have you heard?' said one of the team, a burly man with a huge nose. The grand way he announced it made Narit curious. 'Thanom claims on the radio that we attacked the police and trespassed on the king's palace.'

His skin-headed friend spat, yanking something in a crate. 'That dickhead! I was there, the king opened the gate so we could go in safe. It's the police who should be charged, you know how much tear gas landed in there?'

'That's lese-majesty,' groaned the big guy.

'I doubt that. The government has dug our grave, we're rioters now, no longer students. Now they've got the green light to kill, knowing that afterwards they can make an amnesty blanket to cloak the split blood.'

'As if they've never been caught before.'

Narit took Kwantar by the arm as they resumed their escape. He dodged out of the way of a truck carrying ammonia nitrate and other explosive material. Kwantar was exhausted and could hardly walk. They decided to take cover behind a van. Narit craned his neck and peered around the bumper.

The news must have spread like wildfire. On foot, students came trickling in steadily from Thammasat and the Royal Plaza, provoked and vehement. On free buses, they came from everywhere. Their faces were contorted with disgust, horrified at the nature of the double-cross. Some were unloading the lorry for provisions and makeshift weapons while others ran back and forth, audaciously hurling bricks and stones at the soldiers. After hours of bubbling tension, it had now boiled over and anger piqued out with the steam.

The brigade had just been reinforced and the M14 tanks started to edge forward. The presence of the infantry right at the heart of the city was uncanny. Marksmen had lined up, bowing low on their rifles with the barrels hinged on the bridge's barrier. Behind them came another line standing in formation, ready to provide fire support. Out of nowhere the commanding officer walked forward, his arm hovering in the air for a moment before bringing it down to execute his order.

Cans of tear gas came spinning forward, hailing down with fatally sharp clinks. Palls of fumes shrieked out. The street was quickly turned into a gas chamber as the explosive sound of firing roared deafeningly, submerging all the cries and shrieks. Rounds of bullets randomly drilled into the porous smoke. People ran and crouched low. Car windows shattered as they were hit. Narit snatched Kwantar, shielding her body with his own.

No sooner than it had started, the noise subsided, and a hush soon echoed. While waiting for the smoke to abate, Narit craned up his head to observe, bracing himself for a possible scene of carnage. But all he could see was rubber bullets scattered about the pavement. A number of shell-shocked students tentatively climbed to their feet and began to search for the injured. Kwantar sat hugging her knees, shaking all over. Narit tried to get her up, but her legs refused to cooperate.

Narit did not know if the soldiers had pulled their triggers with steady fingers, but they were still there, looking quite detached from the consequences of their actions.

As the wounded were being carried into the waiting household-van-turned-ambulance, many had dusted down their fear and took up the gauntlet again. Though some had backed off a distance further, no one ran away.

With a vengeance, the students retaliated with a barrage of firebombs—they landed, burned out on their own in the no-man's land before the great forces. It was like throwing eggs at a stone, and yet, it satisfied the pain more than being left to rot.

Narit recognized a brave young man at the borderline. Jira Boonmak, a high school junior, was walking almost playfully, Thai flag aslant on his shoulder and a shopping bag drooped on its pole. 'Hey,' he shouted, 'brothers, we are brothers, aren't we? We are Thais. Let's be friends.' Jira was moving in so close that the soldiers clutched their guns tighter. One of his friends started to yell for him to withdraw, but he went on digging into the plastic bag. Jira lobbed over an orange in their direction.

Hammers clicked, triggers were squeezed, bullets pierced the air. Jira keeled over on the ground. The orange made a high curve and fell.

He lay motionless on the floor as those around him dispersed as the soldiers fired another round into the crowd. The moment the shooting stopped, Narit told Kwantar to wait. Smoke still shrouded the street. He staggered towards Jira and somehow was the first one to make it there. He felt a sudden knot in his stomach. Jira was on his back, his body twisted at an unnatural angle. His hand was crooked, his head tilted slightly to one side with huge white eyes that saw nothing. Narit hurriedly ripped the flag off the pole and tried to press it against the wound. It was clear to all but Narit that Jira was long gone.

A gaggle of desperate men elbowed each other out of the way as they flocked in and collapsed at Jira's side. One started to cry as Narit shook his head in dejection. The young man who had called him to withdraw minutes ago soaked his hand in the growing pool of blood and painted it on his shirt and face. While clearly a symbolic act of grief, Narit nevertheless looked on, paralysed with horror.

Jira was soon hoisted up and placed on the democratic monument's golden tray. Like an angel peacefully ascending to the resting place in heaven that had long awaited him. To see him resting there, wrapped in the tainted flag, the movement was left exposed to an uncontrollable upsurge of outrage.

'Tar!' Narit called out, running back towards the red car, 'You've got to go . . .' But he found her dropped next to a man who lay sprawled on the road. The man was crumpled on the ground, his head resting on her lap, fixing his gaze at her for help. Narit could see a piece of his skull poking through his blood matted hair. Dark liquid seeped into her lap.

Narit tried to pull himself together and quickly went to fetch the medical staff. In a tearing hurry, they came rushing in, lifted the man onto a long wooden board and stretchered him away. On the firecracker tinted asphalt, the insignificant but obtrusive urine puddle ran down.

Still distraught, Narit stabled Kwantar up to her feet. The firing resumed. Not waiting to find out if they were rubber or real bullets, Narit gruellingly bore Kwantar into the nearest building, the Royal Hotel, struggling after some others up the stairs. They barged into a guest room. The door was slammed shut and a table pushed behind it. They looked awkwardly at one another. Each quickly found a spot and cowered. The guns went off again.

Narit propped Kwantar against the bedside and squeezed her shoulder. Her face was as white as that of Jira's. There was not much Narit could do other than hold her closer.

'Do not put any weight on the injured leg and avoid walking on it,' the doctor had said. Narit eyed the battered and shredded cast that still fought to envelop his treacherous foot. 'Shit,' he swore through gritted teeth and looked away.

* * *

The fear was palpable inside the room. Every split second was punctuated by one deadly sound or another. And every time it stopped, stretches of silence would be marked by yells of a discovery and the cries of the wounded. Though there were no quakes, no pieces of ceiling crumpling down, Narit doubted danger would have been any less consummate than if they were sheltering in an underground bunker during World War II. Everyone sat tensely on the floor, sewn together in an inaudible conversation orchestrated by the rhythm of the gut-wrenching sounds outside. Narit grappled with his fear and crept to the window.

The unfolding events seemed like a scene from movie, but this was really happening. It was the sight of people falling down. The sight of the infantry firing as if they were doing a test shoot on some target dummies. On the street, many of those who laid still would never again shift from their horizontal position.

And on the street, the unmistakable trails of blood marked the exit of the wounded.

The students had nothing but numbers. They wept and they fought. Not that they had muzzled their fear, but Narit suspected that it had lived too long and died.

A lad had hijacked a bus before jumping into the driver's seat. The engine roared as the vehicle geared towards a tank. Narit saw the youth wrangle with the steering wheel, jamming in a metal bar in an attempt to set the bus on a fixed course. But the bar shuddered and ricocheted off the wheel in the last minute. He jumped in to take control. The bus accelerated. Narit heard a rifle, and a red flower stained the window. The bus smashed into the tank and went up in flames.

Every time he turned his attention towards a new tragedy, Narit was afraid that he would clock someone he knew. And every time somebody got peeled off the ground, revulsion seeped through his soul. Where were Kawee and Racha? Narit hoped their luck would hold out.

A fresh group of soldiers marched in, reinforcing the existing ones. Little by little they crept in close to an alley beside the Royal Hotel.

A shirtless guy ran out into the middle of the road, shouting, 'Don't come in!' he was stiffly holding a wooden stick, the muscles in his face taut. The alley was strategically important as it provided an access point to the river. The pier was needed to transport the injured to Siriraj Hospital.

The sound of an engine came echoing above and a helicopter swung into view. Narit looked up. Everybody else looked up also and wondered. Their unsaid question did not last long as it opened fire. From the sky, a constant stream of bullets spewed from the machine gun.

Students ran for their lives. People dropped like flies. Some stumbled around like drunkards. Some threw themselves over their loved ones. Others simply froze. Narit wheezed for breath as he saw a girl not much older than his sister, laid on the street with a hole in her throat, clawing at the air with an arm outstretched. At the moment Narit wished humans were less desperate to hold on to life.

To avenge, the public relation department, the government lottery office, and Pan-Fah police station were all set on fire. Thick smoke cast a suffocating layer over the capital. The streets throbbed with heat and was drenched in the terrible smell of burning.

Narit's body had emptied itself of vomit long before. Somewhere within him existed an element of guilty relief that Kwantar and he were safe. He decided he had seen enough and withdrew. Inside, the TV was on.

Kwantar was staring at her blood-stained skirt, but Narit knew she was aware of what was happening around her. As a succession of defamatory statements against the movement wore off with the afternoon, the broadcast was interrupted by a piece of breaking news. Kwantar tuned in, her head turned as a newsreader said, 'Prime Minister General Thanom Kittikachorn has tendered his resignation.'

Chapter 11

15th October

The aftertaste of the scenes lingered. Narit wondered at what point had the telly been turned off? Exactly when did he fall asleep? Passively Narit turned towards the window, his neck crunched as he did so. The red sky, bleats of sirens, sporadic dense smoke, and belching flames, all were still very real.

The toll must still be mounting. More pieces of yesterday. All was ongoing and seemingly insatiable despite Thanom's resignation and a newly appointed PM. Even the king's speech did not work in an instant.

The broadcast was starkly vivid in Narit's memory. The king in his light suit, his face a scowl of grief and concern. His necktie skewed to one side, the right one—a memorable detail that Narit thought marked his unprecedented appearance on the screen amidst the political tumult.

Yet and yet, despite all that, the situation had not decelerated. At this point, the government could at best tend to the spent lies and the supply of the armament that it had. But people's sentiment had gone too far, Narit felt it would not settle for anything less than the heads of the three tyrants.

Inside the room, the others still half-slept. There was heaviness in his body, continuous pulsing and a twinge in his ankle.

The slightest movement could wreck a nerve or two. His eyelids gradually drooped and shut.

* * *

The curtain was becoming lighter as dawn finally neared. Narit reached out for Kwantar's hand as he regained consciousness, but just as his fingers came to rest on hers, the unmistakable sound of boots could be heard on the staircase and rattling again in the corridors. Everyone was alert but frozen where they lay, knowing that now the infantry as good as had the license to kill. The echo got louder and louder as did a voice of someone barking out commands. Then it was dead air.

Bam! Bam! Bam! The door blistered, cracked, and succumbed. A pistol shot, the shower of shrapnel, and the security chain snapped into half. Another kick and the door flung in, ramming into the table, smashing it out of the way. The doorway framed the outlines of soldiers. The light flicked on.

They tore in, pointing their guns at each person in the room and gesture towards the door with weapons. The shell-shocked students stumbled after one another until only Narit and Kwantar were left. The soldiers made way for a smartly dressed man. Distance revealed the familiar features. His oval head, smoothed over by straight hair flecked with silver, his moustache floating high above his wide, paper-thin lips. All completed with a silk handkerchief strangled in his grasp.

'You,' muttered Kwantar who had slipped down the bed and was now cocooned behind Narit's lean yet protective body.

'Good morning, Khun Narit,' Teera chirped, following it with an ostentatious yawn. 'Let's make this private, shall we?' he jerked his head, and a soldier rushed to the bedside, inviting Kwantar to get up. Teera smiled shrewdly, stepped forward, and held out his hand to her.

'My dear Kwantar, come home. Your mother, she's worried for you.'

If Narit caught what had just passed correctly, it was a scornful look upon her countenance that mirrored almost imperceptibly as a hurtful one upon his. What is this guy doing here? How could Kwantar be a priority right now for a man at least in part responsible for the bloodletting on the street outside?

Teera's presence filled the room, he adjusted his shirt collar as his cufflink caught the light now and again. He sighed, 'You know how she's worried about you.'

'She?' Kwantar muttered sarcastically.

'As a matter of fact, yes, she,' crowed Teera nonchalantly and turned to Narit. 'We were hoping that you'd win, boy. And that's my main job right now, praying. Please, not that flummoxed look again.' And Teera strode to the window and peeked outside. 'Revolution takes a lot of people and the innocence of ideology, and believe me, you certainly have played your part. But there are other players at the table. Have you wondered why the military haven't yet wrapped things up?' asked Teera, turning back to Narit. 'Well, that is because they don't have enough bullets. Perhaps somebody, I don't know, chose to disconnect the supply.'

Narit's gaze on the man stiffened. 'What the fuck!? You're a real piece of shit. You used us!?'

'That's quite enough, Khun Narit. Take Kwantar, for example. She knows how to take the news. For crying out loud, can we go home now, my dear?'

Kwantar gave a scornful chuckle.

'Oh Mr Narit, just tell her to behave.'

'It's finished, uncle. I'm not going anywhere. I'm with Narit now.'

Teera laughed. Narit turned towards Kwantar to ascertain that she was aware of what she had just said.

'I doubt that you'll be leaving with this pathetic excuse of a boyfriend. Because you know what my dearest, he's soon going to give you up.'

Narit tightened his grasp on Kwantar's wrist.

'Well, I'd hate to see you cry,' said Teera as he booted a pillow aside and inched his way towards the armchair. He sank down with an arm thrown over its back. All this was perhaps for a reason. His look was too relaxed. His smile was too wide. His voice sounded confident.

The only sound was the humming of the water pump in the loo. Teera glanced at his sergeant and then fixed his eyes on Narit. He slowly exhaled. 'I don't want you to see this, dear. But if you insist on staying, I have no choice. Bring the girl in.'

'Bloody hell!' Narit swore, and in a much louder voice, 'You are not telling . . .' He trailed off as more people entered the room.

Two men were carrying a girl by her arms. Narit's eyes widened. Kwantar shrieked. 'Nuch!' Narit howled and lurched forward. An unseen strike made him tumble. A soldier pointed the barrel of a gun at Narit.

Piyanuch was hanging from the men's arms like a flagging puppet. Her smeared face was covered with strands of hair that clung to her cheek. She barely looked conscious. Her skirt was torn with pieces loosely hanging off around the top. A trickle of blood ran down her inner thighs. Narit choked back tears.

'We found her on the street on the way here and happened to recognize what was at stake, so we saved her. Isn't that so, sergeant?' narrated Teera, his face dropped somewhat. 'Poor creature was wriggling in distress. She's a delightful little thing, although I must admit she's a little worse for wear now.'

Kwantar crept closer and tugged Narit at the arm. Narit raised up his hand slightly. Kwantar looked at Narit, confused. Yet she yelled at her uncle, 'You're not human. How could you do this?'

'My dear, had you not disappeared, we wouldn't need her as insurance. Like I said, your mother is worried about you.'

Kwantar glared. 'You liar, you just want my mother and me to be at your beck and call!'

'Your mother and you mean a lot to me,' Teera replied calmly.

'I want to speak to my father.'

Teera shook his head solemnly. 'Your father is very busy right now, and what I'm doing is in his best interest.'

'He'd never allow this.'

'Perhaps,' Teera smirked.

Narit heard them but couldn't process what they were saying. His head felt like it was vibrating, inflicting a certain hollowness that he tried to stifle. He slumped forward to the floor.

'Khun Narit,' someone called his name. The voice came through clear, but he failed to identify it. 'Khun Narit,' came his name the second time.

'Khun Narit, do concentrate! This is a moment of life and death, yet you have drifted away.'

Narit stared at Teera, his eyes burning.

'You've risked it all, haven't you?' said Teera. 'I thought I'd spare you this, but you've proved yourself to be—for want of a better expression—a real pain in the arse. So, choose one.' Teera observed his watch. His lips were set tightly in a half-smile, a hint of ironic kindness set in the bell-shaped creases at the sides of his mouth. 'Oh, do stop looking hurt and pick your favourite. You know I could take them both by force if I wanted.'

All eyes were on Narit. But the words wouldn't come.

Teera sighed and stood up. He loaded his revolver and flipped the cylinder. 'Too bad, I only need one. Let's go my dearest, Jitramon needs you to be home,' and he raised his arm in Piyanuch's direction.

'No, no! Don't do that!' Narit yelled, holding out his hand. 'I'll do it. I'll choose.'

'That's enough!' Kwantar screamed and burst out crying. She slunk close to Narit, and with a jittering hand, she touched his back. Narit squirmed. 'Narit, listen to me. Please listen to me. Narit for heaven's sake, I have no part in it! I may have known things but not this. So let this be understood, I can't be sorry enough for what has happened.'

Narit shook his head dejectedly. He bowed down towards his palms which was pinned down onto the ground, his body still trembling.

Hesitantly, Kwantar inched closer, pressing her thigh to his. 'I knew you were trouble from the start. But I was the one who was stubborn. So, it's only fair that . . . I started us, and it only right that I end it. At least, Narit, let us part on my terms.'

As Narit shook his head again and gasped for air, Kwantar gently drew him towards her chest and squeezed his body against hers. Narit was as good as lifeless. Her tears fell into his hair. Teera coughed.

'I'm sorry,' Kwantar then held him even tighter as if doing so would leave a permanent mark of her on his skin. 'We knew this could never last. Remember that.'

And she released him.

'Come' ordered Teera, pulling his niece towards him. Kwantar tore her hand away from his and turned for one last look at the man she loved. And she tarried, hoping that he would look her way so she could see herself in those eyes one last time. Narit's forehead remained pressed to the floor. He did not look. Kwantar wiped her tears and turned away. 'Have fun explaining this to my father,' she murmured and walked out briskly. Teera shrugged and followed. The soldiers roughly discarded Piyanuch onto the bed and deserted the room.

Narit frantically dragged himself towards his little sister. The sight of her broken body up close almost killed him. He reeled away for help, tripping once along the way. Outside, hisses of the fire that sparked in the distance had quietened.

Chapter 12

16th October

For a relationship that was as tumultuous as theirs, it had been destined to end badly. Yet Narit could never have predicted this in his worst nightmares. For there it was, his little sister desecrated and broken, and while Kwantar had not been involved directly, he could not help but feel she was responsible to some extent. But then again, Narit had to share that blame. Another day had gone by, and he was not sure what he was thinking anymore.

Piyanuch had just been given all-clear by the hospital and was back at home. She was still trapped in her own private hell and had become, to Narit's disbelief, afraid of him as well as her own father.

Though things had returned to a degree of normality for many Thais after Thanom, Praphas, and Narong left in self-imposed exile, they had not for this family, nor for other families who had been devastated during these last black days. The death toll stood at 77 with at least another 857 injured. A rape case, and probably not the only one, made very little impression on the overall carnage.

Yanee dealt with the present though she could barely cope with it. Often, she broke out crying in the bathroom and wished she did not have to go back in. She had let Piyanuch join the protest. It was her fault. It hardly mattered that she too was scared, that she too was devastated, or her voice kept breaking. It was a must that she told her daughter she would be all right.

Wanchai in this respect was worse off. The first and the last thing he knew about it was a sharp blow to his greying temple. When he woke again on the street, Piyanuch had already gone missing. After having reported the incident to the police, Wanchai kept pacing up and down the house, shouting that he would kill so and so, while at times seeming so dejected, he could not even raise a finger. The police, of course, were useless. The moment they uncovered the fact that military men were involved, they would bury the story until it was forgotten. The love-hate relationship in which the two organizations scratched each other's backs meant Piyanuch would never be given justice.

As for Narit, he sat motionless in a corner. His lips were sealed. Nobody knew about the soldiers. Nobody knew that Piyanuch's life could have been snuffed out and her body buried somewhere in the military fort.

Narit could not bring himself to say how he had found Piyanuch in the state she was in. He had told his parents that a friend in the hospital happened to recognize her and had informed him. 'I'm as clueless as you are,' so he said. Explanations were up in his throat, but he just could not spit them out. Possibly he just wanted to hide from the consequences. He could not accept his role in what had transpired. But if there was something he had learnt from this, it was that pain was how life liked to be defined, while perhaps happiness and ecstasy was how it was gambled away. But unlike guilt that had very little use, pain could achieve a lot.

* * *

Before his red floating eyes was a reeling world. Constant swigs of alcohol and drags of nicotine were alternating rituals. They lightened the weights in his mind and filled him with the purpose he needed. The familiar passing scenes and roadsides disappeared dizzily behind him as the bus hurtled from stop to stop.

The conductor was shouting something as the bus decelerated. Absentmindedly Narit tried to stand up, but the floor shuddered, and he fell back onto his seat. He made a second attempt as the conductor shouted again. Narit took hold of the railings, squeezed his way through the ruck, and hopped down the steps. As one of his legs still hovered in the air, the bus set off. Narit lurched and tumbled towards the pavement. His SangSom bottle slipped from his hand, and without smashing, rolled away. A clutter of waiting passengers edged backwards. Narit put up his hands to ward them off and awkwardly tried to find his balance. He wiped back his hair, exposing the intense colour that flared on his face. Doggedly he limped towards the archway of the gated community at the soi's end.

'I hate . . .' Narit repeated to himself as if to prevent him from losing his nerve. His mind was shooting in all directions, and he needed to concentrate on something. As the sight of the security booth got bigger, his chest heaved mightily inside his loose t-shirt. The security guards were joking with each other. There were two of them; Narit was sure it was not his double vision, although time was irregular and indefinite.

A car blared its horn, rising to a tremendous crescendo when it whizzed past him. Its tires squealed and the wing mirror clipped his arm. The driver shouted something, pushing his horn again and adjusting his mirror.

Narit was swayed sideward by the impact and almost into a nearby bin. He fixed his eyes on the driver, smiled, and took off towards him. Anxious, the man quickly rolled up his window and sped off.

Narit continued on his course. He dragged his damaged leg along, fuelled by the thoughts of yesterday. Nothing could stop him, not his injuries, not the fear nor the disturbance.

A couple of steps more and one of the guards poked his colleague in the ribs and pointed at Narit who was staggering at the same spot, like a boat rocking in the sea. The darker guy came out of his booth, cocking his head at Narit. The gesture failed to get any attention, so he put himself in Narit's way and grabbed his baton. A hysterical wail of a horn exploded again; this time it came from inside the wall. Another security guard who was observing from behind the glass was urged to abandon his position and wheel out the fence barrier.

Narit reached the guard. He pushed him rashly until the man collapsed onto the ground. His pupils now oscillated. Whatever was going on was a mad whirl of dancing pictures. Narit shook his head and tried to concentrate.

A police motorbike came into view. Narit stumbled backwards. The motorcade slowly passed him, and that was when he saw her. A blurred yet unmistakable picture of Kwantar sitting in the backseat moved into his frame. She was sandwiched between two men, gazing blankly ahead. With her short black hair combed to one side, she seemed tame like a lamb yet stern and withdrawn with red lipstick. As always, every first glance of her felt surreal.

The car pulled away so fast that it seemed lines of colours momentarily trailed after it. Narit, who had just been cast in stone, forgot to breathe.

His chest was heaving heavily. The cement could have been where he buried his punches, but not this time. The whole thing was like after an inertia trigger, the gun went click. His head in his hand, Narit wilted under the gentle tug of gravity.

Part III

1988–89

Chapter 1

So much for the faded husks of his youth. For fifteen years he had gone by the name Khatha, outrunning the phantom of his past by a distance that it could never overtake him. Each day more pain would be sifted off Narit until all that was left were archived facts. With Sarvitri as a thread running through both of his personages, Khatha had been a living figure, gradually sculpted by time, growing more assured, realistic, and alive. Because of her, the girl who ran away with him from the capital and to whom he was forever grateful, his life made continuous sense. Yet more than a decade of organized existence built like a labelled bookshelf was now destroyed to pieces of rubble, of papers with no distinct pagination.

They had been so young. He remembered it had been an uncertain one, but it had left a brutally deep scar. Khatha was born from that relationship, and it was a birth of necessity that never brought joy.

But what had happened to her and her influential family? How could her life have become so hard, and now the child, where did she fit in? The child was in the third year of secondary school, that would make her fourteen. Khatha calculated, eyebrows knitted together. Anuwat said the father was dead.

Now there he was, treading his steps back to Kwantar's home, still unable to believe that that rustic, simple place was where she resided. Most people had fallen into slumber, so hers was the only house that still had its light on.

Nothing stirred in the casement upstairs. Not then, not now. That box of light above the empty basement, sombre and melancholic, established a mood which was in keeping with the ambience that dominated the village. Khatha inhaled deeply and knocked on the door. Soon it opened. Sarvitri peeked out just to see her beau faltering away. A plastic bag encasing foam boxes dangled from the handle. Sarvitri shook her head and smiled.

In a corner of the room deprived of light, Anuwat sat quietly. His head hung low; arms pressed against his lap. 'You can eat, Sar. I don't think I can face food right now.'

Anuwat continued to cast his eyes on Kwantar, on that body wheezing under the blanket. His eyes were of a person who, unknowingly, had pawned her suffering as his own. Beside Kwantar, Darin was fast asleep, her torso slumped over the edge of the bed. 'Being a doctor is really not a profession for the faint-hearted, wouldn't you agree?' said Anuwat, as if to himself.

Sarvitri looked at Anuwat. 'She's stable. Hang in there, doctor.'

'Doctor? Doctor is it?' he paused, clenching his fists. 'You know, I used to think there's a retreat of a man within the profession. I thought it would go some way in keeping me whole. How silly I was,' Anuwat clasped his hands and exhaled into the cave between his palms. 'The ambulance will be here soon.'

'At last! Oh, don't worry, I'll stay with Darin.'

He nodded restrainedly. 'Do me a favour, Sar, make sure she goes to school, won't you? Tell the poor thing that I'll pick her up and take her to see her mum in the evening.'

'School,' Sarvitri repeated the word in her mind, the transferring of the food onto a proper dish halted midway. 'Are you sure? If I may. I understand you don't want Darin to see her mum like this and hope that she would look better at the end of the day . . .'

'It's not that,' Anuwat cut in and went on to produce a big, groaning sigh.

With this, Sarvitri slowly realized that he probably needed some space on his own to come to terms with Kwantar's condition. Embarrassed, she quickly reassured him that she would do precisely what he had asked. Sarvitri washed her hands and after having found forks and spoons, carried the meal over to Anuwat.

Anuwat turned towards his nurse and sat up reluctantly, a forced smile carved on his face. He said, 'All right,' eventually taking the tray. But the first spoonful was still in the chamber of his mouth when the red flashing light started to wheel across the walls.

* * *

The door swung back, and teacher Khatha stepped in. He made his way across the classroom. As usual the hushed quietness was only broken by the sound of a textbook being put on the desk and a screech of a chair as he seated himself down.

Before him sat Darin, slouching at her desk. Though it was by his own order that she was there, Khatha started to regret his insistence. He reached out for his cane, and for some time he kept an iron grip on it. He shut his eyes, eventually stood up, and snatched a piece of chalk from the ledge.

'Before we wrap up 14 October 1973, I want to share with you yet another anecdote to illustrate how frightening the event was. A friend of mind stayed three days in the bathroom at Thammasat, can you imagine that? The soldiers were raiding the place and she could not come out in fear that she might be carted off. So, what do you think she did to survive in that cubicle during all those days?' he spread out his arms to help his narration. Dara raised her hand and responded. 'Very good guess, Dara. She drank the fluids in the toilet bowl to keep herself hydrated. Now,' continued Khatha amid the low-keyed marvel of his students. He now positioned himself near the middle of the board and wrote at the top '6 October 1976'. 'Anybody who has an idea why such a date is in the annals of Thai history, raise their hands.' He turned around and leaned against the board.

Vilai shot her hand up.

'Anybody else prepared for this class?' Khatha swept his eyes across the room and sighed. 'Fine, Vilai it is then.'

'Isn't it when Thai state forces and far-right paramilitaries killed the student protesters on the campus of Thammasat University?'

'The Thammasat University Massacre. Excellent as always, Vilai,' remarked Khatha unceremoniously and kickstarted the period with his usual enthusiasm. 'Open your books and turn to page 74. I trust you all remember that following the students uprising, the Thais got a constitution in 1974,' Khatha began. 'Although it didn't last, many historians agree that it was the purest and the most innocent constitution in our history. Why? Because it comes from the will of the people and not some governing body who wanted to bend it for their own benefits. However, in hindsight and with so many people dead . . . There was a man I met on a train totally by chance. He once told me while I was still writing speeches, "Tread carefully and tread quietly. Some goals are achieved much more affectively when you pick your fights and play the long game." And guess what? He could be right.' Khatha observed his students' thoughtful expressions, holding his arms behind his back. 'The 1974 constitution didn't manage to uproot all the problems layered within Thai society. A coup d'état followed, people were divided into far left and far right, and it seemed violence was the only resource to solve the tension. Hence the massacre. Students got killed and were strung up under the tamarind trees in the university. These barbaric acts are not tales. I personally knew many people who had turned communist and ran into the wild before they got royal pardons. I also knew a person who became even more radicalized and ended up with this rope around his neck. He was my best friend, and his name was

. . . his name was Kawee,' Khatha paused. He always mentioned his friend's name in this lesson to give the impression that he shared the story with the students, rather than just drone out facts. Normally he had trained himself to feel nothing, but the past had been opened up again, and so he rather lost his train of thought. Khatha made an attempt to cough and continued. 'Don't worry if somehow you are unaware of this incredibly important event. We will be going into it in more detail in many classes to come. Now, if you look at this excerpt at the bottom here, the press made a huge run of the news . . .'

Darin stayed in her own head, not really knowing if it was an asylum or a dungeon. Either way, her teacher's words seemed to disintegrate mid-air before they reached her. All she heard was the lacklustre scribbling of notetaking. So very little air went in for every deep breath. Like a thunderbolt, Darin sprung to her feet.

All eyes were fixed on her. Khatha paused from turning the page and looked up. The page slipped, curved, and rustled to one side. 'A question, Darin?' he asked flatly.

Darin looked around bewilderedly and on the spur of the moment murmured, 'Can I go to the toilet?'

Khatha jerked his head to the door, 'Go ahead.'

Darin squeezed herself out from behind her row and bowed as she scuttled past him. She drifted towards the toilet. And once the cubicle's door was shut, and the school's bell rang, Darin let out a howl in its resonance.

* * *

'Narit,' she waved enthusiastically at him as he appeared from the lecture hall. It was only him that she saw and everybody else was out of focus. When compared to his peers, there was something about Narit that was different, and despite his awkwardness around others, people gravitated towards him.

Kwantar looked at him as he exchanged jokes and goodbyes with his friends, her smiles which were painted the colour of fuchsia that day refused to leave her face. This man was about to take her to see his family, and she still could not believe it. While this showed an acceptance and a sign of serious intention, she had not really thought about when her time would come and how she would be embarrassed to hesitate. For now, she continued to smile at him as though that alone would draw him towards her.

'Hello there,' he greeted. 'Why are you sitting here all on your own? Anyone would think you're available.'

Her head was at an angle. Through her narrowed eyes, she checked him up and down. Narit looked smarter than usual with his shirt properly tucked into his trousers and a polished pair of shoes. 'Are you the man I meant to see tonight? If not, I'd prefer you leave now, because my boyfriend is very jealous. He could get you killed.'

Narit chuckled. 'You made that up, Tar.'

'Don't ruin my imagination. It's Valentine's.'

'Well, you have your roses and chocolates. Am I missing something?' he said with a sly smile.

Kwantar giggled, 'Why don't you grant me a wish on top of those.'

Narit placed himself down next to her. He kept his notebook aside. His legs were crossed, his chiselled chin in this hand, and his hair tightly pulled back. Eyes half-lidded, he looked at her. Kwantar's face stayed burned. Out of nowhere, she thought she heard something that sounded like 'All right. One wish.'

She almost burst with happiness. Kwantar looked down to hide it and said softly, 'I just wanted to say that I wish in five years' time, we will still be like this, so in another five years I could make the same wish, then another five, and so on, and so forth.' And she looked up, adding, 'Let's hope my beauty can rejuvenate every five years though.'

Narit chuckled again. 'One moment like this is enough for me. It's durable, I guess. You can hang out with this kind of memory forever.'

'You're the least ambitious man I know!' said Kwantar with more than a hint of sarcasm.

'And look, I'm with you.'

Kwantar narrowed her eyes. 'I see you do irony too. I'm leaving.'

'Me too.' And Narit followed her down the yard in his long, confident stride. When he caught up with her, he placed his hand on her back and started to caress the nape of her neck. 'Obviously you know where you're going.'

No, she did not know where she was heading then, nor did she know where she was; yet Kwantar winced, her head felt heavy. It was as if she did not have bones, that her body felt liquid-like. Kwantar squeezed her eyes in an attempt to think. Disconnected flashes of Narit putting down some food on her plate, of his family smiling and talking to her, then . . . then she was somewhere else. She saw her hair raining down onto her gown and Nhamfah consoling her and Darin. 'Darin?' she murmured. 'Dumpling?' Kwantar's eyes were wide-open and started to roll around in search of her daughter. The smell of disinfectant, the blurry white pictures, and the crinkled saline drip that gradually shook into clarity all screamed hospital.

The ward nurse noticed she had regained consciousness and went to notify Anuwat who soon arrived with an otherwise maintained composure, except for the messed-up paper on the clipboard he had with him. 'How are you feeling?' he greeted.

'Ah, doctor,' Kwantar could barely sigh out the words, struggling to turn her neck.

'It's all right. We'll have plenty of time to look at each other later.'

'How long have I . . .?'

'Twenty-eight hours,' replied Anuwat calmly, hoping that his way of delivery could soften the gravity of his answer.

'Twenty-eight hours . . . That long.'

He nodded. 'So, how are you?'

'I think my bones hurt. I tried to . . .' Kwantar coughed violently, choking on the air she took in. The jolt in her chest gave her a burst of energy, enough to raise her hand to cover her mouth.

'Here,' said Anuwat, handing her a napkin.

With a shaking and frail hand, Kwantar blotted her lips and crumpled away the tissue and the blood she knew was inside. Anuwat asked the ward nurse to fetch a pillow which he gently wedged in behind Kwantar's shoulders. He then pulled in a chair and settled down.

'Nu, thank you.'

'Shhh, it's all right.'

'I just wanted you to know,' she replied, gasping for air. 'It's funny isn't it, for all those months you talk of moving out to hospital, and when you're here . . . Actually, Nu,' Kwantar seamlessly added as a thought entered her mind. 'I have a request. It'd be my last, promise.'

Anuwat smiled. 'Go on. Though it doesn't have to be the last.'

'It's Darin, my daughter.'

Despite his usual composure in such situation, Anuwat found his heart beating fast. His momentary pause caused the file's cover to uncoil and close itself. 'It's good you started this,' he began, staring earnestly at her. 'Tar, I'll take care of Darin. With your permission, I want to adopt her.'

'What?'

'What is what?' replied Anuwat wryly. 'I wanted to tell you the last time I went to your house, but you know . . .'

Kwantar blinked.

'Tell me, what is it?'

She looked away. 'Nu, this is really not a burden I can place on your shoulders.'

'Tar, it's really no trouble.' Anuwat became self-conscious as the increased level of his voice attracted the attention of the occupants of the neighbouring beds. He suppressed his agitation and continued, 'Tar, after her high school, Darin will go to university in Bangkok, she will do arts or science, anything she wishes. I'll see to it. Anything at all! You'll be proud of her. Also, I've already looked into the arrangement of a trust fund for her.'

'Oh Nu, this's not right!' Kwantar coughed. 'I have no way of repaying you.'

'Please, Tar, let me do this.'

She turned away. 'Please, just . . .' she paused, 'just help me find Darin's father.'

'Sorry . . . what?' Anuwat stuttered inaudibly.

Kwantar turned back to face him and fixed her eyes on his. 'I want you to find her father.'

'Her father . . . of course, her father.'

Kwantar was dying. The symptoms she had just described confirmed his suspicion that the cancer had spread to her bones. Anuwat grabbed his knees tightly, wrinkling the cotton of his trousers. He searched for words, but he knew he must only say 'All right, I'll do it,' and so he finally did. Anuwat reached for his pen and afterwards brought himself to jot down the information Kwantar painfully parted. 'Call her and ask for the number of Kawee or Racha. Kawee or Racha, have you got that down? Good.' There followed a silent moment during which Anuwat contemplatively pushed up his glasses that had slipped down his nose. 'And if,' he ventured, 'only if, "he" refuses, I just want you to know that Darin still has me.' And with that, Anuwat abruptly stood up and excused himself, saying that it was time to collect Darin from school.

* * *

Khatha watched Anuwat arrive in his car. Over the last few days, fifteen minutes before the school's bell, the doctor had shown up and he would set himself down at the grandstand. When Darin came down, he would wave with a smile like he had just woken up to his best self. It had been the same and each time he had done so without realizing he was being watched.

Today, Khatha gazed at his watch and peered out from his darkened room. A handful of devoted parents were already present in their usual spots. But that part of the grandstand Anuwat had claimed recently was still empty. Khatha let go of the blinds under his fingers and returned to his desk and mountains of sheets. This he did absentmindedly, and just as absentmindedly he catalogued them.

The sounds of doors being slammed excitedly and students' laughter soon filled the school. Khatha had learned to put up with the level of noise and while it lasted, had always gone out through the back door, taming his need for smoke by sipping water. Today however the noise served as a source of notice. He paused mid-routine, went back to the window. After a group of students ran towards Songthaews, squealing with delight as they scrambled into the vehicle, that spot at the stand emerged. It was not Anuwat however but Sarvitri.

Khatha had not been expecting her. On the one hand he felt flustered by her presence, on the other, it was a sense of relief that things must be okay at the hospital that she was free to come this early. Darin and Vilai soon turned up and started to talk with the nurse. Khatha checked the time again and took a long rueful look at the stack of essays. He grabbed his suitcase and took off, leaving the office a little untidier than he should have.

Khatha walked briskly down the corridor and, as he approached, acknowledged Sarvitri who was already looking his way. He then craned his neck to the road that stemmed out from the swishing rice fields, turning to Darin and remarking, 'Your doctor is not here yet.'

Darin didn't reply but looked at Sarvitri who blushed and quickly said, 'I'm told to pick up Darin and take her to the hospital.'

Khatha's steely eyes widened. 'Is there an emergency?' It had been two days since Kwantar had come round in the hospital and Khatha had been on edge, waiting for news.

'The doctor's a little busy today,' explained Sarvitri with a time-honoured flatness of her profession. She then flashed a smile at the girls. Her small eyes reduced to crescents. 'You know, Vilai here is also coming along with us. Why don't you come too? You could just go and say hi to the doctor. He could use that.'

Out of his field of vision, Khatha could still sense his students stealing a glance at him, at their Mr Pedantic, their faces set in a mild wince at the prospect that he might be joining them. Khatha hesitated a moment and then glanced at his watch, 'I've got to go the town hall. Perhaps next time.'

Sarvitri looked confusedly at Khatha as he flitted away. The moment she realized the girls were attempting to read her thoughts, she adjusted her cap and spiritedly embraced their shoulders. 'You're ready? All right, let's go.'

* * *

At the first bed in the long hall where the vertical view was obstructed by the drip poles and infusion pumps, Anuwat was directing his small flashlight. Kwantar's pupils made imperceptible moves following the glare. Anuwat switched off the light and Kwantar's eyes appeared starkly before him. They were like those of a doll, empty, shallow, and rimmed by edgings of winter grey. Although they firmly reflected his image, he doubted she could register his presence. Today had wrung him out emotionally. Anuwat became angry with himself. There was nothing else he could do now but to bring up her blanket and tuck its rim tightly behind her bony shoulders. Kwantar's eyelids shut, and she seemed to doze off.

'Doctor,' Darin called out sternly from behind. Anuwat turned with a practiced smile he had been giving her more and more these last few days. 'Ah, there you are, Darin. I see you have brought your friend. Vilai, isn't it? We met before at the school.'

Vilai shyly greeted him with a wai.

'How's mum?'

'Your mum is . . . She's very brave. She's been waiting to see you.' Anuwat looked down at the floor, then from under his neat and prematurely greyish eyebrows, up at Darin, 'What do you say to taking some days off school and just staying with your mum?'

'That'd be nice, wouldn't it, Da?' Vilai gushed out, 'I can bring you worksheets and help you with schoolwork. That's no problem.' Vilai then poked her stupefied friend with an elbow.

Darin's eyes betrayed the fact that she was clearly distracted. 'What do you mean, doctor?'

'I mean,' Anuwat paused, taking his time to get up, 'your mother loves you and it makes her happy to be with you.'

Darin moved her head in a way that was neither a nod nor a shake.

'Shall we take turns? I'm needed downstairs.'

Darin did not reply. Instead, she hurried to the side of her mum with Vilai following at her heels. And as Anuwat passed Sarvitri, he reluctantly stopped and uttered under a repressed breath, 'We're lucky, she's stabilized. She's good, for now.'

'So I am told.'

'Right. Please do try to get her to drink something. She is dehydrated. Also, the patient in bed 201 needs their bandage changed.'

'Understood, doctor.'

As Anuwat exited the hall, Sarvitri inhaled so hard as if the air would pump up her guts. She clenched her fists and went up to the girls.

Vilai was trying to say hello to Kwantar. Sweetly she called her, 'Auntie, it's Vi,' touching her forearm. Kwantar opened her eyes and turned her head towards Vilai momentarily like a person would when glancing at a clock, then looked away to face the bedside cabinet. Vilai bit her lip, looked at Darin and then the nurse, hoping for an explanation.

Sarvitri put on the most carefree face she could. Much as she hated the secrecy, she could not tell them that Kwantar's heart had stopped, not once but twice, in the afternoon. Anuwat himself said nothing, and she should respect that. The girls kept their eyes on the nurse as she drifted to the other side of the bed.

'Sister Sar,' said Darin. Her voice quavering, her hand timidly touching an intravenous bloodline that ran into the dorsal of her mum's hands. 'What's this blood bag? It wasn't here yesterday. Sister Sar, why can't mum speak?'

Sarvitri's expression stayed as it was, just as it should. She stooped down and reached out for a glass of water. Instead of an explanation, she told them that Kwantar needed help drinking some water and wasted no time as she went on to show the girls how. 'You dip the straw in like this, close one end of the straw, and lift up. Then, gently push it into her mouth. Only when the tube is firmly inside do you release your finger. And don't forget to have some napkins ready; she might not be able to take everything in. Come on Darin, Vilai. Stop looking at each other and show me you can do it.'

Sarvitri, after having supervised the short practice, left to attend to other patients.

Chapter 2

Khatha was standing just outside the ward, peeking in through whatever gaps the glass slats allowed. Amidst a jumble of flashbacks, he was barely there. He was within his own head, hearing an imaginary piece of music that watching her brought on. A soundtrack to the October Revolution. Yes, he would name it that.

Khatha moved back to the bench he knew was behind him. His shaking hand fumbled for the seat as he lowered himself down. A bouquet of white carnations was clutched tightly in the other.

He thought he had mentally prepared himself for this. But now, Khatha struggled to get up and approach the ward again.

Not seeing her the last couple of days meant that now he was in as much shock as when he had discovered her at the house. Kwantar was like a ragged doll, her skin pale, almost translucent, just lying there, staring at the whirling fan on the ceiling. A detached look drifting in and out of her face. Is this how a body winding down and letting go appeared? She would have been unrecognizable if every detail of her face had not been etched into Narit's soul all those years ago.

The corpulent woman with pantomime eyebrows he saw at Kwantar's house the other day was just done with squashing some banana with a fork. She was trying to feed Kwantar whose jaws clenched up as the spoon touched her lips. Khatha raised his hand to his mouth and took a deep breath in.

With a vain attempt to hold back his tears, Khatha lay the flowers onto the bench and began to walk away, an anonymous gesture, the card left blank. The image of Kwantar flickered as he drifted past the frames of the louvre windows. For a fleeting moment, he saw her tugging at the oxygen tube plastered below her nostrils; Darin prompted to grab her mum's hand and keep it down onto her stomach; some textbooks scattered at the end of the mattress where Kwantar's feet could not reach. Then, all that he saw was faded white wall. Khatha wiped his eyes and gathered his pace.

He quickly made his way down the stairs, delving into his pocket. Some coins were clinking. At the bottom at the bright green telephone in the corner, Khatha picked up the handset. Coins impatiently rushed in. After a couple of rings, a woman answered.

'Hi, is Sarvitri around?'

'Please hold on a moment,' said the woman, and in a coarser voice she echoed his question. 'I'm afraid she is on duty.'

'I see. Could you tell her that Khatha will be waiting at the entrance when she finishes her shift?'

'I'll pass on the message.'

The phone soon spat out the change with a clink. But the abrupt sound marked the beginning of a long, inconsolable pause wherein Khatha felt cold and alone.

Had it been on that day, when he was carried there by a raging current of alcohol and revenge, perhaps there would have been a small dark part of him that would have felt perversely triumphant to see her lying like that. But with her presently in that state, he could not comprehend how he could ever want to see her the way he just did and endured it. Khatha gave himself a shake and made his way towards the rows of chairs around the hospital's pharmacy.

Twice he noticed Anuwat. On the first occasion the doctor was wheeling a patient somewhere and as a result failed to see him. On the second, he was striding across the green lawn behind him, deep in discussion about something with a nurse. The doctor just had enough time to do a double take and to raise his hand up to let him know that he was not ignoring him. Khatha nodded back. 'Hang on a minute,' his own voice cut across his tumultuous thoughts. 'Wasn't Tar the one he admitted to putting on a pedestal?' Khatha grabbed his knees tightly. His knuckles whitened as the pressure increased. A bitter chuckle soon broke from his lips.

The hospital had become less hectic as evening neared. The counter, the chairs, the buildings were all throwing their soft shadows onto the ground as though they were falling back into it. That was when Khatha saw the woman he had seen nursing Kwantar coming down and leaving. Khatha checked the time and as he looked up, saw Sarvitri emerging from a narrow walkway, happily approaching him. Khatha's lips stretched out marginally. She stopped before him. He reached out and took her hand.

Sarvitri smiled and blushed. 'Do you still remember the last time you were here?'

'Yes, I needed to use the loo.'

'And this time? Let me guess, you're worried about your student missing class, aren't you?'

Khatha kept quiet.

Sarvitri's demeanour abruptly changed. She leaned toward Khatha and lowered her voice. 'I probably shouldn't be saying this, but I overheard the doctor's taking in the girl.'

'Yes, I think he once mentioned something about that,' he replied.

'I understand him. He has always loved children. He just never found the right person. I guess this is his chance to have someone to call his own.'

Khatha did not respond. Instead, he fumbled for his cigarettes before remembering the 'no smoking' sign he saw earlier. He withdrew his hand awkwardly. 'Who's that woman looking after Darin's mother?'

'Who, Nhamfah?' said Sarvitri curiously. 'I heard she was a friend from a clothes factory.'

'A factory?'

'Yes. You sound very surprised. Factory worker is rather a common job around here.'

'Yes, yes, but her?' Khatha alarmed himself at his own remiss.

She looked at him for a passing second. 'You are very curious about her.'

Khatha measuredly grabbed his briefcase and began to get up on his feet. 'I knew her. A very long time ago,' he said, forcing an air of nonchalance, when only he knew that it was far from the truth. Khatha felt the small of his back twinge and reached around to rub at it. Seeing Sarvitri's concerned face, he quipped, 'I'm fine, or will be, in a minute or two. Okay, shall we? What are you cooking tonight?'

'Your favourite, crispy omelette and cabbage soup.'

'That's what I was hoping you'd say.'

Sarvitri took Khatha's arm. And although he once told her that she looked like an accessory that way, Sarvitri could not care less, replying 'All right, an ugly one then. I can make no man jealous of you for a day, but I'll make all of them jealous of you for a lifetime.' Cherishing the presence of her man by her side, as Sarvitri proudly strolled away with her love, she could not help but think what a small world it was that people who had known each other so long time ago, in another time and place, would cross path again in, of all places, a hospital.

* * *

After having to cover his colleague's shift due to a last-minute invitation to a wedding, Anuwat gratefully returned to the hospital's on-site accommodation, frazzled by the extra work that had stolen his overdue rest. The room sometimes felt more like his home than his own place as he stayed there so frequently.

After fumbling with the door handle, he drowsily entered the room, passed the mess others had left behind, and went straight to his corner. Wearily he drew his cubicle curtain to a close and removed his glasses. Anuwat dropped face down onto his bed. The tension in his body started to evaporate. His tiredness was absorbed by the mattress. All thoughts that came to his mind circulated and powered by their own steam became more and more disconnected.

'Doctor, are you asleep?'

Anuwat did not answer, not even giving an effortless 'hmm'. But just before he drifted off and the footsteps faded, he glimpsed something pushed under his partition, something brown and rectangular. He groped for his glasses, holding them in his hand and peered through them. The sender's name was enough to make him reach down for the envelope.

He sat, perching himself on the edge of his bed, tapping the envelope on his knees tentatively. His initial curiosity was quickly replaced with doubt and worry. What story would the letter be telling him? Would it say that the father was still alive, or even worse, willing to reconcile? The fact that he would think such a thing made him feel more than a twinge of guilt, and he tried to shake it from his head.

Tied to a promise, Anuwat had tried to call the individual by the name of Kawee but had learned that he was dead. He had also called another person named Racha. She was away on some photography expedition. Based on that information, Anuwat had asked a lawyer friend in Bangkok to do some digging for him. He wanted everything written down in case he might need it one day.

Now what he had so persistently sought had finally arrived. But there he sat, looking as though anxiety would sooner kill him than the words in the letter.

'What if this Narit is still breathing?' It would be against her last wish, but he would not want him here now or any day for what remained of her life. It would merely complicate things. It would make dying more difficult. What Kwantar needed was peace, not more heartache.

'What if this Narit . . . oh, sod it,' and Anuwat began ripping open the brown beaten-up envelope. He pulled out a piece of paper and placed its case aside, his heart beating fast while he exposed himself to its contents.

'Dear stranger,

How is life in the backwaters of nowhere? It has been ages since we last met—you have always skipped the reunions, you miserable sod! So, you can imagine it was quite a surprise to receive your call the other day.

Yes, I vividly remember Kwantar, how could I not? Good news is I have managed to obtain some information regarding the father of her child. Narit Chanpradith was born on 1 November 1947, and according to the District Office, he is not dead. He went to Debsirin for high school, then Thammasat for his bachelor's and master's degree in political science. He did not finish his masters though. Apart from that, there is not much about him in terms of records. No TIN, no current House Registration, and the last national ID he had was when he was 21. It is as if he disappeared from the face of the earth. Strangely enough no one has reported him missing. But you know our Registry Office . . .

From what I have learned, his family relocated to New Zealand in 1974 after something terrible happened to his sister. The neighbour said they run a Thai restaurant in a small southern town called Dunedin. No one could say for certain whether he moved there with his family. He disappeared after the uprising of 14 October 1973 (he was the lead copywriter for the Student Fed by the way). Anyway, I called up my acquaintance at the immigration office. He says there is no record of him leaving the country since then, by plane at least. But as you might well know, over the last few decades, politically charged ideologists have fled Bangkok in search of greener pastures—namely the districts—for a peaceful life. Who knows, maybe he's living somewhere in the countryside.

As for Narit's character, Racha said he was an ideologist and often rubbed people the wrong way. He was basically a good guy and popular amongst his friends. Racha enjoyed talking about the past. Unfortunately, she now had no clue as to what has happened to him.

Narit cut quite a figure though, no wonder Kwantar was so taken by him. See for yourself, I have enclosed some pictures I managed to get my hands on. This is the best I could do. I am sorry I could not find him, but I hope this helps. And do not worry about the adoption, you can count on me.

Last but not the least, do come to the reunion next month. Everyone in our old gang will be there. Hopefully you will be too.

My best,

Your friend, Viroj'

Anuwat flipped the paper over, nothing was on the other side. So, he picked up the envelope and slid his hand inside. There were a few sheets, but despite his need to see them, he was tempted to crumple them up. Eventually, he took a deep breath and pulled them out, intact.

The first picture was a close up shot of . . . is this Narit? It was not what he had been expecting. The young man looked every bit the rebel, with a buttoned-down shirt and a cigarette dangling from his mouth. He had misty, jet-black eyes, bracketed by razor-sharp cheekbones, a singular combination that gave him a rugged yet arresting appearance and made him look . . . Anuwat tilted his head to one side before he hastily shuffled to the next picture, then the next. His hands started to tremble but kept on shuffling the disconcerting photographs repeatedly. The more he looked at Narit, the more certain he became. He slumped back on the bed, consumed by disbelief in what he was looking at. Anuwat fought with his stiff yet shuddering arm to take off his glasses. But no matter how distorted his vision became, the reality of the identity of the man in the picture was clear and absolute.

* * *

The morning after and with very few hours of sleep, Anuwat, despite his dark eyes, still functioned just as a doctor should. After a busy morning and a quick brunch in which Anuwat had pondered on how to take the matter into his own hands, he went to his room to pick up a few things before moving on to visit Kwantar. His mind was reeling, but now was not the time to lose his cool. Anuwat had decided on a script. He would recite it to her. It would be a lie, but it would be a beautiful lie. Because given his intention, this could only fall into the good side of deception.

'Tar,' called Anuwat as he settled down next to her. He had asked Nhamfah and Darin if they could be left alone and had drawn the curtain as he would when he performed a medical inspection. Anuwat solemnly squeezed her arm, slightly leaning towards her. This afternoon Kwantar was again sedate. Her eyes half-open, her pinpoint pupils sank in below her eyelashes. Deep inside that tranquillized silence, there was turbulence somewhere. Thank God for the morphine. Yes, he would thank it, even though the need to prescribe it daily meant that he could already see death hanging around.

Anuwat had no idea whether she would rather be in severe pain yet more aware of her daughter and friends and the love they had for her. But he simply could not handle seeing her in agony again. As a dear friend and her doctor, he had chosen for her. And so, to morphine, to self-assurance, and to his professionalism, Anuwat had committed himself. Now, as he gazed upon her lying in relative peace on the bed, he felt his decision was more than justified.

Anuwat exerted a gentle force on Kwantar's arm again. 'Tar, I have some news for you. The father, Narit, he's no longer in Thailand. In fact, the last anyone had heard, he was very far from here. Apparently, the family relocated to a place called Dunedin. Funny name, isn't it? I bet you could never pronounce it right. Not sure if you have heard of the name before, but it's in New Zealand,' and he paused, allowing her to have her turn, but Kwantar did not respond. Deep down, he knew she would not. The spoken word was now beyond her. Anuwat spoke again, 'The thing is he's no longer with the family either. Truth is we don't know where he is. But I promise you, I'll continue to look for him. Though, I've no idea how long that would take, or whether he'd even turn up. And so, we have to put Darin first. She'll stay with me as her guardian. It really is for the best.' Anuwat discreetly slipped out a piece of paper from his shirt pocket and carefully made an effort to iron it out with his palm. Then reaching down, he produced an inkpad from his gown.

Calmly Anuwat reached for Kwantar's hand. He felt a slight tug, but it was quite normal for a sedated patient to have reflex reaction like this. He flipped open the ink pad and now his hand shaking ever so slightly, took hold of her thumb and pushed it down into the blue ink before winching it over to the document. He pressed it firmly onto the paper and rolled it from left to right. Kwantar's fingerprint was imprinted onto the signature line, clear in every friction ridge and from every angle.

'I'll take care of Darin,' Anuwat said softly. 'I'll make you proud of her, Tar, very proud.' He then took out his handkerchief, shook it out, and pored some surgical spirit into it. He carefully wiped her finger clean of ink. His hands were once again steady as if it were a scalpel he was handling.

Having done what he had set out to do, Anuwat methodically checked that everything had been returned to their respective pockets. There they all stayed quietly as he eased himself into the chair next to the bed. He exhaled and closed his eyes, needing a moment to himself while still in concealment. It was not too long before the curtain was opened again, revealing the calming-yet sombre serenade of the hospital ward.

An untouched jug full of water rested beside the bed, the saline, the blood-filled a quarter of the bag, the oxygen was working fine. 'Good,' Anuwat muttered to no one in particular. He glanced at his watch. He had a meeting to go to. Anuwat turned to Kwantar to say his goodbyes. But the words stuck in his throat as he saw that Kwantar was awake. Her eyes were wide open, but they did not focus on him. Her mouth seemed to be struggling with itself as if she was trying to produce a word. There was recognition in her eyes. They were not alone. The reflection almost showed him what she saw. Anuwat spun around. And there was Narit.

Chapter 3

The man before him was no longer Khatha, in fact, he had never been Khatha and the pained expression on his face as he stared at Kwantar was evidence enough of the fact. Despite himself, Anuwat's fear for Kwantar wrestled back control of the situation, and he turned back to her, 'Tar? Tar?' She lay awkwardly, her head hovering above her pillow, her neck taut, her fingers contorted into a snarl. 'Nurse!' Anuwat shouted. And as he attempted to ease Kwantar head back onto the bed, he could not help but crane his head to quickly check the spot behind the louvre windows. Khatha had gone.

'Tar, look at me. Tar, look at me!' Anuwat tried raising up Kwantar's feet to help blood flow to her heart. Her eyes seemed to have congealed into her face. 'Nurse!'

A rotund nurse ran in from an adjacent room, momentarily glancing back at an empty bed she had bumped into, heaving as she made it to the patient.

'She's in shock,' declared Anuwat. 'Loosen her gown and take her legs for me.' It only took him seconds to fetch the oxygen regulator as Kwantar's body began to spasm. 'Tar, please let me. No don't tear it out, please. It's all right. It's perfectly all right. It's nobody.' Kwantar gasped for air, struggling to produce words. She raised her frail arm and pointed to where Narit had been standing.

Anuwat adjusted the valve, looking for signs that she might be stabilizing. 'Shh . . . You need to calm down and rest. You've got to help me, Tar. Now keep taking deep breaths. That's good.'

As Kwantar's breathing became more regular, Anuwat slumped down to sit beside her. What little strength she had was now used up and her body crumpled back onto the bed. Two times she had been resuscitated and now this. It was a matter of hours now, Anuwat was certain. 'Khatha can wait. He can wait,' he muttered to himself as he fought the urge to kill the man. However, his restraint was short-lived when he happened to look up and glimpse him disappearing again.

Anuwat jumped to his feet and dashed out of the room, absently telling the ward's nurse not to leave Kwantar's side. On his exit he bumped into Nhamfah and Darin who had evidently just come back from the canteen.

'Darin, did you see your teacher?'

Looking more than a little bewildered, Nhamfah and Darin stared at the doctor before pointing to the stairs. Anuwat squeezed Darin's shoulder and hurriedly set off in that direction. A half-chewed pork ball still in her mouth, Darin looked at Nhamfah as if an answer to Anuwat's strange behaviour was forthcoming.

Narit's irregular footsteps could be heard in the distance along with the sound of something, possibly his watch, glancing off the steel handrail. Anuwat followed in pursuit, forcing himself to take measured, decisive strides. There was no need to run, he knew Khatha would be slowing already.

And there he was, frantically making his way down the stairs. His loose shirt failing to hide how his shoulder slanted to one side as he put down his weight. Khatha kept on moving, the shock that had propelled him into an escape showed no sign of abating.

The stairs seemed endless. Khatha knew this was coming. He knew that one day it would all resurface. Khatha looked wildly around, agitated. He stopped for a moment to catch his breath. 'What am I doing . . . fuck . . . Kwantar?'

'Khatha!'

Khatha halted. His face involuntarily twitched at the thought
that he had caught his name in the air. 'What?' Khatha tried to
assemble the scattering pieces of himself, arms tightly folded
across his chest with creases around the shoulders. He turned
away from a hedgerow which separated him from the carpark,
there Anuwat stood in his white gown. 'Anuwat? What? Not
now, please.'

'What?' Anuwat raised his voice in disbelief. 'What, what?
What were you thinking of doing up there?'

'What?' Khatha glanced at the flushed face of his friend. He
had never seen him worked himself up so. Khatha was thoroughly
shaken by Anuwat's aggression and that somehow made him
accept that his mere presence up there was fatally intruding. He
tried to lift his shoulders and even at his best, it was hardly a
shrug. 'She, she looked bad, and sick, and I was confused,' Khatha
sputtered. 'That's why I was standing, so just calm down, all right?
What's your problem?'

'My problem! Tell me Khatha, after all you've put her through,
you've decided to give her a heart attack? Really, what on earth
were you thinking of doing up there!?' Anuwat bawled.

'Wha . . .? Wait a minute,' Khatha's face suddenly took on
an incredulous cast, 'what exactly do you mean by "what I have
put her through?" Anuwat, I asked, what do you mean by "what
I have put her through!?"'

'Look,' Anuwat muttered, his hands now jammed in their
pockets as though they were moored there for security. 'I know
everything,' his voice louder and clearer as he progressed. 'Well,
not everything, but enough to know that the life she's living, and
now dying for that matter, has been your fault, your making, all
along. How could you be so irresponsible? Oh yes, I was very
fond of her. Stupid, stupid me. But so be it.'

'Irresponsible?' Khatha repeated in disbelief. 'Anuwat, I asked, what exactly have I put her through? She was a girl I dated in my youth. Please don't tell me you're going nuts now just because I was the first man she slept with?'

A punch landed and it was surprisingly hard, Khatha's head was sent twisting to one side as his chin shot up in the air. He lurched, staggered, but managed to find his balance a couple of steps down the kerb. The side of his face throbbed with the impact. Yet, the numbness almost comforted him. Making no attempt to protect himself from further blows, he braced himself for another strike that never came.

If anyone was shocked, it was not Khatha. Anuwat, rigid as if encased in a shell, looked at his guilty fist, embarrassed and ashamed of himself. Did he just hurt someone? In an attempt to hide his self-disgust, Anuwat muttered, 'I watched her. Little by little, life sucked out of her, her hair falling out, her body covered in sores. The slow cancerous cells sapping her strength; then, then she was bedridden.' Anuwat trailed off, adjusting his glasses, trying still to recover from hearing what he himself had just said. 'How could you? She, who has given so much more of herself than most are even capable of giving back. And you . . .'

'Anuwat, listen. You really have overstepped the mark there. That's a big accusation you're making.'

'You . . .' interrupted Anuwat as he stared hard at his colleague. 'The handsome young man who won her over. Who would have thought that it would be you, the guy who she fell for and ruined her life.'

'Well, listen!' Khatha protested.

Anuwat scoffed. 'I thought you were better than that! I thought you were a man of principles, never run away from your responsibilities. Especially if you have a child.'

'Excuse me?'

'Excuse me,' Anuwat repeated ironically. 'Is that a question or a way of you apologizing?' Having said that, Anuwat caught his breath in a startled gasp at his own blunder. The fingerprint he had secured would never gain him guardianship over a DNA test. He adjusted his coat, hoping that Khatha somehow had paid no heed to his slip of the tongue.

Khatha's hand autonomously lifted up and covered his mouth. The only visible and arresting features on his face now were his haunted eyes.

Anuwat seethed silently. Instead of seeing Khatha as a colleague, a thinking companion, he was now looking at him but did not recognize him at all.

'Are you saying that I . . .?' said Khatha with a hand pressed on his chest. 'You mean Darin, Darin . . .?'

Anuwat made a face and scoffed. 'What you made her believe was the biggest lie in the history of courtship. And you knew it. I suppose none of this matters anymore. The damage is done, she's almost gone. But about the girl, let's be clear, it's better for everyone that I take her. I am adopting Darin. And from now on, Narit—yes, that was your damn name, wasn't it—I forbid you from coming to this hospital. Piss off before you make things any worse than they already are.' He paused for a moment and opened his mouth as if to speak again. Then shaking his head, he thought better of it and with that, turned and started to make his way back up the stairs.

'Wait!' Khatha shouted after him. 'Darin? How!?'

'Go home!' Anuwat bellowed back as the tail of his white coat fluttered and disappeared up the stairs. Seconds later, however, he angrily backed down a couple steps and shouted, 'Actually, you know what, you're so damn good at rationalizing everything, why don't you do yourself a favour and figure it out for yourself this time?' And he was gone.

Shaking, Khatha suddenly lost his hold over his footing but managed to shrink back against a wall nearby. Weak-kneed, he slid down the panel to a squatting position. What started as a laugh quickly changed to tears.

* * *

Back in the ward, Kwantar squirmed uncomfortably. Flecks of blood disseminated back into the oxygen tube that was inserted into her nostrils. The bedsheet, the pillowcase were all soaked through in sweats. Condensed vapours clung inside her mask and then expelled from the holes on both sides of it as she heaved for air. Kwantar's chest rose and fell intermittently. Her struggle to breathe had the intensity of a person running a marathon.

Nhamfah frantically rubbed her friend's chest. 'Oh, Tar, you're a fighter, you really are. But it's time to let go . . . let go my dear, let go,' she thought. At times Nhamfah touched her friend's feet. When they felt cold, she put socks on them, and when they felt hot, she took them off.

Darin mopped her mum's tears, she talked to her, then she mopped her own tears.

'Darling, try not to cry. You'll make your mum sad. She hears everything, still.'

'Does she?' Darin looked up, a flicker of hope in her eyes. 'Really?' A part of her face was eclipsed by what was left of a tissue she had blown her nose with.

'Well, that's what the nurse said. Now, why don't you tell your mum about your new room at the doctor's home? She'd love to know that you'll be all right.'

That evening there were a couple of visitors—one being the local grocer, the other the go-between who gave Kwantar sewing work. They all took turns talking to her and encouraged her on her way. 'Don't forget to wai the monk, Tar,' they all reminded her. Whatever they said, every word extracted tears from Kwantar. The kind, comforting condolences and sanguine conversations flowed against the constant groaning that still defied the assuaging effect of morphine.

'Aunty!' Darin shrilled, clutching Nhamfah's arm as Kwantar suddenly stiffened. Her blanket got swept to one side, and she began to shudder as if she were terribly shocked to discover herself for the first time in a hospital, or more likely to still be alive and once more see the people she knew. She looked at Darin pleadingly with watery eyes, but it was unclear to all as to what she wished. Violently shivering, Kwantar fought hard to raise her index finger and curl it down.

'Oh no, you are not dying!' cried Nhamfah instinctively, the sign having drawn the blood from her face.

'Ho . . . home,' croaked Kwantar, her legs lamely kicking at the thin blanket.

'Tar, don't do that . . .'

'Narit . . .'

Kwantar shook her head, and for the briefest moment, the tears caught the light, adding lustre to her eyes. Her anaemic lips parted for some air, in vain. She persevered again. Her lungs puffed out, her mouth still gaping, chin slightly elevated with the tension. Then, with a palpable, unconscious exhalation, her body went limp. Her head, from the inclination of the pillow, rolled to the side.

'Mum?' murmured Darin, no louder than a whisper. 'Mum? Mum . . .' she squealed, throwing herself at what remained of her mother. 'No, no, no! Mum!'

'Oh, my little imp,' said Nhamfah, seemingly composed while, on the inside, her emotions were no less all over the place. She got to her feet and stooped over. 'She's gone. Your mother is gone.'

She gave Darin a mindful yet futile rub on her back. Darin who was hardly aware of anything except for her loss continued to weep.

Hearing a cry in the distance, Anuwat rushed back, dispersing the circle.

'Doctor, help!' Darin begged through her tears as Nhamfah tried to peel her off her mum. 'Help!'

Anuwat did not hear Darin, even if he had, he would not have comprehended it. Instantly he took Kwantar's wrist and felt her pulse. He shifted his thumb around and applied even more pressure. The beating was not there. Kwantar's hand in his grasp was growing cold. No more reviving. She was dead. She was dead. Anuwat blinked hard. Her wrist slipped through his fingers and flopped onto the bed.

'How, how is she?' Darin struggled in the embrace of Nhamfah. 'You've got to bring her back. You're a doctor, you can bring her back.'

Anuwat fidgeted with his thumb. His eyebrows crowed in. 'I'm sorry, Darin. I am sorry.' It was not long before he managed to regain the weight of his heart and proceeded to remove the oxygen mask, replace the pillow, and arrange her head back at the centre. His gaze never shifted from her face. It was a blanched, unreadable mask that was no longer bathed in fear. He must be happy for her. She is in a better world. And so, he reached out and passed his hands over her face to close her eyelids. 'Sleep now, Tar. That way you won't be so tired taking the very long journey ahead of you.' Anuwat then gently brushed away a stray eyelash off her cheek and methodically began to pluck out tubes, needles, and everything else that had lost their battle to save her life. 'Forgive me, Darin. Forgive me.' But no sooner had he finished apologizing than Darin fell onto the ground. She was soon gently placed onto the chair where she continued to droop.

As equipment was being withdrawn and rolled away by the nurses, Anuwat gave a discreet cough, hands awkwardly pushed into the pockets of his gowns. 'Nhamfah, have you got the clothes she liked? The clothes on the day she was admitted would do. We haven't got much time before the body stiffens.'

'I'll fetch some from the house,' replied Nhamfah. 'I'd like to go and get some flowers too.'

Anuwat forced a nod in agreement. 'Darin,' he called. But Darin did not move, still clutching desperately at her mother's robe. The doctor glanced at her and knew what it was like. So, he looked away reservedly. 'Right . . . and the rest of you, thank you, you can all go home now. There's a number of documents I'll need to attend to, and I'll let you know as soon as I can contact a temple and make arrangements for the funeral. Excuse me.' Then, after briefly mentioning something to the nurse, the doctor escaped the ward.

Once again, the curtain was drawn as the nurses turned up with water bowls and linen to clean Kwantar. And when Nhamfah came back with her friend's best apparel, stockings, and shoes, they helped her put them on, not forgetting to slip some banknotes into her friend's dress pocket. 'Go to wai the monk, Tar,' she prayed and sewed the pocket to a permanent close.

Then, after a layer of powder, a shade of black was pencilled in to bring out her eyebrows the way Kwantar always did. A touch of light brown eyeshadow. A hint of pink contoured on her cheeks, and a splash of red painted onto her lips. Her hair now combed, her hands were laced together on her chest, where a beautiful jasmine garland now rested.

Looking from afar, Kwantar seemed restful, a slight smile on her lips etched into her face eternally. And although her visage was still one of beauty no less than pride, half of it would always be those wrinkles that defined her sacrifice until this day. The mother showed no fear as she was wheeled into the mortuary.

* * *

In the pub, dust swam in the misty air where the pale light beamed. There was an elemental feel to the décor, or the lack of it, with bare hoary walls on all sides. Low-key sympathetic chats hummed away in the background. Groups of men huddled in their favourite corners with their dark pints of beer and food, and their chess pieces made of carbonated drinks' caps.

Upon staggering in, Khatha signalled with his index finger to the young lass behind the bar. He took an obscure table at the side, throwing his pack of cigarettes on its top. Over a wobbling stool facing the wall, Khatha straddled and buried his head into his hands.

A glass of rum and ice soon landed before him. The thud urged Khatha to look up. 'No, no, give me a bottle,' he ordered to the surprise of the waitress.

The boxing was on the telly. He was sure it was Thai boxing. 'Yes, that's right. That ritual. That dance. It must . . .' But with his eyes failing to focus, Khatha concentrated on himself.

Rum lazily swirled in his rocks glass. His head throbbed. Khatha took a swig, draining it down his burning throat. He brought the glass down with a thud and slumped forward on his stool. 'Fuck Arse' was carved into the table. Khatha snorted, laughing through his nose. He filled up the glass, emptied it again, then a smoke, then another glass, then a smoke, and soon the room started to spin. 'Drown thou empty selves Drown . . . hmm . . . selves,' Khatha babbled as he tried to push a cigarette into one of his ears and began to laugh. 'Ha, a wife died, a female doesn't, doesn't make one pity so much as one spills a drop of alcohol,' he repeated the saying between hiccups.

With all the dregs sliding out of the bottle with a help of a gentle, unconscious shake, Khatha, now chewing on his cigarette filter, waved at the waitress and once again signalled her with an index finger.

Khatha's body swayed as he struggled to stay awake. But at last, he succumbed, leaning forward at an awkward angle before eventually collapsing over the profanity on the table. His lanky arm, pushed out by the fall, toppled the glass. It rolled, gushing out liquor and ice before spinning to a stop.

* * *

How long had it been since he first met her on the university trip to Rayong? The bus was bringing everyone back home after a long day of activities. Narit was making his way to the front of the bus, and it was then that he first noticed the rosy-cheeked Kwantar asleep. Her face was moist with sweat. There was something about her face that was marked by an element of undone insouciance. Without giving it much thought, Narit slid the window open to let the heat out, but all it did was wake her up. Kwantar turned to thank him, though added that she was, in fact, allergic to the fumes. Narit was taken aback. Yet he replied dismissively, 'It's just the construction site. You'll find it better to have the wind in.'

She raised her eyebrows.

'You may very well do that, young miss.'

She sniggered before throwing her eyes to the view of ocean that was presently rolling out from behind the seawall.

Chapter 4

One Year Later

The ironic comforting embrace filled the back of his throat and a tendril of smoke crept up his finger. A light breeze blew away the expelled wisps, their trails partially shrouding his worn-out face. Discounted books laid in piles on a metal table just outside the shop. Khatha shuffled through them. Not finding what he was looking for, if indeed he had anything in mind, he stacked them back up.

'You're late today. I'm closing,' the shop owner roared in his gravelly voice as he emerged from behind the counter inside the store, a miserable greeting which Khatha waved off as he entered through the half-shut doors. He passed the second row, going straight to the third one undeterred.

His head slightly at an angle, his eyes running through lines of book spines, his fingers shudder as they trailed his gaze. He continued to pull out books, flicking through them and scanning the back covers. 'Why do you have the sign "new arrival" if there's nothing new here?' Khatha said to no one in particular. 'All these have been here forever. I don't know what to get her now.'

'Get her something pretty,' shouted the owner as he jotted down some squiggles into his account book. 'Fifteen this year, you said? Really, stop being a teacher and start being a father sometimes.'

'What? No, no, not another experiment,' said Khatha anxiously, stopping midway, pulling out the blue book, leaving it at a slant. 'A father, honestly?' He muttered. A train of thought shunted its way to him. His mind soon drifted to the last visit.

* * *

Standing on to the step of the white house under the navy clay roof, he knocked, a brown package snugged tightly under his arm. The door soon opened and Anuwat's face emerged through the gap.

'Good to see you again,' he greeted with a glass of coffee in his hand. As usual, his words prompted but a nod. 'She's in the garden. Well, actually, Khatha, can we talk?'

Khatha looked at him. Although, his face did not give away much, the question had him rattled. It had been such a long time since they had last exchanged more than just a few words. 'Right,' he conceded and was soon taken to the dining section of the house.

The clock ticked monotonously on the pillar as Khatha made his way inside what was now her home. The books he had been giving her lay in small piles on a table. Dust particles hovering in the narrow beam of light filmed their covers. Khatha approached his stack and carefully placed the new package down next to its predecessors. A draft of cigarette smoke steeped behind him still.

The greyish living room soon revealed a humble yet bright kitchen where some food lay, halfway prepared. Kwantar's portrait remained on the shelf by an overhead cupboard with a glass of orange juice and canna lilies that were the day's offering. A new metallic table reflected the sun that spilled in from the yard, blinding him for a second as he navigated his way to the inside. There was something about the table setting that seemed to indicate that he should sit at the end of it.

'Tea or coffee? I also have orange juice if you want.'

'Thanks, but I'm okay.'

Anuwat raised his eyebrows and walked over with his cup of cooling coffee. He pulled up a nearby chair and settled at a reserved distance. He drummed his fingers on his knees a few times before looking up at Khatha who was now absorbed with himself, alone in a brown study.

A carefree but restless figure had leapt into his vision in the window frame, now gliding further towards the end of the backyard. Khatha followed Darin with his gaze, and for a split second he was in 1973. She was wearing one of her mother's dresses, a dress burned into his memory, the flowing polka dot that Kwantar wore the day he gave her the present. She had grown up so much this past year with a figure that already filled out the dress. She was a young woman now. Her back was facing him. Part of her hair was pinned up, the rest rolled over her shoulders, almost grazing it when her head inclined a little. She was sitting on her knees, picking some ivy gourd leaves and placing them carefully into a basket. She looked beautiful. Khatha clenched his fists, digging his nails into his palms, fearful that the moisture in his eyes would betray him.

'How—how's she doing at her new school?' said Khatha, casual as if they had been shooting the breeze for a while. Without turning to face Anuwat, he continued, 'I heard private education is more yielding to a learner-led approach. By the way, has she set her mind on doing art for her tertiary studies?'

Anuwat shifted his coffee to the other hand, and instead of addressing his companion's questions, forced himself to speak in the general direction of the wall. 'Look, Khatha,' he paused. From the corner of his eyes, he could see Khatha turn around. 'Look, I wanted to apologize if I had accused you of anything in the past. Please . . . hear me out. This has been playing on my mind for a long time now.'

'I don't know, Anuwat. I don't see the point of reopening old wounds. What happened, happened. Let's just leave it at that.'

'Please, just give me five minutes.'

Khatha gave a resigned sigh and ran his hand across his brow. 'Go ahead.'

'I've got to tell you something. I think it's important that you know,' said Anuwat, shifting his coffee back again to the other hand. He leaned across the small table. 'I . . . I forged Kwantar's signature to obtain guardianship of Darin,' he paused. Khatha said nothing, he did not even shift his gaze from Darin. So, carefully, Anuwat revisited his mental notes and ventured on. 'Well, you know, something of that kind. All right, I took her fingerprints, there you go. You have to understand that I had a pretty bad opinion of you when it all happened back then. And I simply couldn't risk it. But I understand now that something must have happened that parted you from her. And that you had no idea about the baby then. To be honest, I was selfish. I wanted a part of her to remain close to me. I needed to solidify the girl being under my care before I tell you this. I am so sorry.'

Khatha looked down at his hands and said nothing. For a few brief suspended seconds, it was as if his brain was floating aimlessly in the sea, like the time when they spent on Koh-Samet Island. Here was a man who had stepped up and was cut out to be a perfect father figure, yet here he was, apologizing for taking on the responsibility. He would never contest him for being that role model. Perhaps this might be for the best. For a moment Khatha thought he would share a story in return, a story that would tell him the reason why they could not be together. But he decided against it. It was best that past times stayed in their respective graves, to be visited with token flowers and, perhaps, a secret, fleeting smile as time passed. Anuwat did not need to know.

'Kwantar once said to me,' Anuwat mused, braving a reluctant smile. 'By wanting to erase pain, you are erasing the experience.

She never wanted things to be otherwise, you see. That was how much she loved you.'

A moment of observed silence. An unlikely revelation. Khatha was shaken. 'She . . .' He thought. 'Is that . . .?' Khatha adjusted himself in the seat and looked at Anuwat, eager to hear more.

'Anyway, enough reminiscing. There is this parent-teacher meeting coming up, would you like to go?'

Khatha sighed. 'Anuwat, I don't think she's ready for that. I'm not asking for much, you know. I only wish she could speak with me normally. Not just to me. And definitely neither fidgeting nor struggling to find somewhere to look.'

Anuwat shuddered internally but did not pursue the topic.

'If you don't mind,' said Khatha and suddenly got up, hand still holding on to the edge of the table as if it would keep him on his toes. He navigated his way to the backdoor. Anuwat followed him. Khatha grabbed the doorknob, hesitated, slowly turning it so as not to make a sound.

'Darin,' called Anuwat from behind him.

'Yes, dad?' cheerfully she replied, rising up and turning around only to realize it was Khatha standing there.

He saw the guilt in her eyes.

'Afternoon, teacher.'

'Darin,' said Khatha. 'Shouldn't you be studying?' It was meant as a joke, but it did not come out like one. He instantly regretted it.

Darin gave a nervous laugh and looked down at the basket on her arm. An awkward silence fell within the small space they now shared. Khatha stood in the kitchen in his jeans and loafers, scanning her new guitar.

'Khatha,' called Anuwat from behind him. 'Why don't you stay for dinner?'

Darin who was now pretending to be busy putting on her apron did make an effort to look up at him but he averted her gaze. 'Maybe . . . perhaps next time. I just wanted to drop off something. A CD, Tina Turner's. They said she's famous. Well, I've put it on the pile, you know. Sorry I interrupted you. Both of you.' He then quickly turned and headed back into the house, his face twitching with self-loathing as he left.

* * *

Khatha inhaled some more smoke deep into his lungs at the recollections, wincing visibly as a sharp pain shot through his left leg. He slowly slumped onto the floor against a rickety shelf, causing it to grate out of its neat block. A number of books were dislodged with the impact, and a few fell off in a series of thuds. Alerted by the noise, the shopkeeper stopped counting his cash and darted to his customer's rescue. He was however quickly rebuffed. 'Don't be so dramatic, Wat. I'm fine. Leave me be,' Khatha muttered. 'I'll put them back up. Don't worry.'

'Don't be silly. I'll get you a chair,' he snapped back before disappearing into the storeroom.

Amidst the sweet, musty smell of paper that penetrated the air, Khatha attempted to stand up but thought better of it. He squeezed his eyes so tight that the soft lines around them dug deep into his cheekbones. The picture of Darin, of her expression, of him being called a father still lingered and hurt him. Although he had secretly looked forward to his regular visit, he dreaded the thought that he was going there today, especially after that embarrassing attempt at humour the last time. He had once been so good with young people. His sister had adored him. He could make her laugh like no other, and she had trusted him. And he . . . and he . . . Khatha winced. As things were, his sister remained yet another source of happiness that he had to deny himself. For now, Khatha was somewhat consoled by the knowledge that Piyanuch was happy with her full schedule at the family restaurant.

Rows of books shimmered in the last gleam of the evening sun as though they were queuing up to clock off for the night. The streets were quieter. Khatha shook his head and leaned forward to massage his ankle. The rattling noise of furniture being moved could be heard in the other room. The lower half of his face now sank in the grip of his palm. His forehead slick with sweat, cigarette still straddled between his fingers, Khatha silently chuckled to himself in a weak attempt to shed a sadness that hung over him.

The shop owner reappeared from behind the partition, with a chair lugged behind him. The books were no longer on the floor and had been placed back on the shelves. A couple of banknotes and a few coins had been left on the counter beside his old calculator. As he looked out through the opening of the shop, a hint of black smoke could just be made out along with the sound of a motorbike's engine quietening into nothing.